I0550150

CRIMSON MOON

The Strange *Rumors of*
Georgetown

———————

WESLYN TRIMMINGHAM

CRIMSON MOON

Copyright © 2025 by Weslyn Trimmingham

All rights reserved. No part of this book may be reproduced or transmitted in any form or by any means without written permission from the author.

For more information or to book an event, contact:

Email: superwessy@gmail.com

Email: findinghopepublishing@gmail.com

Cover design by Camille Glasgow

ISBN: Paperback: 978- 1- 0691090- 6- 4
ISBN: Ebook: 978- 1- 0691090- 5-7
ISBN: Hardcover: 978- 1- 0691090- 7- 1

First Edition: October 2025

DEDICATION

First and foremost, I must express my gratitude to God for providing me with health, strength, Wisdom, and creative ability. This book is dedicated to my siblings, who have been my greatest allies. They have consistently pushed me to put forth a valiant effort, not holding back any ideas and providing me with honest critiques to help me improve.

This dedication is also extended to my parents, who have provided positive inspiration to my life, particularly in my writing endeavors, and to my cousin, who assisted me in completing this work's final version. My heart goes out to you.

Thank you, dear readers, for making this excursion advantageous to everyone who received this book. Thank you for allowing my words an opportunity. Additionally, I want to thank the innumerable books that molded my life from yesterday to today. Finally, I thank myself for appearing, pushing through, and completing what I began. It is essential to keep in mind that unspoken tales await us tomorrow.

THE STRANGE RUMOURS OF GEORGETOWN

TABLE OF CONTENTS

CHAPTER ONE

O n the seventh day of every month, the moon turns crimson. This phenomenon is exclusive to the town of George. And because of this, a legend, or some say rumors, that the town of George is filled with many mysteries. On the seventh day, no one is allowed to linger outside their houses due to auspicious things happening. Lately, these legends were proven to be true, seeing that several bodies were found dead these past days, some ripped apart, and others brutally mutilated, their unrecognizable bodies completely dried out with various peculiar signs.

On a cold summer night, a young girl named Wendy Granchest was walking the streets. Despite the news spreading throughout town, she was unaware of it because her childhood had been sheltered, and she was also a realist who loved to reason through everything with logic. She did not believe that anything could exist which could not be defined by humanity and science, so such ideas never crossed her mind. While she was walking late into the night, she stumbled upon a small cavern that consumed much of her time, and the moon, as usual, turned crimson. Inside this cavern were strange engravings resembling prophecies, but she could not read them.

Nevertheless, they looked intriguing, and her curiosity was piqued. After looking around, Wendy traced the symbols along the cave wall with her fingers. It was rough yet somehow soothing. A strange chill danced up her spine, not fear but recognition. It felt...familiar.

She couldn't understand why, but her instincts screamed at her to remember this place, remember the engravings, but she knew she would forget. Every carving seemed to whisper as her finger tingled with every touch made.

Suddenly, she blurted out, "This means something to me, but what?" She stared at the stone, unmoving.

As time passed quickly, she realized she had to return home. After leaving the cave, the feeling lingered. It was as if fate had reached out and marked her.

She made her way home and began to hear the sounds of howling, crickets chirping, owls hooting, and other strange noises. Suddenly, the sounds ceased, as if something terrifying was approaching and had scared them away.

Without a second thought, she quickly grew afraid and started to run. While running, she encountered a strange man. "What are you doing out here all alone?" he asked.

"I was just heading home," replied Wendy as she gasped for air. "You're shaking a lot. Let me follow you home," replied the man.

"Where do you live?"

She pointed, "Just beyond the hill." Wendy replied to the man without fear. She didn't even second-guess herself. Telling a strange man where she lived. One that can do her harm. Instead, all she knew in that moment was that she "You live very far away.

Why didn't you go home earlier?"

"I got caught up in the market," she said.

"So, you're telling me that you don't know about the rumors in this town, especially around these parts?"

"What rumor?" replied Wendy. "And before you do, can I know your name?"

"Oh, sorry, my bad. My name is Eithan, what's yours?" "My name is Wendy. So, what is the rumor?" she added. "Several people have already died," replied Eithan.

"What!" exclaimed Wendy. "It's true. That's why no one is on the street at night—especially when it's a crimson moon—let alone by themselves, because that's when the predators appear. You're a brave one, I must say." Eithan continued, "BEWARE! BEWARE! OF CRIMSON GEORGE!" He dangled his hands in front of her while making a scary face.

Wendy began to laugh and replied, "Crimson George... that's a combination of the moon and town, right?"

"Yes," Eithan replied.

"So, what about the predators that seek their prey at night? Are you one?"

"Yes," Eithan said. "A vicious one too," he added with a laugh. Wendy joined in the laughter with Eithan, but little did she know that he was dead serious.

Curious, she then asked Eithan, "What are you doing out here late at night?"

Eithan paused for a moment, smiling in a somewhat eerie way. "I always come out late at night for a run," he replied.

After hearing what Eithan had to say, a chill ran down her spine. It was a tremor unlike any she had ever felt before.

With a trembling voice, she said, "Eithan, can't we walk a little faster? It's getting darker, and I really need to get home. My parents must be worried about me."

Then from the darkness came a growl. Wendy's pulse spiked as a pair of glowing red eyes emerged from the shadows. Then, before she knew it, more red eyes appeared. Wolves—they were wolves. Wendy couldn't believe her eyes. Something was playing tricks on her as her mind struggled to keep up with what she was seeing. Huge wolves—bigger than humans—showed up and began chasing the two of them. Eithan grabbed Wendy's hand, and they started running together. The moment he took her hand, he felt a strange yet soothing connection, a spark of electricity between them.

Luckily for him, he also enjoyed the sport of running. Deep inside, he wanted to smile, but tried his best to mask it with a frown so as not to cause a scene. On the way, Eithan picked up more speed, forgetting that he was holding the hand of a young human girl. As soon as his instincts were back under control, he slowed down and turned around to look at Wendy, whom he assumed to be out of breath, but she was not. In fact, she had no trouble keeping up and looked just as fit as he, which piqued his curiosity.

"I can't believe she managed to keep up, he thought.

After all the running, they both slowed down and hid behind a stone next to a tree.

"Hey, Eithan," she whispered. "Now I see why you come out to take a run every night. The speed that you were running, you might as well be the fastest man in the world."

Eithan smiled and scratched his head. "It's fright. Fright does things to a man—even the impossible. Besides, if I were the fastest man, you would be the fastest woman."

Wendy smiled. "That's true."

But in Eithan's prideful head, he thought, Of course I'm fast. Who can make me afraid? Not even death.

Deep into the conversation, forgetting that they were running from something, the wolves caught up.

"Run, Wendy!" he said with his pretentious, loud voice. "I'll distract them as bait, then catch up to you."

Wendy took off and left Eithan, causing her to feel heavy-hearted and guilty. Eithan had thought that Wendy would be happy to have such a handsome, gentle, and caring man performing a noble sacrifice for her, but Wendy was thinking differently. As she ran, all her thoughts were on him. She was wondering if he was all right. Then Eithan's face flashed through her mind. When he said to run, there wasn't a hint of hesitation or fear in his eyes. It was as if he was enjoying the thrill of it. Furthermore, Eithan had been running every night, so he was bound to meet up with a few troubles now and again, wouldn't he?

Questions started to emerge from Wendy's mind as her thoughts spiralled from what she had just experienced. After all the running, her legs finally gave out, so she sat for a while. She was already out of Eithan's sight.

11

Meanwhile, the thrill Eithan felt quickly disappeared. He was filled with extreme anger, and his eyes glowed the same color as the moon, just like the wolves. He began to growl at the pack.

"Just go away!" he barked.

Two members of the pack, Mandy and Jason, transformed into humans. "We saw that you were having fun running in your human form, so we decided to chase," said Jason. "We've been smelling something strange for a long while. Your personality is a little twisted, though. You used us, and now you want to throw us away when we are no longer needed."

Eithan smirked.

"We haven't seen you this happy in a long time," added Mandy.

Suddenly, there was a scream in the distance.

"It's Wendy!" Eithan exclaimed. "Sorry, guys, I have to go."

Eithan ran full speed ahead until he caught up to her. When he got there, he saw Wendy lying on the ground. It turned out that she had fallen and bruised her leg.

He stared at her, fully taking in her dishevelled appearance. The panic on her face answered his pending question. The darkness scared her so much that it caused her to faint. Eithan smiled as he gasped for air, recovering from his brief sprint. It only took him five seconds to reach her.

This was only his first time meeting her, but there was a magnetic force that made him feel like she was the one. He had to protect her.

"I am very sure this is not me imprinting on this girl," he whispered under his breath.

He picked her up and held her in his arms. Her house had to be somewhere nearby. The hill was drawing nearer and nearer, but the further they went, the more Wendy's leg began giving off a sweet, pungent smell. The vampires that were near began tracking the scent that was making them lose all sense of reasoning and driving them into insanity. Using his supernatural hearing, Eithan heard footsteps coming in from a few blocks away and picked up his pace until he found her home.

Surprisingly, Wendy lived in the Granchest manor. No one tried to interact with the family that lived in that house. They developed a reputation for being the weirdest people you could find, even though they had a history in the town. There were rumors that they believed in demons lurking in the dark that walk among us during the day. Because of this, people tended to keep their distance from them, intimidated by their presence. They were also known to be quite a powerful family.

Bell rings."Uhm, hello? Who is that?" said Elena. "This is Eithan."

"I don't know anyone by that name. Please go away. It's extremely late at night, and we are quite busy looking for our daughter."

Elena quickly yet reluctantly opened the door. "Why didn't you say that earlier?" she roared with relief. "I told her that she must come home before it gets dark, but she didn't listen. We were so worried."

Eithan placed Wendy on the floor, and as he was about to

turn around and leave through the front door, he paused.

"Next time, don't allow your daughter to roam the streets or anywhere by herself. She's too naïve about the world. She doesn't know the dangers of it. And as you can see, she's easily frightened."

Elena held back her anger. "Thank you once again, but that advice is not necessary. Though we were worried, we trusted our girl."

"All right," said Eithan. He could sense the hostility within her voice that would intimidate others.

However, Elena sensed that Eithan was not afraid one bit, and she was the one who was starting to feel intimidated. Immediately, she disliked Eithan.

"For taking care of my daughter, I will allow you to stay here for the night. It is late and dark outside. I can't allow you to go back."

"No! It's all right. I can go. I'm not afraid of the dark."
"That's good to know, but I insist."

No matter how Eithan said no, Elena kept on persisting, and he eventually relented.

Eithan sighed. "Wendy's injured on her leg, so she should get that looked at."

"Yes, don't worry about her," replied Elena.

"So which way is the guest room?" asked Eithan. "It is on the second floor, on the right."

14

"Thank you, I will be going now."

As Eithan headed for the room, he suddenly remembered how Wendy had managed to keep up with him when they were running in the woods, even though he was surpassing the limit of any ordinary human. He stopped and turned around.

"Has Wendy always been a fast runner?" he asked Elena.

No!" she said. "Wendy has been an extrovert at times, but she is clearly an introvert. Her father and I always pamper and shelter her, so I don't think she has time for things such as sports."

"Oh, that's quite sad," said Eithan. "She should think about it." "Why do you say such things, sir?"

"I say such things because when I saw her tonight, she was running at such a rapid speed that I don't think ordinary humans would be able to measure up."

When Eithan said this, Elena's face went sour, as if sucking on a lime. "I do not know what you are talking about, but I guess you can say that she's a fast runner. Maybe she hid her talent from us."

"Is that so?" asked Eithan. "Yes… I guess."

"Alright, I am off." Eithan headed off to the guest room. On his way, he saw strange paintings, writings, statues, and petroglyphs. Moreover, the writings to the left of the corner were written strictly in black. Before Elena left his sight, he quickly asked her about it.

"What is that?"

"Don't you think that you're a little too curious for a guest?"

15

Elena responded.

Eithan replied with a smile. "I don't think so. If I'm staying at someone's house, I should at least know about certain things."

Elena walked away, leaving him with their butler, who provided some answers.

"That's just a short inscription engraved above the sword that says Praecisa Omnium Creaturarum. When translated, it means 'to cut through all creatures.'"

The butler continued. "These words that are printed on the wall are to remind the Granchest family that the sword 'Incasera' must be presented to defeat the evil things that are unnatural to the world."

"What!" Eithan shook his head. "Tonight has been one crazy night," he muttered under his breath.

He turned and looked the butler straight in his green eyes. "Isn't the sword Incasera a myth?"

The butler laughed. "Don't you know that there are a lot of strange things in the world today?"

What can be stranger than this?" said Eithan sarcastically.

Not long ago, he was telling Wendy about the strange things that were occurring, and now he was being schooled by an old, grumpy butler who looked no younger than fifty.

"It is also written that 'the swords and claws are one,' but no one knows what that means."

Hearing whispers in the hall, Elena returned, having heard

enough.

"Enough of that. Go to your room and forget about what the butler said."

This time, Eithan went straight to the guest room. He did not sleep a wink all night. The whole night, he thought about Elena's hostility and uncertainty, the weird butler, Wendy's father, who had gone MIA, the inscriptions, and all the weird-looking things around the house. Though he himself was not an ordinary man, he found the people living in this house to be bizarre.

The butter was exceptional at what he did. Sometimes, William wondered if he was something more than he appeared, but his scent was distinctly human. Elena, Wally, Wendy, and even William all relied heavily on him. This level of trust and reliability earned him access to most areas of the house.

Observing the butler, Wally noticed the difference in treatment. The butler was more affectionate towards his mother than any other person in the house, but he paid it no mind.

Elena, on the other hand, was thankful, but didn't give anyone access to her little lab. It was her secret, and therefore off-limits.

That night, after the butler escorted Eithan to his quarters, he returned to his own.

"Another wild soul enters the den." He chuckled to himself. "Like moths to a flame."

Shredding the crisp uniform, the transformation began. Underneath the formal black and white layers was a chiselled body that defied his age- Lean muscle, taut abs, and a youthful face. His green eyes dulled, replaced with the brown beneath contact lenses.

Wrinkles faded as he peeled off a lifelike mask, revealing a younger face.

After slipping into his loungewear, he picked up a black Motorola and dialed a secure number.

"Take over for me," he said. "I'll be gone for several weeks; handle everything while I'm away." As the butler spoke with authority, the voice on the other end accepted the commands without question.

Though the butler may have looked and served like a servant, it was evident that he was much more than a butler and pulled more strings than anyone suspected.

The next morning, Wendy got up and did her daily routine. She entered the bathroom in one of the guest rooms because hers was broken. Coincidentally, she entered as Eithan was taking a bath. Before entering, she took off her light pink pyjama top, then the pants. Lastly, she took off her bra and entered the bathroom. As she turned the door handle, she heard the shower pipes turn on and saw the shadow of a male figure standing behind the shower curtain. She quickly picked up her clothing, which she had dropped on the floor, clutched it to her chest and privates, then ran out screaming.

Hearing the scream, the butler ran towards her in a panic. "Are you alright?" he asked as he stormed towards her.

"Yes, I'm okay. I'm just a little surprised."

"That's a lot of noise for someone who is just surprised," said the butler.

She was trying to catch her breath. "There is… a strange…

man… inside the shower."

"Oh, that is why you were screaming. That strange man happens to be Mr. Eithan. He saved you yesterday, so your mom told him that he could stay in one of the guest rooms because it was dark."

Wendy tried to remember the events from yesterday, but they were a little blurred. Then she remembered the guy she met.

"Eithan! Oh, the old guy I met last night. He brought me home. I must express my gratitude."

The butler stared at her, wondering if something was wrong with her eyes.

At the same time, a deep and raspy voice spoke. "Who are you calling old?"

He was already dressed and ready to go.

When Wendy saw the figure to whom the voice belonged, her mouth dropped.

"Close your mouth, you'll catch flies." The butler wanted to smile, but he remained stern, showing the traits of an exemplary butler.

"What! You are him!" she exclaimed, looking shocked, surprised, and every other emotion her face could muster. "How can you look so—so—so handsome? Your beauty is out of this world. I thought you were an older person who jogs at night to keep his body fit. I am sorry for my mistake."

"Take a breath," said Eithan. Too many questions. "That's okay, no need to apologize. As for looking handsome, I was born that way."

Wendy could see the smirk on his face. She wanted nothing more than to knock it off. But who was she kidding? The guy was a specimen among men.

"I'm heading off now. I'm grateful that your mother let me stay the night. Also, I appreciate the kindness that your butler showed. I will be on my way."

"All right," replied Wendy. "I am incredibly grateful to you for saving me last night. Come to think of it, without you, I do not know what would have happened to me."

"Where is your father?" asked Eithan.

"My father and elder brother are away on a business trip, but they will be back today."

"Good for you. I also have an older brother and a sister who are around the same age as me, and they'll be returning in a couple of months. Anyhow, take care of yourself and remember not to walk that late at night."

After Eithan had gone on his way, Wendy thought about him the whole time she was up in her room.

"Wendy! Aren't you hungry? Come down and eat breakfast," shouted Elena.

"Alright, Mom, I will! Just a second."

Elena continued. "Remember that you said you must see Michael and Afeisha in the afternoon. Your dad and brother will be coming home for dinner, so stop idling."

"Yes, Mom! I know."

Once Wendy completed her tasks, she headed downstairs to have breakfast before meeting Michael and Afeisha in town. Meanwhile, Eithan returned to his residence.

Interestingly, Eithan came from a well-known wolf family but preferred not to flaunt his wealth. He chose to dress modestly to appear like an average person and wore glasses to conceal his remarkable attractiveness.

As he sat at home, he recalled the brief conversation he had with his friends Mandy and Jason, whom he had met along the way.

"Hey, guys. Did you spend the whole night outside hunting?" Eithan asked.

"Yes, we did," they both replied.

"The vampire was actually following Wendy's scent," Jason added. "It turns out that her scent is quite a delicacy."

"There's something not quite right about her," said Mandy. "And I'm not just saying this because I'm jealous. There seems to be something...weird going on with her."

"So, you noticed it," Jason said.

Eithan frowned. "What are you going on about?" He didn't like the way they spoke about her, as if she were something that needed fixing, a problem to be solved.

Seeing his irritable expression, Jason quickly added, "Calm down, bro, we don't mean anything by it."

"I know," Eithan said. "She is a little different from the ordinary person, and I know that her family and house are quite bizarre. Nevertheless, she's quite the looker, and she has a sense of humor. I like her."

Mandy let out a short laugh. "You? Interested in a girl? That's new." She twirled a strand of hair around her thin fingers, but her voice gave away how she felt. It was too light, too casual.

Jason smirked and patted Eithan on his shoulder, then he touched his forehead to his, as if checking for a fever. "Since when do you talk about girls like this?"

"Did I mention that her family can be quite weird?" said Eithan, to divert the subject. It didn't work, and he became embarrassed. He slapped Jason's hand away.

"What are you doing?" he demanded in an angry tone.

"Do not be angry," said Jason. "It's just that ever since I have known you, you haven't spoken about any females—not ever. So, hearing it from you now, I'm a little surprised."

"Well, I really do like her," Eithan admitted. "I can't put my finger on it, but being around her puts me at ease."

Jason was genuinely happy for his friend. Still, he raised an eyebrow and smirked. "If that's who you want, then you go for it."

A moment of silence filled the air as Mandy's sour attitude heightened. She was clearly not pleased with what she had heard.

Eithan tried to break the tension. "I slept over at her house."

"What! Already!" exclaimed Mandy. "Don't you think that is

moving a little too fast?"

"What is moving fast?" replied Eithan, feeling confused.

Mandy folded her arms to her chest. "Think about it for a minute. The girl just met a stranger who happens to be in the woods, and he saved her. Suddenly, he was asked to sleep over. Doesn't that sound a bit funny to you? Especially since this is George, we're living in."

Eithan hesitated, then nodded. "Now that I think about it, her mother was quite adamant that I stay the night."

"That makes it even worse," scoffed Mandy. "It's like they weren't afraid of who they might let in."

"I get it," replied Eithan. His annoyance grew, but he knew deep down that Mandy had a point.

"Can we go now? I'm starving."

Meanwhile, Wendy made her way into town. She had previously spoken to her mother about how their house was too far away from town, but her words fell on deaf ears. Instead, her mother dismissed her concerns, saying, "That's how it has been for a long time now."

As Wendy walked, fragments of her memories from the night before began to resurface. She remembered the rumor that Eithan had told her— other creatures besides them were lurking in the woods. But she quickly shoved the thought aside and continued her way to meet her friends.

Eventually, Wendy met up with her two friends, Michael and Afeisha, and the three headed to a diner called Feistus. This was a place where people go to relax, chat, and enjoy themselves. They were also regulars at the café. Feistus was a three-in-one place of entertainment. Wendy and her friends chatted for quite some time and had some fun dancing and singing. Wendy hesitated to talk about what was on her mind, but before long, she needed to discuss with her friends what she had heard.

"Do you guys know anything about the strange rumors going on around town?" She felt ridiculous for even suggesting it, but the events from the night before still lingered in her mind.

"I thought you were the type to dismiss those as crazy talk," said Afeisha. "Wendy! Since when have you been into such rumors and things going on in George? I have not thought of you as that kind of girl. I thought that you were a realist and did not study such things."

"Stop being sarcastic, Afeisha. I'm serious here. Recently, events have occurred that have opened my eyes to the world. I think that I am being a little too naïve and ignorant of the things that are happening around me."

Michael chuckled and shook his head. "Looks like my girl is growing up."

Wendy punched his shoulder.

"It's good that you are taking things seriously and being cautious. You never know what is out there at night," replied Michael.

Wendy faced Michael. "Do you know of any guy around these parts named Eithan?"

Michael's hand froze in the middle of stirring his drink. His smile slipped from his face for a few seconds, then he plastered on a fake one. Casually leaning back in his seat, he said, "Eithan, huh?"

He let the name roll off his tongue slowly, as if he were testing it.

"No, I don't think I know him. However, I have heard it somewhere, but I can't seem to remember."

This was the first time that Wendy was asking about a man, and it didn't sit well with Michael. The red tropical colada mocktail he drank was supposed to taste sweet. Instead, he couldn't even taste it. His sense of taste dissipated, and his tongue was no longer working. It felt like lead in his mouth.

Afeisha, who had been quietly observing the display, smirked to herself. Wendy can be so oblivious at times. Why can't she see the way Michael looks at her with so much passion burning in his eyes? I am starting to get a little annoyed, seeing that Michael never looks at me, no matter how hard I try.

Afeisha broke the silence. "Yes! I have heard that name before."

Michael's expression darkened as he looked at her, which made her quiver. He looked upset.

"How do you know him?" he asked.

"I just happened to see him in the road looking all shabby when a girl named Mandy called out to him."

"So does he have a girlfriend?" asked Wendy. "Is this Mandy chick his girl?"

"I do not think so, but why are you so interested in this guy?" teased Afeisha. "Is there something I should know?"

"No, it's nothing," said Wendy.

Michael's mood soured upon listening to the girl's banter. "It's time to leave," he said abruptly. "Your father and brother are returning today, and I do not want you to arrive late, seeing that you live extremely far away. It's already three."

Wendy nodded. "That's true, I don't want a repeat of yesterday.

Goodbye, guys."

As soon as Wendy was out of sight, Michael turned to Afeisha, his expression filled with disappointment. "Couldn't you have said something different?" he muttered.

"What did I do? I just told the truth." She watched Michael closely, feeling a twinge of sadness. "No wonder we're all friends," she spoke softly as they separated. "We're all completely and utterly clueless when it comes to love."

Along the way, Wendy met another of her so-called friends, and this time it was Sheila Andrews. She just happened to be walking around when they bumped into each other. Sheila Andrews was a tall beauty. Her hair was long and black, her skin was as pale as snow, and she had an attitude as bad as dirt. To make matters even more complicated, she had a crush on Wally Granchest, Wendy's elder brother.

"Wendy!" she called in a sweet voice. "I was looking for you!"

"Why were you looking for me, Sheila? I am quite busy today and will be heading home now."

"Wendy, it's not like that." "Like how?" asked Wendy.

"You should know that Wally is coming back today, and your house is quite huge. I want to spend the night at your house. I was heading to your home before I met you on the way."

Hearing this, Wendy started to doubt if this was even a coincidence. She put both hands on her face.

"Look here, Sheila, you cannot just stay over at someone's house without informing them first. My brother already has a girlfriend."

Her lie failed to convince Sheila, who became agitated and annoyed. "What more do you want? Look here, Wendy!" she roared. "I have already informed my parents that I'll be staying over at your place. You would not like to make me angry. You know what I can do."

Wendy sighed and almost bit her tongue. Sheila was a lost cause, and Wendy had no choice but to give in.

"Don't blame me if something bad happens," Wendy warned Sheila.

Their conversation had gone on for thirty-five minutes, and they both decided to go on their way before it got dark. Sheila continued to torment Wendy on the way to her house, but Wendy kept silent. She kept to herself and ignored Sheila. Suddenly, a switch flipped in Sheila. She pushed Wendy, causing her to trip and reinjure the same leg that she had injured before.

"Sheila! Why did you do that?"

"I am sorry," she said, without a trace of guilt. "I was talking, and you were not even listening. I want you to introduce me properly to your parents."

Wendy glared at her painfully. "You have not convinced me one bit that you are sorry. Furthermore, how are we supposed to get to the house early when you made my injured foot hurt once again? You said to introduce you properly. What introduction do you need, apart from Sheila, a schoolmate?"

Sheila was disillusioned. "I can walk slowly to match your pace, but I will not be carrying you."

"Fine!" exclaimed Wendy angrily. "You have such a bad personality.

Just what did I get myself into?"

Sheila turned to her, and she stopped talking. "No wonder my brother doesn't like you. It would be a nightmare if he did. Luckily, he can see straight through your façade, she thought."

The girls continued to walk, but they were not getting any closer than they had been.

"Wendy!" Sheila suddenly screamed, causing Wendy to jump. "Can you please walk a little faster? Night is closing in, and we have not even covered half the ground yet. You should convince your parents to live closer or in town."

"Maybe you should have thought about that before injuring my foot," Wendy replied. "And don't you think I've tried that? Stop complaining. Because if you had just behaved, we would not have been in this situation."

"It is childish of you to be pointing fingers at such a time," replied Sheila. "I'm exhausted... let's stop for a minute."

This girl is crazy, Wendy thought. "It's getting dark, you know. Let's hurry and get out of this forest. I am the one who should be tired. Besides, haven't you heard about the rumors?"

"Of course, I have heard, but I'm not you," said Sheila. "I am not sheltered, I'm tired."

Sheila stopped to rest, but Wendy wanted to go before encountering another experience like the night before. Little did they know that some visitors were travelling thirty miles per hour so that they could latch on to the delicacy that emanated throughout the whole forest.

"Sheila!" yelled Wendy. "I can sense something bad is going to happen.

Let's go!" Wendy had a horrid look on her face.

"What are you talking about, Wendy? You can be such a dork at times."

"I am telling the truth. Let's go."

"Fine, fine. Let us go."

It was not completely dark, but the amount of time spent in the forest arguing and resting made it seem like it was at least seven o'clock, and the predators couldn't resist such a smell. Wendy and Sheila began walking once again, but the environment became lonelier the farther they went. As the girls thread deeper, they pick up speed. Both girls were facing forward, so they couldn't see what was behind them. This scared them even more, not to mention the rustling trees.

Suddenly, the girls heard whispers behind them. They turned around, and there they were: the creatures of the night. Their eyes were red and shining, as if they were pearls. Their fangs looked as sharp as branded knives in the shadows, ready to pierce through their soft and tender flesh. Upon seeing them, Wendy's ideology slowly shattered. It was bad enough that there were wolves larger than humans. Now, there were human beings—well, people who looked like human beings—with extra sharp, pointed teeth. Or were they fangs? Something within her screamed danger.

"Run!" Sheila shouted, her don't-care attitude rapidly shifting as the things that Wendy spoke about quickly sank in.

Both girls began to run. Wendy forgot about how painful her leg felt and was running for dear life. It was the first time both girls had experienced such a thing in their entire lives.

CHAPTER TWO

"Wendy, wake up!" said Wally. "You don't want to be late for the first day of school!" he shouted, pulling the covers off her.

"Just five more minutes," Wendy muttered.

"No! You are going to be late. Now get your lazy ass up and get ready."

Walking out of the room and shutting the door behind her, Wendy did her morning routine, then headed down for breakfast. As she walked through the house, the smell of pancakes, fried bacon and eggs hijacked her senses, luring her in as if she were under a spell. With her senses under arrest, she sat at the table and began digging in.

"Slow down, Wendy," said Wally. "It's like you haven't eaten in days!

You'll choke. The breakfast isn't running away."

Paying no heed to his words, Wendy devoured her meal, savouring every bite. With the same energy, she grabbed her things and dashed out of the house, school the only thing now on her mind.

After what felt like an eternity, she was standing in front of the school building.

"Wendy!" shouted one of her best friends. "What kept you so long!" "Ahh, come on. It's the first day of school. Can't you be nicer? A little smile will do," responded Wendy with a smile.

"Okay, fine. I know you didn't want to wake up this morning," replied Afeisha.

"Let us head to class before it is late," Michael interrupted.

Meanwhile, Eithan was heading to the teacher's office to get his schedule, but he lost his way.

"Ouch—ouch, that hurts," a blonde girl whispered under her breath while trying to pick herself off the floor.

"I am so sorry," Eithan responded. "Here, let me help you." He picked the fallen books up off the ground.

"Thank you," she said with a smile. "I am Kylie." She held out her hand for a handshake, not paying attention to his face.

"I am Eithan," he said while shaking her hand. "It is nice to meet you. Can you help me find the teacher's office? I lost my way," Eithan said with a shy and embarrassed look.

"Yes, no problem. This way."

While in class, Wendy and Afeisha chatted and had fun with the other students. Suddenly, everyone became quiet and took their seats.

"The teacher is coming," Afeisha shouted to the class.

After a few seconds, the teacher entered the room and was

greeted happily by the students.

In a hoarse yet raspy voice, he said, "We have a new student who will be joining us today, and I expect everyone to treat him nicely. He has not been here long, but students should learn to get along with their fellow students."

While the teacher spoke, Wendy had her head on the desk, too lazy to listen to the teacher. The teacher continued, gesturing with his arms, "Come in."

When Eithan entered the classroom, the class was in awe. Who was this breathtaking human being? The girls started to squeal and scream. This was something Eithan was accustomed to. He knew his features weren't ordinary, jet black hair with blue eyes, a face surpassing any Greek sculpture, and he was at least six feet two inches in height. Eithan was so handsome that the girls could not believe that such a man existed. Before they knew it, their innermost desires began to spill. This was the effect his charm had on people, specifically girls. As his eyes met with theirs, a few girls from a clique—Ashley, Gabriel, and Eliza—couldn't contain their feelings.

"Marry me," said Ashley.

"Will you be my boyfriend?" asked Gabriel.

"You just shut up because he is mine, all mine," said Eliza.

These three girls were very beautiful and had the confidence to back up their words. Nevertheless, this did not stop the other girls from shooting their shots. They were all moonstruck, becoming straightforward to the point of making grammatical errors in their speech.

Eithan, on the other hand, was quite annoyed by the girls and their silly behavior towards him, but he tried his best not to show it.

Bam-Bam! Mr. Sam, the teacher, slammed his hand onto the desk.

"Can you all just shut up? This isn't very pleasant. Everyone knows he is handsome." He looked at him again and added, "I suppose."

He then placed his hands on his head, scratched it, and let out a deep sigh.

"I really do hate this bloody job and these annoying kids," he muttered under his breath, hoping not to be heard.

Eithan was shocked at the teacher's reply to the students.

"Hey, new kid, don't worry," said Johnny with a smile. "He's always like that. He won't get fired anyway, so don't waste your time trying. It is better for him to state his mind. After all, teachers fall into two categories: enthusiastic teachers who love teaching and those who are interested in money. Don't get me wrong—they both teach, but there is a difference in the learning. Not to mention that children are stressed, you know?"

That caught Eithan off guard, and it was a lot to take in, but he knew Johnny was right.

"Introduce yourself," said Mr. Sam, annoyed at the time that had passed. "Everyone, my name is Eithan. Nice to meet you. I hope we all can get along."

"Is that it?" Mr. Sam asked. "Yes," Eithan responded.

Mr. Sam shook his head and continued with the introductions. Meanwhile, Wendy, who was lost in thought, dozing off, suddenly lifted her head off the desk when she heard a familiar name. Eithan... could this be the Eithan she knew? Surely not. There couldn't be such coincidences. Facing denial before opening her eyes to see who it was, she nodded her head left to right, then started to bow her head back down towards the desk.

However, Mr. Sam gestured towards the empty seat beside Wendy. "Your seat will be next to Wendy," he said.

Hearing this, Wendy hesitated for a moment before raising both her head and right hand to indicate where he should sit. Their eyes met, and for a second, both were frozen in shock. Eithan at seeing her again, and Wendy at the realization that this was not only her Eithan, but that they attended the same school, were in the same class, and sat directly next to each other. This has to be fate, she thought.

With the introductions out of the way, the lesson began. Time flew by quickly, and before they knew it, it was lunchtime.

Eithan, who only knew Wendy, leaned in and whispered to her softly in her ear. "Let's grab lunch together."

"But I have my friends," Wendy replied.

"Then we all can eat together," Eithan countered.

She reluctantly gave in as the eyes of the other girls were becoming unbearable. Like a thousand invisible daggers were stabbing her.

After meeting Afeisha and Michael, who didn't seem particularly pleased with his presence, Eithan decided that the guys would buy lunch while the girls found seats. The girls agreed, handing over their orders before heading to the cafeteria.

Meanwhile, Orsha and her crew sat watching, their expressions dark with jealousy. Orsha, the self-proclaimed queen of the school—thanks to her father being the dean—couldn't stand seeing Wendy getting Eithan's attention. To add to this, there was another reason why she hated Wendy. The first time Orsha saw Wendy was on the second day of school. She already had a thing for Wally, not that he noticed the other girls, but his sister. He was an exemplary example of what the Japanese would call a Siscon.

That morning, like every morning after, Wendy walked the hall like she owned it. Hair perfect. Smile effortlessly, and the boys turned their heads.

Orsha wasn't impressed until fate humiliated her. In that moment, a boy carrying his drink bumped into her while staring at Wendy. Water splashed her chest, and this added to her annoyance. What took the cake was when she turned to leave, she slipped and fell on her behind, books flying, skirt soaked.

The worst part? Someone recorded it, and it spread throughout the school like wildfire. Someone added gasoline to the flame with a ridiculous video title, 'The girl who wet her skin in the Hall.' It was utter humiliation for a senior to be disgraced by a junior like that. Since that day, she has blamed Wendy.

"If I ever get a chance, I'll make her pay."

Present Day:

While Wendy and Afeisha were sitting and chatting at their table, Orsha and her clique strutted over. Without warning, she walked up to Wendy and poured a glass of water over her head.

The water felt like ice, hugging her skin like shame. But what stung her was not the ice, but the silence. Every eye on her, every smirk from Orsha, every second stretched like punishment. A lump began to build up in her throat, but she swallowed it down, flexing her fingers to remain calm. She wouldn't break—not here, and certainly not in front of them.

She couldn't believe what was happening, as water dripped from her face to the floor. This was the first time that something like this had ever happened to her, but she was not about to back down.

She flinched then stood slowly, eyes burning with defiance. After shaking the excess water off her clothes, she did not ask any questions. Instead, she raised her hand and struck Orsha hard across the left cheek. It echoed throughout the cafeteria, and gasps rippled through the room. Without missing a beat, Wendy went to a nearby table where someone was eating.

"Sorry in advance," she muttered.

Wendy took the student's lunch—who was later identified as Brooks— along with a bottle of grape juice and poured it all over Orsha's head, taking her pound of flesh.

Beholding the scene, Eithan and Michael rushed towards the girls, drawn by the commotion. As they got near, Orsha stood motionless, clenching her cheek with a pained expression. She was utterly humiliated.

Afeisha, who was standing beside Wendy, flashed a proud

smile.

"You go, girl. I always knew you were a bit sheltered, but I never knew that you had that kind of fire in you."

Afeisha's words caused Wendy's mind to drift to something that her mother had once said around the dinner table: "Survival is for the fittest." That day, she decided that she would not be prey for anyone.

"Why did you slap her?" Michael asked, his tone laced with curiosity.

Meanwhile, Orsha—ever the actress—played the victim, batting her lashes as she swooned dramatically in front of Eithan. That was a grave mistake.

Eithan did not spare her a glance. Instead, he sidestepped her completely. But Orsha wasn't one to give up easily. Well known for her relentlessness, she quickly picked herself off the floor and tried again, this time attempting to seek refuge in his arms.

Eithan's patience snapped. With a swift yet firm push, he put distance between them. He didn't say a word, his cold dismissal making it clear that Orsha's antics were beneath him. Yet she continued embarrassing herself, desperately trying to get his attention.

Wendy turned to Michael and exhaled sharply. "Do I really need to explain why I slapped her? You know that I would not do anything without cause."

Michael studied her carefully. He could see it: a lioness, barely restraining her fury. He sighed. "I'm sorry, Wendy. I know you wouldn't. I guess I've just been feeling a little irritated today."

Wendy raised her eyebrow. She saw that he was sorry, but what does his irritation have to do with this? She was puzzled. Afeisha, however, gave Michael a knowing glance and smirked. She knew exactly why he was so irritated.

Orsha, who had made a mockery of herself, refused to back down. She scoffed and crossed her arms. "Wendy, aren't you behaving too arrogant lately? You're not even a senior, yet you always seem to have guys swarming around you. First, it was Wally. Then Michael. And now, Eithan. What tricks are you playing?"

Wendy smirked. "Aren't you the one playing tricks here, my dear senior?" Her voice was dripping with sarcasm. "You act vulnerable when you're anything but. As for the guys, they're just my friends, nothing more." Her eyes flicked towards Eithan for the briefest moment.

Orsha's face twisted in frustration before she spun on her heels and ran off.

Meanwhile, Michael, who was silently observing the exchange, clenched his fist. His expression darkened. "I have lost my appetite," he muttered while walking away.

Wendy rubbed her temples. "Today was going so well until she ruined everything."

Just as Wendy tried to shake off the bad luck, the lunch hour was interrupted by an announcement over the school's sound system.

"Wendy Granchest, please report to the dean's office. I repeat, Wendy Granchest, please report to the dean's office."

The words rang out throughout the school, sending a shiver down her back. She wondered if the mess that had just occurred had already reached the dean's ears. As she made her way to the office, she noticed two police officers stepping out after what seemed like a long discussion.

The dean adjusted his glasses as she entered. "Ms. Granchest," he began, his tone unusually serious. "The police officers wanted to speak with you about the disappearance of one Ms. Sheila Andrews."

A cold chill ran through Wendy's veins. Her palms turned clammy, and a bitter taste settled on her tongue. Swallowing hard, she said, "Officers, how can I help you?"

One of the officers stepped forward, gazing at her intently, searching for anything that might give him a clue as to what she might know or was hiding.

"We have been informed that you were the last person seen with Ms. Andrews yesterday before her disappearance. We're not accusing you of anything, nor am I trying to intimidate you. However, we need to understand what happened and where to look. Her parents are worried sick and have been looking for her ever since her disappearance. They said she stormed off, claiming that she was going to spend some time with her friend at your place."

Hearing this, Wendy's heartbeat quickened, but her expression remained composed. "I am sorry, sir," she said carefully. "Sheila never made it to my house. Both of us were walking to my house, and suddenly Sheila disappeared. I assumed she went home, but I guess she didn't."

Wendy knew this wasn't the truth, but it wasn't a lie, either. Sheila Andrews did not make it to her house. With this, all taste had left her mouth.

The officer studied her closely before nodding. "Thank you very much for your efforts. And if you remember anything—I mean anything—be sure to inform us. The officer repeated the last part with emphasis, as if her response didn't entirely convince him. Wendy nodded slowly with a heavy heart, signifying she understood.

During this time, Eithan had been listening to the conversation from the stairs. Furthermore, as soon as the news travelled around about what happened during lunch, he quickly made his way over to the dean's office, abandoning basketball game plans. Wendy was heading back to her class when she heard the footsteps of someone racing towards her, like a herd of donkeys. There was only one person who behaved like that when it came to her well-being. As the person started to visibly appear, she could make out a familiar figure. Sure enough, she was right. It was Wally.

"Wally, why are you here?"

"I heard about all the things that happened today. I am sorry that I couldn't protect you."

"It is all right, brother. I am no longer a sheltered kid. All these things that have been happening lately have opened my eyes."

"So, did you see Sheila's body after the incident?" asked Wally.

"No," replied Wendy with a grim look on her face. "The body

completely disappeared. I just hope that things get better."

Wally swiftly changed the subject. "I noticed that you have changed lately. I can't exactly put my finger on it. But you look stronger, fiercer, and even prettier. It's quite a good change."

She was uplifted by what her brother said. He always had a way of changing her moods.

"This afternoon is physical education. I am looking forward to seeing if you've become athletic, too, as you were so bad at it."

"Brother!" she exclaimed while pouting. "Do not underestimate me. I may look like this, but I can run just as fast— no, even faster than people my own age. Look out because this time, here I come. I am bringing home a medal." She said all this while remembering her first time meeting Eithan.

"I guess this time you will." Wally gently patted her head and smiled. "I like your change. It's a good thing you're this optimistic."

Wendy laughed. "I have the skills to back it up."

"Well, we will see," Wally replied, heading off in the opposite direction.

It was finally time for the afternoon classes. For Wendy, that happened to be physical education. Her brother, Wally, had gathered up a lot of people for this very class. They were betting on who would win the races. A lot of girls bet on Eithan. Many people, including Wally's friends, had all placed their bets on Johnny for boys and Alliah for girls, seeing that they were the fastest of their year. However, because Wendy was optimistic, he decided to place his bets on his one and only sister, although his friends thought otherwise.

The races had now begun. For the one hundred meters, Wendy took first place. For the two hundred meters, Wendy again took first place. For basketball, netball, and gymnastics, Wendy took it all. Her brother was shocked, even more so than the teachers. His tongue almost fell from his mouth.

Everyone watching could not believe their eyes.

"What did Wendy do to become that strong?" said Orsha, who seemed to be unable to leave Wendy alone.

"She took steroids," replied one of the members of her clique.

One of the teachers became suspicious and asked Wendy the exact same questions. Everyone thought the same, that a girl who was not even good at sports became a pro in one day, making and breaking records.

Wally, who had earned everyone's money, defended his sister with an angry tone. "Do not talk such nonsense! It's unthinkable, for my sister will never do such a thing."

After Wally became angry, everyone turned to Orsha and her clique, accusing them of defaming Wendy's character. However, one of the teachers defended them by saying it's understandable why they would think that way, that they just weren't being tactful. The students dropped the subject once the dean's lackey spoke up.

Eithan also won every match, which made Wendy even more attracted to him. As usual, Michael saw their gazes at each other and felt quite down about himself. After all, a broken heart is not easily mended. Everyone who participated in the races had lost to Wendy and Eithan. They acknowledged them as the fastest within their year, but sadly, not everyone agreed.

Minutes after basking in their glory, coming into the school's compound, walking in style, and looking more beautiful than ever was Miss Perfect.

"What are you doing here?" Shouted Afeisha.

"Wendy, miss me?" she cooed with a sweet yet venom-laced smile, while spitefully ignoring Afeisha. For some reason, her voice carried an unexpected bitterness that clashed sharply with her saccharine tone. It was an unsettling contrast that unnerved Wendy, who was still reeling from the horrors of the night before. She could hardly believe that Sheila was standing in front of her unharmed, as if nothing had happened. The sight made her tremble not just from fear, but from a deep aching dread that twisted in her gut like a knife.

"Just when the day was about to get better," Wendy whispered. She mustered the courage that had run away from her. "Wha–what are you do– doing here, Sheila?" Wendy stammered, her voice still faltering before she forced herself to reclaim the confidence that almost slipped through her fingers.

"What do you mean?" Sheila replied. "Is this not my school?"

"Yes," said Wendy, as she remained composed. "It's just that people were out looking for you. If you are fine, you should inform the authorities."

Sheila walked off, still remembering to throw a kiss at Wally, who knocked her kiss away with a scornful face. Under his breath, he muttered to himself. "As beautiful as she may be, that does not change her snake-like personality. She looks more venomous than before."

Wally may have been an idiot at times, or at least he might've seemed like one, but he has always had good judgment when it came to a person's character and could see through the act.

Afeisha walked up to Wendy, waving her fingers up and down in a curious gesture. "Since when are you so close to Sheila?"

"I am not," she replied quickly. "It's just that… an incident had happened, and I'm surprised to see her."

Wendy's heart churned with mixed emotions. She was relieved that Sheila was alive. On the other hand, she was still frightened—terrified that maybe she was talking to a ghost. Silly Wendy, she caught herself. How could it be a ghost when others were seeing her too?

Wendy froze, diving deeper into her thoughts. "Wendy, Wendy!" shouted Afeisha, snapping her back. Suddenly, she replied. "Yes, what is it?"

"Are you okay?" Afeisha was concerned. She didn't like the expression Wendy was making.

"I am."

"All right, I believe you. But you'll tell me about that incident." "I'm sorry, Afeisha, but I can't."

"Alright," Afeisha replied with a sad face, but decided not to press the matter. When it was time, the right time, she knew Wendy would tell her. However, Wally's case was different. After Afeisha had left, Wally grabbed Wendy and asked her what the deal was with Sheila and why she was alive. But Wendy herself had no clue. Everyone who knew the lie was astonished to see her, except Eithan and Wally. Although he was there with Wendy that night and witnessed all that happened, there were only two possibilities: that she was dead, or she had become one of them. Since this happens to be the town of George, nothing is impossible.

To make matters even worse, tonight was a full crimson moon. During this moon, one's sanity is completely lost. And Sheila is new to this whole thing. Her craving for blood will be at its peak, unknowingly taken without knowing the rules of one's own nature.

After class, Eithan met up with Wendy and her friends. Wally had desperately told Wendy to come home earlier than usual, seeing that she lived pretty far away. His dad had instructed that no matter what happens, Wendy is to be home early. Although she said yes, she went out to the cafe in town with her friends. There was a lot of tension in the air between Eithan and Michael, but that was not about to stop them from having an enjoyable time. At the cafe, Afeisha was persistent in subduing Wendy to find out what happened to her and Sheila, but she constantly changed the topic.

"Can we talk about something else, like what he is doing here?" Michael said as he glared at Eithan, but Eithan paid him no mind.

"Finally, you break the silence," Eithan teased with a smirk. This made Michael feel like Eithan had some ~~sort of~~ superiority, and he was furious.

"Let us order!" said Wendy. They ordered, ordered, talked, and talked. Suddenly, Eithan remembered that the full crimson moon was tonight and reminded her of what her brother had told her.

"Oh!" said Wendy. "Thanks, Eithan. I am sorry, guys, I must go." "So early?" replied Michael.

"Yes, it was not only my brother but my father as well who wanted me to return early, and I have an unbelievably bad feeling, so I think that both of you need to go home as well."

"Okay," replied Afeisha, "I will listen because every time you have a bad feeling, something really does happen."

Eithan then bursts in. "I will walk home, Wendy, seeing that my house is in the same direction. You can follow Afeisha home. We cannot have young, innocent maidens going home by themselves now, can we?"

Michael was reluctant but had to agree. He may not have liked Eithan, but what he said was correct. He had his own share of the moon and knew what could happen. At the same time, he knew that Eithan was taunting him, so he was not about to let him get the upper hand. "No problem. I have something to buy on my way there, so it will be like killing two birds with one stone."

Wendy, not having a clue as to what was happening between the guys, chimed in. "I hope you get through with what you want to buy and make sure Afeisha gets home safely."

"Do not worry, I will," said Michael as he patted her head with his hand.

Eithan felt annoyed, but he did not show it. Afeisha could see what was going on and could not stand what she was watching, so she headed off first while saying goodbye to Wendy and Eithan. Michael quickly followed behind her.

"Hold up, Eithan!" said Wendy, "I never knew that you lived

in this direction. I have never seen any house while walking home before."

"It is because it's on the opposite route of what you take."
"Oh, well, that makes sense."

The two of them were chatting happily on their way home. It was surprising to Eithan to see how far he could fall for a girl he barely knew, but the things he experienced were beginning to make sense. The feeling of liking someone and them liking you back is quite a splendid feeling. He thought not knowing whether she liked him back would leave a bitter taste in his mouth. He continued to be himself. But what is not to enjoy with his super good looks, incredible physique, confidence and great personality, and gentle smile? Although they both were chatting for quite a while, Wendy had no idea what was going through Eithan's head. Meanwhile, Michael, who was following Afeisha to their house, kept silent for quite some time.

Suddenly, Afeisha said, "How long are you going to pretend that you only see Wendy as a friend? I know you love her. Why not tell her?"

Michael looked at her scornfully. "If anyone knows how I feel, it should be you, after all. Don't you feel the same?"

Afeisha held her head down for a minute and stopped talking. Though she was secretly happy to be walking with Michael, that was an insulting thing to say to her, even if he was annoyed. Wait, what? I'm sure Michael just told me I was the same. Does he know I like him? Questions began to overflow Afeisha's mind, leaving her speechless. They walked for hours, but no one said anything. "This is my stop!" she suddenly said to Michael. "Thank you for walking me home."

"No problem," replied Michael as he walked off.

"Hold up!" She cried out. "Didn't you have something to buy along the way?"

"Oh, that! I do not want it anymore."

He apologized for his earlier outburst and then walked off, waving her goodbye. Afeisha smiled, inside she was happy deep down that he had followed her home, but then she remembered that the person he really wanted to accompany home was Wendy. The betrayal clawed at her heart, and with a devilish smile, she masks her pain. He did follow her home, which was enough because she knew he didn't have anything to buy in the first place. Eithan and Wendy, on the other hand, had almost reached home. She realized that walking with Eithan was not only nice, but they covered the ground rather well. Wendy suddenly stopped and asked Eithan if, after the incident, he still ran at night. Eithan paused before answering.

"Yes. It's a routine that I always do, so if I try to stop myself, I'll probably keep doing it unconsciously."

"I wanted to tell you not to go out tonight, but seeing that you will go anyway, I will leave you with a piece of advice. If you go out, do not stop too long outside. I have a feeling that something is about to happen."

"All right," replied Eithan, "I'll take it to heart. Now go inside."

Wendy thanked Eithan for dropping her off, unaware that Eithan had already sensed the weight behind her words. He knows precisely what occurs under the moon. However, the fact that she cared about him enough to offer that little piece of advice moved his heart once again. He smiled as he headed home.

Running through the forest in a panic, the girls were beginning to separate. Although Wendy's leg was in pain, she was running so fast that she was far ahead of Sheila. "Wendy!" Sheila shouted as she gasped for air. "Aren't you running too fast for a girl with an injured leg?"

"It is fear. Now run!" Wendy said. "These creatures are toying with us." Wendy slowed down and grabbed one of Sheila's hands, picking up speed again.

Sheila could feel that she was going so fast that whatever creature was hunting them could not keep up anymore, and neither could her legs. "Let us stop and hide, Wendy. I'm tired." Sheila recognized the limit of a human, holding her chest and gasping for air. It was as if she was about to die, hearing her heart beating like drums in her head. "I cannot keep up any longer."

Wendy agreed with her, but not before alerting her to be extremely quiet. They both hid behind some grass, camouflaging themselves so they wouldn't be seen. However, that didn't work. As Wendy took a second glance at Sheila, she disappeared into nothingness.

Wendy began to panic and ran off, screaming Sheila's name, pushing her aching lungs beyond their capacity. As she flew through the forest, every branch was a threat, every breath a gamble. Sheila wasn't welcome company, but Wendy didn't want *this* to happen to her.

When Sheila disappeared, it was like the air left the forest. Something deadly had entered, but Wendy didn't have the time to pay attention to this. Her voice crackled as she screamed for

Sheila, desperate and raw, but the only voice she heard back was her own. She began to break, her voice trembling.

"Just one... word. Please! Anything! Even a sound would be good.

Sheila! Where are you?"

But silence answered her louder than her scream. Realizing she couldn't find Sheila and was now alone in the forest, her fear turned inward. However, she was overtaken with fleeting relief as her injured foot was now fine. This relief went as quickly as it came.

She continued to look for Sheila. This was one of the worst moments of her life. She was filled with a selfish urge to go home. After all, who invited Sheila to her house? Not her. Who made her late by re-injuring her leg? Not her. Who quarrelled all the way? Not her. Everything she thought about landed Sheila on the blame end. This made her want to be selfish and bold, but her conscience gripped her so tightly that she couldn't bring herself to do it. She spent more time in the forest looking for Sheila, and before she knew it, night had already approached her.

Meanwhile, Eithan and his companions were going into the forest to do their usual runs, but this time was a little different. Each party took on its original form, and its animal instinct was at its peak. They began smelling strange scents and were running towards that smell when he smelled   blood. Ryan, one of the wolves who thought of Eithan as a rival, said, "Don't you smell that? There are not only strange scents, but I think it's about three people." "No, five," replied Eithan. "And I can sense a familiar smell."

At that time, Wendy was still searching through the forest and calling for Sheila, even though she was tired. After clearing the bushes in front of her to make a path to walk, she spotted Sheila.

"Sheila, are you there? I was searching for you. This forest is not safe. We need to get out of here. Sheila, are you listening?" As soon as she came out in the clear to grab Sheila, she saw the three vampires who had blended themselves in the darkness, feasting on her. She grasped both hands over her mouth, eyes wide open. This had to be a dream because what she was seeing wasn't—she was at a loss for words. Suddenly, a vampire who was hidden came up from behind her and bit her neck, drinking all that was left of her. It was as if he was enjoying some delicacy.

Wendy pinched herself, trying to wake up, but her body went numb.

What was she really seeing? Wendy screamed. Her voice travelled in the air and echoed through the entire forest.

"Are you hearing that?" Mandy asked.

"I am hearing it," said Eithan with a displeased face. He re-transformed into a human. He and his pack headed in the direction of the scream. While running, his heart ached. There was something familiar about the sound. Back at the scene, Wendy was so surprised and terrified that she could not even move. The vampires then turned towards her.

The leader of the vampires, Jeremy Boswin, turned to Wendy. "It's you—the girl who smelled tasty. I can't believe I've finally got to meet you. I missed you the other night, but here we are again. Fate is indeed a cruel thing."

The other two vampires then turned towards Wendy and

smelled her; they were quite intoxicated. But to her surprise, even in fear, none of the vampires seemed to want to bite her. Upon smelling her, Jeremy could not contain himself any longer. He moved in to take a huge bite as he smiled with satisfaction, but as soon as he was going to pierce her tender white skin with his fangs, he stopped once more.

"What is up with you, Jeremy?" "This is so unlike you," said another.

"Don't you think I know that? What's up with this chick? How come every time I try to bite her, I suddenly feel like I am doing something wrong?" Turning to his friends, he said, "Hold her down." He watched and observed her carefully, thinking about what the problem could be. Then, it finally hit him. "We vampires have an unspoken rule that we must abide by no matter what, and that's killing our own without a cause, which includes biting as well. This is to prevent our kind from becoming extinct, seeing that we are few. But you, I cannot believe it. It is indeed rare, but I've found something amazing myself. In any case, I'll just take a nibble to see how it tastes." Wendy couldn't believe it. She was listening to a lecture, a vampire lecture, before meeting her demise. "Is there a better way to go down?"

After saying all this, Jeremy geared up with excitement to take a chunk of Wendy's flesh, even though he said it was just a nibble.

All the reasons had flown out the window. Just as he was about to bite, Eithan and his pack arrived and intervened. He pushed Jeremy off, and the pack of wolves dealt with the other two. After separating Jeremy from Wendy, all of Eithan's thoughts were cast upon Wendy. Furthermore, Jeremy had already made a run for it, so it was no use chasing him.

"Are you all right, Wendy?" he asked with a grim look on his face. What would have happened if he had reached her too late? He didn't want to know.

Wendy replied with a shaking voice. "I am all right, but Sheila isn't," as she cried.

"I am sorry," replied Eithan. "I did not get here fast enough."

"It is not your fault, Eithan. You told me not to travel so late in the night, and I disobeyed, even causing Sheila to die. She was bitten on the arms, foot, and neck like food, and that scoundrel ran away with her corpse."

"That is enough," Eithan added, fully knowing what would happen to Sheila. "We'll walk you home." All the members of the pack had returned to their human form, and they all followed her home. This made her feel at ease. Mandy, of course, was angry, but what could she have done? After the long walk, they had finally reached their destination: Wendy's house. The lights were on, and you could have seen the figures in the house sitting and waiting as if they were panicking.

"That is a first!" said Eithan. "Why do you say that?" she asked. "Oh, it is nothing."

Wendy rang the bell, and a figure approached the door in a hurry and stepped outside. "Dad!" shouted Wendy. All her nerves and pain washed away as she saw his face, reassuring her that he was home. Now that he was back, she wouldn't have to suffer another night.

Her dad quickly grabbed her and hugged her while feeling relieved. "Where were you?" he asked with a face filled with worry.

"I was coming home after having a long day with my friends, and on my way, something bad happened, but my friends brought me home." She omitted half of the event that took place. "I will introduce you." But when she turned around, she saw no one. "Where are they? They were just here some seconds ago." Wendy turned and looked all around, but they could not be found. This was okay. After all, it had been a long day, and she just wanted to go inside and rest.

"Alright, sweetheart, you've been through enough for one night. Let us have dinner. You're my favorite, not to mention my one and only daughter, and your brother was worried waiting for you." She nodded in agreement. "Let's go inside and have dinner."

Wendy went inside first, but her dad stayed a little while on the porch looking around. He could sense them even though they were hiding in the woods. In one moment, their eyes met, and he stared straight into Eithan's eyes. Then, he went inside. Mr. William called Wally from up in his room because he was pouting about not getting to see his little sis. "Let us all go and have dinner," he said. Everyone gathered in the dining room around the table. Elena had cooked a scrumptious dinner and could not wait to please William, or Willy, the pet's name she gave him. That is how she refers to him, but he doesn't like it. They had a hearty discussion when Wally demanded, in an overprotective tone, that Wendy tell him what she was doing out late. Wendy, who sees her brother as someone she can trust and confide in, told everyone the story and made sure to add the pieces of Sheila. Wally never liked Sheila. For some reason, his spirit never quite took to her. He did not know that she was a two-faced and terrible person, but if there was one thing he knew, it was that there is something called karma, and it catches up to those who do bad. Along with that, he gave Wendy a curfew because he heard that this was not the first time such strange things had happened. Elena sat there the whole time, showing little concern about the situation. She wanted the dinner to be splendid and to get her husband's attention but felt that Wendy had taken all the spotlight during the dinner. William looked at her, noticing her quiet and carefree attitude, which she displayed around the table. She looked at William, gazing at her.

Suddenly, Elena spoke. "Sweetheart! I know that you feel sad about Sheila dying and you surviving, but you should know something: survival is for the fittest, and because you survive, that means you were the fittest."

For a minute, Wendy sensed the coldness within her stepmother's words, and Wally could not believe that there wasn't a hint of sympathy for Sheila in his mother's words, nor was there any sympathy for Wendy.

William became upset at such words. "Are you saying that if my daughter had died, then she wasn't strong enough, that she wasn't fit?"

"No, I didn't mean it like that," said Elena.

Wally watched her with a distasteful and disappointed look that made Elena even more upset.

"You all are my family, and I love you. How can I mean such things? Please cut it out before you ruin dinner. Tonight is supposed to be a happy occasion."

"Summer is finally over, and tomorrow is another start of a brand-new semester," said William. Wally and Wendy smiled.

That night, Elena was so angry at Wendy that it did not fade until the morning. Sadly, Wendy was oblivious to what was happening around her.

After Eithan and his pack had gone back to their home that night, Eithan still could not believe that Wendy's father was one of them. That explained why Wendy can run so quickly. But what he did not understand was why he was keeping Wendy in the dark and why he didn't notice Elena's lack of love for Wendy, even though she is her daughter. So many questions filled his mind that he could not even rest properly for the big day tomorrow.

CHAPTER THREE

After going into the house, she met her dad. "Are you alright?" asked Wendy.

"I am fine, honey. You can go to your room now."

"Where is Wally?" He is already in the house, and your mom is in the kitchen preparing food.

"Alright, I am going to head upstairs." Wendy could sense the impatience in her dad's voice, and the house was silent as if everyone but her was preparing for an incoming storm. It was dinner time. Elena called the children and her husband for dinner. They all gathered around the table and ate.

"Dad, are you alright?" Wendy asked once more. "You do not look well."

"I am alright, honey," he said as he watched Elena and him.

"Eat your food, Wendy. And you ask too many questions. He is all right."

Wally watched his dad and then looked at his mom. "I am feeling a little bit weird. I do not know what it is, but I'm feeling like I want to run around and rip—" He paused.

"Ripped what?" "Nothing," said Wally.

"Why is everyone acting all weird tonight?" William couldn't believe what he was hearing. If anyone was acting weird, it was her. How can she not feel anything? Perhaps it's all for the greater good, he thought.

"Mom, I may not have asked you, but you look just as terrible as Dad." "I am fine, it's nothing."

"Please go to your rooms after eating dinner," said William.

When they had finished eating, Wendy and Wally went to their rooms, leaving Elena and William in the kitchen to discuss important matters. "Not only are you feeling it, but Wally is feeling it too," said Elena.

"I am surprised as well. Even more so that he feels it more than Wendy." "What are you talking about that child for? Not only is she not feeling it, but she is completely fine," roared Elena. "I do not know what that child is!" Elena exclaimed.

William tried to hold on to what little sanity he had left. "Do not think I overlook your dislike for my daughter. Let me tell you this: she's my precious daughter, and if you love me, you'd better get good with her."

"What are you saying, Willy?" This added to his fury. She continued, "Of course, I like her. It is just that she looks too much like that despicable woman."

"Be careful!" roared William. "That despicable woman is the woman I loved, and without her, you would not have been here. I honor her wish by taking a second wife since she died during childbirth. Wendy is a miracle created between me and her, and I will not let you sully that."

"Fine," she said in a disgruntled manner, "Calm down."

"I am calm!" he roared, smacking the tables to shambles. William could not contain it any longer.

The moon was just too strong. Suddenly, out of the strange clouds was a big, majestic moon colored red. It enveloped the whole sky, illuminating its surroundings with its color. The moon was so strong that it affected the weakest supernatural being, excluding Wendy, of course, or so they thought. William could not hold out any longer. He turned into a gigantic, fierce, big, hairy wolf and stormed outside the house, knocking the door off its hinges.

"What was that sound?" exclaimed Wendy. As she was about to open the door, she remembered the words of her dad and quickly pulled back her hands from the doorknob. Elena ran outside after William, the love of her life, but could not find him. She beheld just how scary the forest can be for a house so far from society. Immediately, her thoughts ran to Wendy and what she had endured the two nights. Her conscience pricked at her, leaving an intense yet fading pain. Suddenly, her thoughts went back to William for just a second. Lost in her thoughts, she looked up in the sky and beheld the crimson moon, a bloody super moon. She became startled, taking two steps backward, dropping to the ground, and letting out an inviting scream.

She was well informed about supernatural beings, as she was a friend of Wendine, Wendy's mom, and William when they were young and was a part of a unique family. She quickly ran toward the house. That was part of what made her hate towards Wendy grow stronger: they were all different from her. Though she had the skills of an excellent hunter, she was not a supernatural being.

"What was that scream?" Wally shouted as he quickly ran towards the noise. He was so focused on the scream that he did not even notice that he skipped almost every step on the staircase and came outside in a rush. "Mom! Why are you screaming?"

"What are you doing here outside, Wally? I came to look for your father.

Wait!"

"What are you doing here?"

"Go inside now, please! Go inside!" shouted Elena hysterically, "And whatever you do, do not look up at the moon. Go now!"

"Yes, mom." Wally left his mother, who was on the ground in front of the entrance of the forest and headed back towards the house.

There, he saw Wendy making her way out the door, looking at the hinges that had been ripped off along with the missing door. "Wendy! Get back in the house right now!"

"What is up with everyone tonight? And why is the door like that?" "Enough of the questions, Wendy. Just do what I say." Wally's head was becoming a bit fuzzy, and it became hard for him to engage in intelligent speech. He could shout in an effort to keep her safe and unbothered. Elena, who mustered some courage, feet regaining energy, stood up and began walking toward the two. She saw Wally informing his sister to go back inside. Wally's head was becoming more and more distorted, and he could not think anymore. To clear his head, he looked up at the moon, forgetting what his mother had just said. That was a mistake, the breaking point. The last thread of sanity he clung to finally snapped, and the changes began.

He felt his bones breaking, his clothes stretching beyond their limit, straining against the change with immense pain. Then he transformed with a scream. He became like an animal, a beast with raw instincts, but this did not deter him. Surprisingly, if it's one thing Wally could brag about, it was his ability to control himself. He was still fighting whatever urge had taken over. Suddenly, whatever god, man, or self he begged, he re-transformed, but not fully. The pain, oh the pain, was too much, and the moon delighted in every second of it.

Though his body was still human, his mind was that of a ferocious beast because he was only half-wolf. Witnessing the drama Wally displayed, Wendy was shocked. She couldn't find the words to describe the situation. The only thing left for her to do was to grab a bucket of popcorn, put on her best glasses, and watch the show. It had to be one, she thought. But no words escaped her mouth.

Elena got mad seeing Wendy. She walked up to her and grabbed her by her collar. "You did this to my son!" She yelled and cried. "If it weren't for you, my son wouldn't have headed off into the forest." After hearing Elena utter nonsense, Wendy couldn't take it any longer. She had known of Elena's dislike towards her, but not to this extent. This was becoming ridiculous. Something had to be affecting her brain to hold her liable for Wally's situation. But wait, she did have some responsibility. If she had just gone back when he said, he wouldn't have looked at the moon. Then again, what was that transformation? Was that really her fault? Things were becoming more puzzling as her brain worked, so she just stopped thinking.

Elena was still filled with worry and turbulence. "You also

should look at the moon," she said as she gripped the back of Wendy's head with force, turning it up towards the moon. This made Wendy let out a pained sound, but she didn't care. Aggravatingly enough, nothing happened to her, even after staying motionless for ten minutes.

"Oh, I forgot," Elena said sarcastically and with a laugh, as though she had taken drugs. "You're daddy's special princess. It should be you to look for them."

Although the moon did not affect Wendy physically, her instincts were also at their peak. Elena went into the house and forbade Wendy from entering unless her brother and father had returned. She had to enter the forest by will or stay on the porch until the moon displayed its mercy. She then remembered that Eithan takes midnight jogs every night, so she stormed off into the forest, hoping that she would meet Eithan and that they would find them together. Wendy knew that something was up, and she was not about to miss what was about to happen under the blood-red moon.

After running in the forest for hours, she finally found Eithan, or at least it looked like him, but he was not looking too good either.

"Run, Wendy!" Eithan said. "Run as far away from me as possible. Didn't I tell you not to come to the forest tonight?" Eithan's face was wrenched with agony. Usually, he has no trouble changing, but this was different. Something compelled him, and he didn't like it. It was that bloody moon.

"I know that," replied Wendy. "But my father and brother are missing." Wendy failed to grasp the urgency of her situation. Beasts at their peak don't think. They just kill their prey and whatever is lying in front of them, not for food but for sport, and now she was prey to them. Every being in the forest was prey to the strong, and no one was safe. "I had no choice," Wendy said.

"Wendy, I said to run!" roared Eithan in his blended wolf voice. "Before something bad happens."

"Eithan, you are scaring me."

"RUN!

Wendy slipped by Eithan, running into town, running as fast as her legs could carry her. This was the first time that she had ever felt so scared, and this time, it was because of her family and Eithan, or rather, this bloody moon. She stared once more at the moon, hurling curses. After her heart felt better unloading what she was feeling, she took a deep breath, then yelled, "Everything is just because of a big bloody red moon."

Realizing she was now out of the forest and into town, she looked around, beholding something even more frightening. Bodies and more bodies piled up on each other, scattered in all directions and in all positions. "What is going on?" she muttered to herself. The further she went, the more bodies she saw. As if that was not bad enough, the town was lonely because the people who she presumed to be alive had shut themselves in safely so they would not fall victim to whatever this was. She then saw a figure standing over a guy digging into the neck.

"Wait a minute," she said to herself recognizing the figure for who it was. "Isn't that Sheila? Why is she out here?" She was about to shout at her, but the image of her dying came flashing through her mind, and yet now Sheila was doing to a man what was done to her. Her face grew pale as if she and the man had swapped positions, and her blood felt as though it was being drained. Wendy watched, hoping Sheila didn't notice her taking a gander. It looked like she was devouring the man completely, "Is she that hungry? This is no time for that," she said as she held her breath. But Sheila had already noticed her from a distance. After draining the guy completely of all his blood, she said hello to Wendy in a sadistic tone.

"Did you miss me?"

Wendy did not reply. Instead, she whispered a few words, "And this is why they say curiosity killed the cat."

Sheila laughed. After the incident, she now had impeccable senses. She heard every word Wendy said, smelled every smell, and saw her clearly when she exited the forest. "I see you have a sense of humor," she added to Wendy's smart whisper. "Do you want to join me? It's quite delicious."

"No," responded Wendy, "You are crazy. Why are you killing all these innocent people?"

"I killed them because I am hungry. No, that's not quite right. It's fun, but no, that's not it either. I don't know. Yes—that's it. I don't know. This feeling, this urge, I can't control it. And now it's your turn."

Upon hearing this, Wendy ran for shelter anywhere she could, if it meant getting rid of that lunatic.

"Oh, Wendy, where are you hiding?" Sheila taunted her like it was a game of tag. If it was, then Sheila was "it". Wendy continued to hide as Sheila taunted. "You have always been a fast runner. Lucky how one finds out more about a person when they are in danger." Sheila flipped over a vehicle. "I can sniff you out, you know. My sense of smell has increased.

"Oh, then try to find me. If you do, I am all yours." As Sheila was trying to catch her scent and following her snide remarks, she could not grasp anything. She was confused. What was going on? Everyone has a distinct smell, but not you. Something was wrong. Luck seems to always be on Wendy's side.

"Wendy, you win. You can come out now!"

"No," replied Wendy. "Do you think I am stupid?"

Sheila tried to follow Wendy's voice in her direction by constantly taunting her, but she did not know that Wendy had a plan of her own. She had used an instrument to echo her voice across to her while moving. Sheila got angry and suddenly started her mental abuse.

The Truth That's Hidden Behind the Lies

Sheila's screeching laugh echoed through the street like a curse. "Where are you, Daddy's little girl? You know, I've always wanted to rip you to shreds." Her voice was laced with venom.

Not wanting to get caught, Wendy pressed her body tighter against the brick wall, doing all she could to prevent her heart from pounding too loudly.

Sheila continued to tease her. "You're too privileged. You have Wally, the person I love, who's always protecting you. You have Eithan, that hot one, by your side. And you even have Michael. You are quite the vixen, aren't you? Wanting everything and never wanting to share."

Hearing these words, Wendy gripped her chest tightly. What the hell was she protesting about? She decided to give Sheila a taste of her own medicine. "What are you talking about, Sheila? Aren't you Miss Perfect? Perfect little Sheila wants to order everyone around to do her bidding. Why don't you get up off that high horse and clean your mess yourself?" The anger in Wendy was gushing out through her voice. This was not wise.

"When I get my hands on you, I'm going to kill you."

Wendy was hiding behind the cafe that she frequently visited. Before long, Sheila had stopped taunting her. This is my chance, she thought. Her chance to get out of here. As she got up, she looked around one more time and saw no one, so she took the opportunity to go out. As soon as she exited from behind the cafe, she collided with Sheila.

"Found you!" Sheila said. "Did you think that you could escape me?" "I had hoped so," replied Wendy sarcastically.

Sheila, feeling patronized, took her hands and placed them firmly around Wendy's neck, trying to choke the life out of her. Wendy, gasping for breath, took her two hands and started pulling Sheila's hands from around her neck. There was no way she was about to be killed at the hands of Sheila.

Sheila was astonished at such strength, thinking that Wendy was a human. "Even if you managed to be in my clutches, you are still going to die tonight. I just tried to give you the painless way out, and yet you refused."

"Psychotic bitch," Wendy shouted. "You want to kill me because you cannot get your way."

Sheila screeched. "What did you call me?" She hissed her fangs and directed them towards Wendy, but she was caught off guard by the dustbin that was headed her way.

She held her head for a mere three seconds, collecting herself from the blow. But when she looked down, Wendy was already gone. Instead, there was another figure approaching.

"Michael, what are you doing here at this hour?" asked Wendy.

"I was outside buying something when I came across a lot of bizarre things that night. And was that, Sheila?"

It was apparent to her that he was telling lies, trying to evade the subject.

She gave in, "Yes, it was. Why?"

"She looks a little too vicious, don't you think?" he responded.

"Of course, she is," Wendy smirked. "Did you see when she tried to kill me back there?" Michael pretended to be perplexed. Wendy disregarded the conversation, "You need to go home right now. A lot of strange things are happening. I am looking for my brother and father, but I guess I'll head home."

"Are you sure you don't want me to follow you home? Michael asked. "Yes, I am sure," replied Wendy, who didn't want to drag Michael into her situation.

Michael didn't want to leave, but he reluctantly hurried off, and Wendy went on home through the forest. On her way home, a lot of things crossed her mind. What's going on with my dad? Is Wally alright?

Thinking back, she saw that there was a shadow tailing her, but she could not place her finger on it. It was like Michael's build, that is. Wendy then asked herself, was it really Michael stalking me all along? No, it cannot be. She doubted.

Meanwhile, on Michael's way back, he met up with Sheila even though he had taken a different route. Sheila appeared in front of him in a split second as though using a flash step.

"Was it you?" she asked.

"Was it me, what?" Michael replied. He did not appear to be shocked.

Instead, he was calm.

Sheila, on the other hand, was quite irritated. "I am going to ask you for the last time. Was it you who threw that dustbin into my face?"

He was beginning to get irritated. "Good timing," he said. "Yes, it was me. And I was looking for you, too."

Sheila laughed, "I will wipe that smug look off your face." Sheila then bared her fangs at Michael, not realizing that she was inferior to him in many ways. As soon as she closed the gap, leaping toward him, Michael, who had always suppressed his aura and killing intent, let loose for the first time. It did not even take an hour, but Sheila was already defeated and, on the ground, gasping for air as her chest went up and down, trying to steady itself. Michael was going to terminate her, but then he laughed and looked at her as if he were a madman. "I am going to spare your life," he said. "But only because you're a necessary piece in this chess game. I can't have you dying too early now, can I?"

Sheila began to shake with fear. "Why are you pretending to be what you are not? Why are you hanging around that Vixen? You will never be with her, you know?"

Michael walked up to her, holding back his urge to shatter her face. Instead, he grabbed her mouth, tilting her head upward towards him. "Watch what you say," he demanded. "I am just enjoying myself. Besides, what do you know? I love Wendy, but my love is different from that of her brothers and that nut job who calls himself Eithan."

Sheila looked at his expression. He really had lost it. "There is nothing I don't know, so don't get in the way," he added. Michael then walked off toward home, and his eyes began to turn red.

Eithan, who was running to the forest with no care in the world, saw something ferocious. In fact, this was the first time in his life that he was so scared. What he witnessed had him at a loss for words.

There it was: a big, black, ferocious demon wolf. Its eyes were dark red, and yet they were the same color as the moonlight surrounding it. Its sanity was stolen entirely. Out of fear, Eithan quickly ran, but the demon wolf was right behind him. It saw him and wasn't about to give up. It was today that Eithan had met his match. No, he met someone, something even stronger, scarier than him. At the same time, there was something vaguely familiar about it. Who was he kidding? There was no time to get familiar. He had to go. The demon wolf, he chose to call it, was just too fast for him. Even though Eithan usually ran at night, and he knew the forest like the back of his hand, the only thing left to do was outsmart this wolf since he couldn't outrun it. Upon running, he realized that it was not only him who had knowledge of the forest routes but the demon wolf, too. In fact, more than him. He quickly hid behind a tree, waiting for the moment to escape. It was as if the demon wolf could not differentiate between wolves and vampires, friends, or foes. He hid their patiently until it was gone. Suddenly, he heard footsteps, and they were getting closer.

With his guard up, he watched and waited as the footsteps came closer and closer, and what he saw was indeed trifling. It was none other than Wally. After reverting to his original form, he whispered, "Wally? What are you doing in the forest? Don't you know it is dangerous?"

Wally was still in a confused state. It took some time, but eventually, Wally snapped out of it and came back to reality. The power of the moon was fading. Wally then looked at Eithan. "I should be asking you that. What are you doing here?"

Eithan was bewildered. This wasn't a time for conversation. Nevertheless, he replied, "I am on my usual run, and you—you should not be out here. It is also too dangerous for you."

"Yeah, I hear you." Wally didn't have time to argue with Eithan. There were more important things to do. Then suddenly, Eithan grabbed Wally, and they both hid. "What are you doing?" asked Wally.

"Hush," he said. "Just watch."

After listening to what Eithan had said, he yielded. Minutes later, he saw a huge beast, a frightening one. This was also the first time that he had witnessed such a creature that defies logic.

"This cannot be right," he whispered, "I hope that my—" he stopped. As soon as he said that, the beast heard and went in the direction they had hidden, but fortunately, they had already moved. Eithan and Wally silently sighed. We're lucky. An encounter like that can only mean the reaping of one's life.

At the same time, a gang of undutiful and thirsty vampires were swooping by when they beheld the creature. The leader of that crew was knowledgeable but not too informed to know when to run. They surrounded the monster and began to attack it. Unfortunately, while they were striding swiftly through the forest, the demon wolf was the only creature that they had seen. There was a scarcity of animals. Wally looked at Eithan, "This is our chance, so let us run."

Puzzled, Eithan thought that it was weird for Wally not to say anything about the vampires, but in the end, he ruled it out as fear taking over and clouding his judgment. Wally couldn't believe— not in his wildest dreams— that Wendy was in the forest. He didn't expect his mother to be that cruel. Both boys left the vampires with the demon wolf and headed towards Wally's house. On their way, they met Wendy. In a fit of rage mixed with fear, Wally said, "Haven't I told you that you should stay inside the house? Why are you here? Never mind, you will tell me when we get out of this forest."

The three of them began running again. Immediately, Wally grabbed Wendy, who tried to grab Eithan but missed his shirt. They hid behind a huge tree once again.

"It seems like the vampires are not enough to hold him off," whispered Eithan.

"Let go of my hand. You are squeezing me too tightly," Wendy said in a soft and serene voice as she leaned toward Wally.

"I am sorry, Wendy, but whatever you do, don't look." Wally had forgotten the nature of a human, that whenever you say not to do something, it makes them want to do it even more. Wendy looked at the creature and gasped loudly as if she needed air.

"Wha—what was that? That thing." She went white. Someone—no, something was draining her of her energy. It's not like she didn't have an inkling of what was happening. After all, she had witnessed Sheila and even Wally, but this was too much. Water began to flow from her eyes as her senses screamed danger. She thought that the thing, the demon, could massacre them all, and yet she felt this familiarity. The mixed feelings she felt toward the beast were more confusing.

"Stop crying," whispered Wally, "We will be alright." He knew just how she felt, but now wasn't the time.

As Wendy tried to stop her tears, Eithan stared at her. Something was gripping him. He understood the situation, but there was nothing he could do. With a frustrated look, he said, "It seems you shouldn't have looked." But she didn't hear. The demon wolf, who had quite a strong nose, smelled fear, not from Wally but with the keen sense that came from Wendy. He quickly headed in that direction. Eithan, who had sensed it, shouted and ran. The three of them ran toward the exit of the forest with everything they had, but the wolf was just too fast. Each headed horizontally in the direction that led to the exit of the forest. On each end were Eithan and Wally, and in the middle was Wendy. No one held hands because they believed that they would all escape the forest faster, on time, and unscathed. With the trio, hope was shining brightly, and the exit was even more exciting. They could all see the light. However, whose idea was it that the demon wolf could not exit the forest? After all, it was a crimson moon.

The demon wolf stopped, clenched its teeth, and breathed in the scent of the forest. Something was tickling at its nose, and it immediately began heading toward Eithan, but luckily for him, the exit was just up ahead. Wally and Wendy made it out fine, but huge claw marks were left on Eithan's back. The wolf had caught up to him. Nevertheless, they all made it out safely.

"Are you all okay? Is everyone safe?" asked Wendy. "Yes," said Wally, but Eithan stayed quiet.

They all investigated the forest to see if the demon wolf was still present. After scanning left and right, there it was, the pair of red eyes staring at them from the darkness. It was something to behold.

"Guys," said Wendy. "Can the demon wolf exit the forest?"

Both Wally and Eithan stared at her. They were shocked. This frightening yet straightforward question didn't even cross their minds.

However, before they had any time to think, it disappeared. Their calm returned, and their breaths steadied as their chest went up and down. As Eithan's breathing normalized, he started feeling a slight pain in his back. He knew the wolf struck him, but escaping was his first priority, and now, healing became the present. However, the pain in his back remained, and he found that he was not healing. His leg gave out due to the built-up tension he had with the added pain, and then he fell on the floor. Wally and Wendy had to take him to their house. On the other hand, outside was still as bright as day. The unusual red moon that enveloped the sky was beginning to   lose its color. As more and more time passed, the color faded bit by bit as it moved across the sky. It looked as though it was taking a stroll. It changed from a crimson moon to a normal full moon, which started to hide once more behind a grey, punchy cloud.

CHAPTER FOUR

After all that had happened and the return of the full moon, William woke up inside the forest. "What am I doing here? And naked at that?" He could not remember what had taken place some hours ago. He was perplexed. With nothing to do, his best option was to go home, and he went home as quickly as he could. While approaching the steps, he saw that the door was missing from its hinges. "This can't be safe." He stopped and glared at the doorless entrance, then toward the yard where bits and pieces of the remaining door lay. Rubbing his head, he went inside speechless and still had no idea of what was going on. He found his wife and two children, as well as a male figure who looked like he was in pain, all in one room. This was even more puzzling.

"Honey, you are back!" Elena squealed, happy to see William unhurt. "I am," said William, wondering why the sun had landed on her face in such a gloomy atmosphere. "What happened?" His voice was a bit hazy.

"Dad!" Wendy exclaimed with joy. "Where were you? You all gave me a shock last night. Dad!" she said once again, "Thank God you are home." Wendy failed to mention what Elena had done to her.

"Honey, go and put on some clothes, and then we'll talk." Luckily for William, he was still in his expandable underdrawers.

William heeded and went into his bedroom. He hurriedly gathered any piece of clothing his hands had landed on, put them on, and started back at Wendy's room.

There, he saw a male on the bed lying on his stomach, along with five deep scars placed diagonally across his back. On closer inspection, they were claw marks. Claw marks that had taken up his entire back. "Who is this boy?" asked William.

"He is my classmate and friend. He saved us when we were in the forest." "The forest?"

"Yes, Dad, the forest," Wendy retorted.

Elena cut in. "This was the same young man who had brought her home that night."

"Oh, well, we must save him," William said, but Wendy's remark did not leave his mind. If the forest was that dangerous, what were they doing outside the house? Where's the door? As more and more questions emerged, he turned his gaze to Wendy. "Come to think of it, what were you doing in the forest, Wendy? Didn't I tell you to go and stay in your room?" His head and memory were becoming clear.

"Now's not the time to talk about this, William," said Elena. "I would like to know as well," said Wally.

"I was going back inside when Mom told me that I could not return unless I found you two," Wendy answered. She had no intention of mincing words. After all, she almost died. Not once, not even twice, but three times. Thank God for her luck. It was evident that Elena only treated her well when her dad was around.

Wendy continued. "She blamed me for Wally's sudden

disappearance, and I found out that I was not her daughter last night." Wendy exaggerated. Though she was right, this wasn't news to her. She had known for a long time that she wasn't Elena's daughter. It was evident in the way Elena and her relatives treated her. Wendy continued with tears in her eyes and began recalling the events that had happened during the crimson night.

"I could have died," she blurted out, her voice cracking as the words tore from her lips."

The room went silent as her eyes shimmered with tears, her shoulders trembling. This was too much.

Wendy's gaze locked with Elena's. "Sometimes I feel like you just tolerate me because you have no choice," she said, in fury.

Elena stood up, frozen at her words, which hit like daggers. William glared a deathly stare at Elena with extreme anger. He could have snuffed the life out of her that very second. That was the angriest he had ever been with her. "Elena," he called to her in a furious tone, "I cannot believe you would do such a thing. So, you want to kill my daughter, eh? Answer me!" he roared.

Elena jumped to attention when William shouted at her. She was afraid. This filled her with even more hatred towards Wendy. Right now, she had reached her breaking point. Tears flowed down both her cheeks. "Yes! I did all that. What is the problem?" she said with confidence. "Isn't it the truth? I told her the truth so you people would stop lying to her."

Before fury overtook him and he accidentally snapped her neck, William sent her out of the room, but she refused to step outside. He then asked Wally to accompany her, telling her that he would deal with her later. His children were present, and he didn't want to do something he would regret—not in front of his children, especially Wally. William regained his composure and turned towards Eithan's back. When he saw his back, he could not believe it. What vicious animal could have done this to a child? For some reason, he felt sorrowful yet guilty. As he traced his five fingers over the scars, being careful not to touch his skin, he sensed that Eithan was the same kind of creature he was. He had to save him. William reminded himself of this because Eithan had spared his daughter and brought her home. Who knows what else? William had decided to help him. He stared at his back once more and traced the marking on his back with his hand again. It was a perfect match.

His head began remembering, and vague pictures of him began resurfacing in the forefront of his brain. He could not remember anything, but he knew one thing was definite. "He had caused Eithan's injury. He was the reason for Eithan's pain- and suddenly, everything made even more perfect sense. William is a powerful Alpha, and for him to fully transform and do something like that, it would be hard for any Alpha like Eithan to heal. What he still could not figure out was what triggered his transformation. It was like I was forced into changing against my will. All these things went through his head, and the only conclusion had to be the unusual full moon. After regaining sanity, he felt like crap. Like he was just dropped from being the main character of a movie to some helpless beggar on the street. William made sure Wendy left the room. Now, it was only him and Eithan. William took out his claws and sank them into Eithan's back. His intention was to give him the same amount of pain, informing Eithan to use the pain to heal himself. Eithan cried until he heard a wolf cry and then passed out.

William came out of the room. "He will be fine. Let him rest." Frankly, William was tired. It had been a long day. He had no intention of fixing the door. Instead, he covered the entrance with a cupboard, its back facing outside and the valuables inside. William headed toward his bedroom. He was too tired to deal with Elena that very night, but he did.

Days passed by, and Eithan was getting better. Wendy had given him her room. Every day after school, she would rush home to see him and take care of him. Through all those days, a bond had developed between them, and they were more intimate than before.

Three days after the full moon, on Thursday, Eithan was still at Wendy's place healing. His friends and parents were worried about him, but because of the trust they had in him, they allowed it for a few more days. His friends were the ones who delivered the news to his family. A lot of things had happened. The only three people inside the house were Wally, Wendy, and Eithan. William had to go on a business trip, and he could not postpone it because he had to meet up with some extremely important people, and this time Elena had to tag along. She had been pushing it off just so that she would not have to meet her family members. Her family had been a generation of renowned supernatural hunters for years, and because she had fallen in love with one of the very beings they had sworn to destroy, a wolf, it was hard for her to keep up with them, causing her family bond to slip. Nevertheless, her dad had grown fond of William at the time, and they had established a treaty called the Billsman Treaty.

This treaty states that they do not hunt unless it's necessary. Once an unnatural course is causing a disturbance to society, it becomes a necessity, hence the first visit.

81

After they both went on the trip, William felt guilty leaving his children, especially Eithan, knowing that the cause of the problem was him. Wally and Elena headed off to school, leaving Eithan in the room. His wounds were almost healed.

Mandy and Jason were scouting the forest, looking for Eithan, but he was nowhere to be found.

"We should go and search that girl's house. He might be there, you know?" said Mandy.

"Who, girl? Are you talking about Wendy?" he retorted.

"Yes, her, I am guessing he's there. After all, that moon didn't only affect us, you know. A lot of strange things have been happening lately." For once, Mandy was making sense.

"Well, I guess we should," replied Jason.

They both headed towards the house and caught the scent of Eithan. "I told you so," said Mandy.

"I heard you," replied Jason with an annoyed expression. "Can we go now?" He started walking in front of her. She was lagging. After coming across the house, both went up towards the new front door. Jason, who happens to be qualified to pick up any lock, unlocked the door and headed inside. As he looked around, careful not to make any sound, he said, "This house is beautiful but strange."

"Tell me about it," Mandy agreed.

"What are all these strange things?" asked Wendy rhetorically. She wasn't hoping for any answer. Just filled with amazement.

"Forget about the things, and let us go search for Eithan," said Jason. While searching, Jason and Mandy came across a hidden door, but there was no way to access it. There were no locks. Mandy concluded that it was part of the house's interior to give some illusion, but Jason didn't believe it. As Jason stepped forward, he accidentally tripped on something and grasped a statue of a gargoyle for balance. This triggered a door to open, revealing a room filled with chemicals and various unknown substances.

"Look at that," said Mandy. "I guess you can pick any lock." She smirked, but Jason only grounds his teeth.

"Is there a scientist living in this house?" Jason became curious, but Mandy just wanted to find Eithan and leave. Looking at Mandy, Jason placed the statue back in its original position and headed straight to Wendy's room, where they saw Eithan lying on the bed.

"Are you alright?" asked Mandy as she rushed towards him to hold him. "I am all right," he said. "I will be going home in three days' time."

Eithan was trying to sit up from his lying position to communicate better.

"You do not have to push yourself," said Jason. "Your mom has already written you a leave of absence from the school, and the pack misses your presence."

Eithan laughed. "By the pack, you mean you, right?" Jason smiled. "What happened? And why are you here?''

"It is a long story," Eithan replied. "But I want you to know that I am fine." After telling them all that transpired during the

83

crimson moon, they could not believe it. But seeing the faded claw marks on Eithan's skin had given them confirmation. Mandy was unhappy that she was not there during all that happened, but she was even more jealous that it was Wendy who was nursing him back to health.

"Alright, Eithan is staying. We will tell your mom everything that has taken place. Do you know any scientists living in this house?" Jason couldn't help but ask.

"No. Why do you ask?"

"Nothing. Please remember to be careful." Both Mandy and Jason headed off, leaving Eithan alone in the Granchest manor.

Back at school, Jeremy had transferred in. He was positioned in the class opposite Wendy, and she noticed that the school had started to grow weird. It was becoming a breeding ground for the unknown. Wally told Wendy earlier that he did not want to leave her home by herself, but he had somewhere to be and would be arriving home late. Hearing this, she was filled with excitement, but she tried not to show it. Finally, she would get some privacy. For once, her overprotective brother had given her some space to be with Eithan, the one she had fallen in love with.

After the school day was over, Wendy rushed out to go home. She saw Jeremy from a distance but pretended not to notice. For the first time, everything was going her way. She had a wonderful day at school without encountering troublemakers like Sheila. Her brother was coming home late, and her pathway home was clear of obstacles. Not to mention Eithan, who was at her home waiting for her return. He wasn't waiting on her, just recovering, which made it all the better. There he was, in her house, in her bed. Well, technically, not hers, but that hardly matters.

When she arrived home, she saw that the front door was open but paid no mind. Her thoughts were filled with Eithan and only him. She hurried through the door and up the stairs. She went into her room to check up on Eithan and saw him sitting on the bed, staring out of the window. She stood there for a while, gazing at how beautiful he was. It was like looking at a painting.

Breaking the silence, "Are you alright?" she said.

This made Eithan turn around slowly. "Yes, I am all right," he smiled gently. His wounds had healed to perfection, and thus, his wolf abilities were back to a hundred.

"I will prepare something for you to eat." She was busy scrambling for words, yet repeatedly uttered, "My brother will be coming home late, so tell me what you want, and I'll make it."

Eithan did not know what he wanted to eat. He just gazed upon her. Her heart was beating fast, and she gasped at every word he said. Eithan knew, after all, that she was thinking of him. He picked up her scent, heard her footsteps and her beating heart as soon as she was in range.

"I'll eat anything you make. This will be the first time tasting your cooking," he said while scratching his head.

"All right," she said with an embarrassed smile. Wendy went into the kitchen to fix dinner and placed it on a timer. She then went up into the room and tried to hold his interest by improvising a conversation on what had happened during his absence from school.

"Tell me all that happened today at school," Eithan vocalized. She told him that Jeremy, the vampire that he had met in the woods, had transferred to the opposite classroom and that the teacher was asking about him. Eithan smiled as Wendy's expression when delivering the events was quite ecstatic. They continued to speak more and more, and the conversation grew from classroom events to intimacy. This gave Wendy the courage to ask the question about which surety was needed.

She bit her lip. "Eithan, is there a girl you like? I mean, someone who is special to you?" Eithan paused and looked at her passionately. This was an unexpected question from her. He never saw her as the straightforward type or as one who would broach sensitive topics first, knowing its impact on her.

He waved it away, instead asking, "Is there a boy or someone that you like?"

Her cheeks flushed, and her face lit up. "I asked you first," she retorted. He gazed upon her, her face flushed with contentment, but he didn't utter a word. She felt a little down with the silence, and Eithan saw it. He chuckled, placing his hand to his mouth.

"The girl I like is you," he said. "You are the girl who stole my heart in a matter of minutes. There is no other girl but you."

Her eyelids fluttered. The words she so desperately wanted to hear. The simple, soft yet earth-shattering words wrapped around her like the warmth after the storm. It was as if her heart was freezing in the cold, and just a few words melted the ice, changing the season from winter to summer.

Her lips parted to respond, but no words came. All she could do was stare at him, praying that he didn't see how much those words rattled her.

While towering over her, he repeated, "Who is the guy that

you like?" He knew she liked him, but like her, he needed words to be sure.

She shied away at first, taking some time to regain her composure before responding.

"You are the guy I like. I've liked you for a good while now."

Eithan was pleased with her response. He started to think that being clawed in the back was a good thing. They both stared into each other's eyes, which were filled with passion and vigour. The room was getting hot; her cheeks were flushed, and her body tingled. She tried to unearth the words buried deep within, but it was proving too hard to breathe, and she couldn't. Instead, Eithan spoke.

"Are you feeling that?" He placed his hands on her chin and tilted her head upwards towards him. "I know I'm feeling it," he said. The room became tense. The edges of her mouth tilted upwards, and she smiled. It was too hard to speak, and the heat from Eithan's hand travelled through her skin. He pulled her closer to him, leaning her slender body against the length of his. This made the heat even more invigorating. He opened her mouth, and they began to kiss passionately. It turned fierce as tongues intertwined. Little by little, their sense of reasoning began to slip away, and their hormones got in the way of all rationality. Eithan had never kissed, but the feeling was too great. Every kiss sent a shudder through him.

This made his wolf wake. The things he wanted to do to her, the things he could do to her, teach her, and mark her. She was his and his alone. Eithan's wolf side started to emerge from within. His eyes changed from blue to red, and his claws came out. Things were becoming difficult. His attention was on his claws, and he tried not to sink his claws into her smooth, soft flesh. Wendy, who was drowned in ecstasy while deepening the kiss, did not notice the change that Eithan was taking on. With mustered strength, Eithan quickly pulled away from Wendy and looked away. He retracted his claws, returned his eyes, and let out a huge breath. It was a struggle that he had won.

While Wendy was breathing heavily, Eithan was trying to calm down. Not wasting any time, Wendy started to take off her clothes while staring at Eithan with lust-filled eyes. Eithan was in trouble, his face exposing his lust for her. He groaned and asked Wendy if she was prepared for what was about to take place. They reconnected their lips, this time kissing more intensely and deeply. Eithan placed Wendy on the bed, caressing her thigh and massaging her clothed breast with his other hand while sucking on her bottom lip. Wendy was a moaning mess by then. Not wasting any time, Eithan ripped off his clothes while Wendy admired his toned abs. His body was perfect. Just by seeing his body, Wendy was even wetter.

Eithan, trying to be gentle, reminded himself that it was her first time, their first time, and he needed to make it suitable for them. He moved from her lips to her ears, gently kissing and caressing her breast that he held in his hand. He slowly moved toward her neck. This made her chuckle, as she was a little ticklish in that spot. He then went back to her breasts, one at a time, kissing and suckling. Wendy let out a moan that was lovely to his ears. Yes, she liked it, and he could tell. With every squeeze and suck, she uttered his name in pleasure. Heat filled her body, and she started to feel it below. She knew she needed something but didn't know what it was.

Eithan, whose wolf was intervening, was rock hard.

Anymore, and he would be a goner. He ripped off Wendy's bra that hung below her breasts, along with the rest of her clothing and underwear, leaving her utterly naked. This swift movement caused her to cover herself with her hands and look away in embarrassment. He tilted her head towards him and slowly removed her hands from what he craved to see. He wanted to see her in all her glory. She was beautiful. Her long curly black hair covered her back, and her brown eyes with a hint of green glowed. It was as clear as marbles. She had voluptuous breasts and curves in all the right places, and her skin—God, her skin—was dark, smooth, and soft. She was ripe for picking.

"Do not be shy with your man. You're beautiful." He said every word with conviction, and she believed him. She smiled and kissed him while his hands continued their work on her body. He made sure she was wet enough before positioning himself between her legs, centering himself. He then thrust into her with one fell swoop, embedding himself to the hilt, breaking her innocence and causing her to scream in pain.

"Relax your body," he said gently while looking at her lips. "It's okay. It'll soon turn into pleasure. It's only this one time. I won't hurt you again." He said this to her while wiping her tears, kissing her lips, and waiting for her to adjust to his size.

Wendy relaxed her body beneath him; her pain had turned to pleasure, just as Eithan had said, and she moved her hips, causing Eithan to thrust into her with a steady yet inviting rhythm. They were a moaning mess. The only thing that could be heard in the room was the slapping of the skin, the creaking of the bed, and the sounds of pleasure that swept over the room. With one last thrust, he pumped into her with his might, then landed atop her, sinking her deeper into the bed. His skin felt nice against hers. After the vigorous workout, they had forgotten all about dinner. They didn't even hear the timer, which had rung nearly two hours before. Luckily, the stove had an automatic shut-off feature.

With a satisfied look, Wendy said to Eithan, "That was the first time I had ever done something like that, and now I'm extremely happy."

Eithan looked at her and smiled, feeling pleased. His love for her had grown even more, and no one was going to get in the way. He had never felt such love, such possession of any other being before. After another thirty minutes of resting, the door opened downstairs, and a loud voice protruded through the hall and up the stairs.

"Wendy, I am home. I am sorry that I stayed out late today. Something came up." Wally went into the kitchen. Something smelled nice. He hovered over the stove, staring into the pot to see that nothing had been eaten. In fact, nothing had been touched. He swiftly remembered that Eithan was also in the house, and the unthinkable flashed through his mind. "Oh no!" he said as he ran upstairs.

Simultaneously, Eithan and Wendy had heard Wally's calling, and they started to dress. It was the fastest anyone in the world had ever gotten dressed and escaped. Heading up, the first room Wally went into was the guest room, which Wendy had been staying in, because if she had not been there, there could have only been one other option. But luckily, she was in bed there.

As Wally looked at her on the bed and around the room, he concluded that she was fine. Wendy pretended that she had just heard his voice and had awoken from a slumber. She yawned, stretching her hands above her head, and opened her mouth. It was true that she was tired, but certainly not from sleeping. After seeing her, he felt relieved.

"Why hasn't anyone eaten dinner?" asked Wally.

"I am sorry, big brother. After coming back from school, I cooked and took care of Eithan, but I was a bit tired. I had asked him to call me when he was ready to eat, and I came into my room and fell asleep."

Wally, who was quite perceptive, did not respond because she had given him the idea that nothing had happened. But for some reason, the phrase that she had used, "I took care of him," made him ponder because Eithan was not sick. He only had fading scars. In other words, he was in good health. Wally then told her to eat something, and all of them ate that night. But Wally sensed something different about Wendy, although he couldn't quite put his finger on what it was. After all that catastrophe, he said, "All's well that ends well."

CHAPTER FIVE

New Beginnings

After all that had happened, Eithan, Wendy, and Wally left for school that morning. They arrived at the front of the college and split up, taking different routes to their classes. Seeing

Eithan's face was a reassurance for the girls at the college. Everyone was wondering what had happened to him because he had been absent from school for some time.

Mr. Sam entered the room. "Good morning, class. And hello there, Eithan." He singled Eithan out with a wave of his hand. "Are you feeling better?" He asked with concern in his eyes.

"Yes," Eithan replied. "Lately, the school has been getting quite a few transfer students. Here they are approaching, yelling my name." When the students approached Eithan and Mr. Sam, the first student introduced herself.

"Lily Peters, nice to meet you. And I hope we get along."

The second said, "Same here, my name is Jeremy." He glared at Eithan with a hint of a smile. This made Wendy curious. She stood to attention and headed towards where they stood. Before she could say anything, Jeremy turned to her and said, "Wendy, starting today, we will be classmates." Wendy was muddled. The last time she checked, he was residing in the opposite classroom.

Jeremy looked at her face and read her expression through. He giggled, placing his hand over his mouth, "Yes, Wendy, I'm in your class." Wendy was dumbfounded, and Eithan was growing perturbed at their interaction and what was to come.

Another partner felt left out. "What's going on, cousin?" Wendy turned to the figure. Her hair was black, shoulder-length, and she had a small, round yet angled face with green eyes. It was Lily.

"Go and take any available seats," said Mr. Sam. The students took their seats, and the class proceeded as usual.

During lunch, Afeisha saw that Lily was looking lonely and went up to her, asking her if she wanted to sit with them.

"Are you sure that it's okay?"

"Yes, it is no problem," said Afeisha.

They all met up and sat around the table. "Where is Eithan?" Michael asked.

Wendy replied that Eithan was coming a little late. He was at the office doing something for the teacher. Michael felt relieved hearing that, but something about Wendy made him think otherwise.

"Why are you looking at me like that?" she asked.

"It is nothing." But in his mind, it was as if the veil of innocence had been removed from Wendy. However, she was still the same as ever. For some strange reason, there was a lump in his chest, and he disliked Eithan even more. They started introducing themselves to Lily, from Afeisha to Michael.

After the introduction, Lily said to her, "I was about to look for you after this."

With a surprised look, Wendy asked, "Why?" "I'm staying at your house," Lily said.

Wendy was baffled, but then Wally came running towards Wendy and saw Lily.

"Lily, what in the world are you doing here?"

With excitement, she jumped to her feet and started hugging him. "I just moved with my mom and dad, along with Grandpa and a few others."

"That—that sounds great," said Wally, repressing a sigh and welcoming the intrusion.

"I haven't seen you in a long time," she continued.

Wally intervened and motioned to Wendy. "I see you have already met Wendy."

"Yes, why do you ask?"

He turned his face to Wendy. "Lily here happens to be your cousin. She is my mom's elder sister's daughter, and they will be staying with us in the meantime."

Wendy looked at him and studied him closely. "I already know that. We may not have interacted a lot, but I do remember her physical features, even if it has been a while. Also, we are classmates, and everyone wanted to reintroduce themselves to her."

While everyone was eating and talking, Eithan came in,

walking with Jason and Mandy. "I am sorry I took so long. I was doing something at the office. Let me introduce you. This is Mandy, and the other is Jason. They are two of my best friends." He glanced around, eyes landing and stopping on Wendy. Wendy stood up and shook their hand.

"Nice to meet you. My name is Wendy, and I have heard much about you."

"I, too," replied Jason with a smile.

Once again, everyone introduced themselves, but when it got down to Lily, she was lost. Seeing Eithan, she immediately fell for him. It wasn't his looks or his demeanor; there was something about him that had hooked Lily, like his very being commanded respect. She stammered, trying to bring out the words. She said her name, and they all sat at the table.

Eithan sat next to Wendy, and everyone noticed the intimacy between the two.

"Are you dating my little sis?" asked Wally.

Eithan replied with confidence. "Yes, we are dating. I love your sister, and she loves me."

Wally still couldn't shake his unease from the other night, but he managed to force a smile. If that's what his sister wanted, then he could only accept.

"Okay," he said in an uncomfortable tone. "I have already told my sis that whoever she likes must be of standard, and besides, you're a brave one."

Hostility filled the room.

"I am happy for you," said Afeisha.

On the other hand, Michael was in a trance. He couldn't believe what he heard. With a masterful expression, looking somewhat genuine, he smiled and said to her, "Good for you," but he could only hear the walls of his heart breaking and water flooding his eyes. He couldn't hold it in. Michael stood up from the chair, glanced at Eithan, and then headed off. It was abrupt, but Afeisha knew.

Lily, who was heartbroken the very minute she found love, was not about to let anyone take what belonged to her, so she just smiled and stayed silent, attracting Wally's attention. Wally stared at her. They might not have seen each other in a long time, but her character was seeping through. Her fake smile gave her away.

Also sitting at the table was another broken heart. Mandy, not delighted by the news, was also filled with anger and stayed silent. It was the best thing to do.

Wally looked around at the table. A straightforward piece of news did massive damage and broke four hearts. Noticing all this, Wally said to Eithan, "You'd better treat my sister well, or you and I will fight."

Eithan laughed while hugging Wendy. "No problem," he said, unaware or simply without care for the tension sitting at the table. Jason just smiled. The tension, however, was short-lived as Sheila entered the room. Her gaze landed on Wally, and she started her few strides across the room to their table.

"Wally, do you want to come and sit with me?" she asked.

Wally immediately refused, igniting Sheila's wrath. "Sheila!" he exclaimed. "You and I... are a wilderness apart."

These words pierced through Sheila's cold body, stabbing like knives, even though she did not feel as strongly as she once had. It was evident that she had changed, but her feelings for Wally were just too strong. Sheila remained calm.

Jeremy, who was following behind her, asked, "Is that the guy that you're dying to have?"

Sheila gave him a reproachful look, then replied in a confident tone, "Yes! He's Wendy's brother, and sooner or later, he will be mine."

"Why are you wasting time when you have the power to make him yours? Just give him a single bite." Sheila had never thought of biting Wally and putting him through that kind of agony, but the way things were progressing, it was like she had no other choice. Jeremy's voice kept ringing in her head. She looked in Wally's direction.

"Wally, I want you to go on a date with me today. If you do, I will no longer bother you."

It was an enticing offer, one that made him feel ecstatic, and so he agreed. Wendy, whose thoughts only had Eithan, stared over at the two, her gaze holding with Jeremy's. "I do not think that you should go to where Sheila is directing you for a date. It isn't safe." Wendy knew what Sheila and Jeremy were and what they were up to, forgetting that her brother also wasn't an ordinary man.

"It's good. I know how to take care of myself," he replied, glancing a smile at Wendy.

Lunch break was over, and they resumed their usual studies after school. Lily went home with Eithan and Wendy, who had their arms interlocked, while Wally headed in the direction that

Sheila had given him for their date. As it turns out, their date was in the middle of the forest, close to a huge tree. In fact, it was the place where Sheila was bitten. Wally, on the other hand, just wanted to go home, and this dating spot happened to be a good choice as it was closer to his house.

"Sheila, what do you want?" asked Wally. Though he liked the spot, it was evident that a sane person would not have asked to have a date here, even if she wasn't entirely normal.

Sheila smiled at him. This time, she decided to be her true self. She only had one chance. "I have decided that our date will be a little picnic. We can eat surrounded by nature and enjoy ourselves."

For the first time, Wally smiled at her. "Where did you get time to prepare such a feat?"

She smirked at him. "A lady has her way."

This caught Wally off guard. He stared at her for a few minutes, unable to pull his eyes away from her. It was a date that he didn't want, but it was turning out to be a pretty fine one. They spoke on surprising topics, as they had common ground. They like music, art, and even history. Sheila was proving to be more than just a face, more than a character. She was a person and, for once, a normal person. Wally could see himself spending time in her company, but before his mind wandered too far, he collected himself.

"I'm sorry about this afternoon's outburst," he said. She felt his sorrow and forgave him.

The conversation took a quick turn, and it was Wally who initiated the change. "Why do you hate my sister?" he asked.

Sheila paused before answering.

"I don't hate her. In fact, I would say that she's quite intelligent, kind, charismatic, and practical. However, your love for her is overwhelming. I guess that my jealousy of her having a brother like you, having you—to be precise, turned into dislike and obsession, and for that, I apologize."

Wally was shocked that she could utter so many nice descriptions to depict Wendy yet be so distasteful towards her. This made him want to know why she had feelings for him.

"And why do you love me?" he asked.

Sheila blushed. "This is quite an unexpected question," she said while looking for the words. She cleared her throat. "I love you because you are kind, capable, and can tell others apart just from looking. You have a friendly demeanor with others but don't tolerate nonsense, especially when it comes to your family. You protect those you care about, and still, there is so much more than your frighteningly handsome face, brown eyes, and scary but sexy build. You might not be a perfect guy, but you took up my gaze, then my heart."

Wally couldn't believe his ears. Sheila's heartfelt confession and her view of him touched his heart. He chuckled at her words. "Frighteningly handsome, eh?"

She smiled. For the first time, he saw her for who she was, not the pretentious character she had built for herself, and he loved it. She saw him for who he was, and a strange heat was building inside him.

"My goodness," he said. He stared at her. "Wendy is my only sister, and I love her dearly. This means that anyone who hurts her will answer to me."

Her expression changed. She knew of the hurt she had caused her.

Wally grabbed her cheeks and tilted her head towards him, looking at her with fervor. He pulled her towards his body, which she described as scary, and gave her a peck, but that wasn't enough. He started kissing her lips, inserting his tongue into hers. Though she was a vampire, her lips were soft and smooth, and he liked it. He wanted to devour her right then and there, and she was feeling wicked. If he took her into the forest, she would let him. However, they were greeted with uninvited guests, and he pulled away, regaining his composure. Surrounding them were three other vampires, one of whom was Jeremy.

"Jeremy, what are you doing here?" asked Sheila. "I'm here to help you," he said.

She scowled at him. "I don't need your help. Leave!"

This annoyed Jeremy. Since she didn't want to do it, he would do it for her. He moved towards Wally as the two other vampires held him down, and Sheila took a bite. Jeremy's words from earlier rang through her head. She could make him hers. One bite is all it took. She said no with conviction, but she was becoming less resolute as Jeremy taunted her about all she had done for him and his dislike for her. She was returning to her old self. Not wanting to wait any longer, he compelled her.

"I have given you my love, but you threw it in my face!" she said. "I have given you a chance! But you kept on refusing me! Why is that?"

"It's because I saw your intentions," Wally replied. "They are as bad and visible as day. You think I don't know what you have been doing to my sister? And right now, you're even trying to do something bad to me."

"Well, I am tired of chasing. It's your turn to chase me." Jeremy was enjoying the scene.

"I will not!" roared Wally hesitantly as seething gripped his heart. "This is the last time you will call me out for such things." Wally shrugged off the two vampires pressing him and walked off with his hands in his pockets. Suddenly, Jeremy held him by his shoulder and tossed him to the ground.

"Who do you think you are talking to, human? A bit arrogant, I see." Sheila had the two other vampires hold him down once more. She had concluded that the only way to possess Wally was for her to bite him. Her thoughts got the better of her. Wally stayed on the ground and pretended to be weak and defenseless. As Sheila approached him, she bore her fangs. With an unknown strength, he shook off the two vampires and held her by the neck, careful not to bruise her, and lifted her off the ground with one hand. Anger took over him.

"Who do you think you are?" he bellowed. "Are you trying to turn me into one of you? You have picked the wrong man." He tossed her to the ground, and his heart ached. He looked at her on the ground, then looked at his hand, too ashamed of what he had done. "Do not repeat this act ever again."

Sheila was surprised at the strength that Wally possessed. Even Wally surprised himself. With venom in his voice, he warned her sternly to keep away from him. Some date this turned out to be. He chuckled at himself for allowing the situation to get this far, running his fingers through his soft hair, and with a final glare, he turned and walked away.

When he was out of sight, her compulsion broke, and her true self returned. She was sad. Her first intimate moment with Wally, her hard work that had borne fruit, was ruined in a split second by Jeremy. Nevertheless, Sheila was determined. She felt his lips, and God, she wanted more. She wanted him.

As for the three vampires who were knocked out cold, Jeremy soon regained consciousness and ignored the others. Immediately, Jeremy figured out what he was, which confirmed half of his theory about Wendy, and he disappeared. After Sheila had gotten up off the ground, Jeremy was nowhere to be found. He was gone, abandoning her to her fate. "Fate is quite something," she added as she walked away. Meanwhile, back at the house, Wendy met Lily's parents: Laura, her mother, and James, her dad.

Wendy also took that opportunity to tell them that Eithan was now her boyfriend and that she was going over to his place to meet his parents. Elena did not want Wendy to go, but she had no choice, for her father was happy. They had all approved, including James and Laura. Their spirits took a liking to him, but when they saw the look on their daughter's face as she watched Eithan, they were filled with discontentment towards Wendy, for they valued their daughter's happiness over all others.

Nevertheless, she went with Eithan. Her father gave his approval, and that was all that mattered. While everyone was eating and talking, Wally walked in the door.

"Are you alright, Wally? I thought you were going on a date." He turned to his father, "It turns out that I could not make it."

Elena turned to him. "That is okay. Go upstairs and have a bath so you can quickly join us at the table."

"Thanks, Mom. It will be drifty."

While upstairs, Wally's mind ran to Sheila. He thought back to what had happened. He replayed it over and over and then realized that Sheila was under some spell. This made him feel guilty. He quickly cleaned himself up and then went back downstairs.

"Wally, you remember Aunt Laura and Uncle James, right?" Elena said with satisfaction.

"Yes, I remember."

"Good. They both will be staying here for some time." He looked around but didn't see Wendy.

"Where is Wendy?"

The room became a little dark at his question.

"She went out with her boyfriend to visit his parents."

"Things are progressing fast, I see, Dad. I am surprised that you are allowing this so easily?" Wally said with a smirk.

Elena jumped in. "Right? Why are you allowing your daughter to visit another man's house?"

"I trust Eithan. He is a nice guy," said William.

"I'm happy to hear that, as I feel the same," said Wally.

Part of the reason was that he felt guilty about what he had done to Eithan, and he knew Eithan knew. "Enough of this," said William, let us eat.

Laura was in her seat, filled with anger and hatred for Wendy because she thought she had stolen the only thing that mattered to her daughter, Lily, who hadn't even been here for a day.

Meanwhile, on their way to Eithan's house, Wendy could not believe how surprisingly close their homes were. Eithan was living at the other end of the forest, opposite their house. Upon opening the door, the first thing that they saw was Mandy and Elia fixing the table to set dinner. Elia had a crush on Mandy, and she had told Elia a lot of terrible things about Wendy, making him dislike Eithan's new girlfriend even before they had met.

Elia saw her son and Wendy preparing to enter the house. "Hello, and welcome to my humble abode. I'm Elia, Eithan's mother, and I am guessing you must be Wendy. It's nice to meet you." Elia's dislike for Wendy did not stop her from being polite.

"It is my pleasure," said Wendy happily.

"Uhm, I am going now," said Mandy with a sour look on her face. "Don't you want to stay for dinner?" asked Elia.

"No, it's all right."

"Be careful on your way. Eithan, can you go upstairs and fetch me my bracelet? It has been missing for some time." Eithan realized what his mother wanted to do, but because he loved and believed in Wendy's capabilities, he did what she asked.

Elia wanted to get more acquainted with Wendy, so she called her to the kitchen. Both spoke while setting the table, losing track of time.

After observing her, she realized that all Mandy had said about her was a lie. Through interaction, she came to like Wendy, and her spirit took her. The bell rang. "That must be Cam. He is home."

"Whose Cam?" Wendy asked.

"Cam is Short for Camron, Eithan's father."

Eithan, who had been upstairs lazing around, decided to come down, and there he was.

"Dad!" he shouted with excitement. "You are finally home."

Camron looked at his son with a warm smile. "I haven't seen you in a long time. Who is this beautiful miss standing next to your mom?"

"She's my girlfriend. Her name is Wendy Granchest. I brought her to introduce her to mom because you were on a three-week trip. However, I see that mom also had a surprise for me."

He turned to Wendy, and she flashed him a grin. "Hello, sir. My name is Wendy. Nice to meet you."

"The pleasure is all mine," Cam replied in a gentlemanly manner. His stomach growled, and he turned to Elia. It was as if the sun had landed on him. "I am hungry. It's been a long trip, and I missed your cooking." The three sat around the table, ate, and talked. It was almost as if they were a family. Camron liked Wendy very much and was happy with his son's choice, but even happier that he had found a girl he liked, because when a wolf imprints on someone, that person becomes his for the rest of their lives, which is why they must be careful.

After eating, Elia told Eithan to take Wendy for a tour of the house before he took her home. The house was massive, which Wendy had not noticed because she was filled with nerves about meeting Eithan's parents and impressing them. She realized that it wasn't necessary, that being herself was more than enough. He took her to many parts of the house, and she was ecstatic. There were a lot of things for one to behold. To sum it all up, it was extremely beautiful. The last place that he took her was his bedroom. His room was painted blue and large. It had many photos of him and her, a bathtub large enough to fit two, brown leather couches, a large Vizio television on the wall, and an even larger bed covered with soft silk sheets.

"Where did you take all these photos, Eithan?" "Well, I took them secretly."

This would have been creepy if it were someone else. Nevertheless, the pictures were quite good.

"When did you start liking me?" She had to know.

"The first time we met, you were drooling over my body." "I was not."

"Yes, you did."

The two of them were giggling and playing, their hands all over each other. Suddenly, Wendy hit her left foot, slipped, and fell on the bed. The mood changed again, and they began having another intimate dance.

After a while, Elia and Cameron noticed that Wendy and Eithan had been upstairs for quite some time, but they did not say anything.

"Eithan, I must go home early today. Do not forget that there are people staying at my house."

"I know. I will follow you home in thirty minutes, but let's stay like this for now and cuddle." These words were pleasing to her ear, and she agreed. The pair stayed like this and fell asleep, surpassing the thirty minutes. Wendy woke up first.

"Oh no! I must go. It is already late." She tapped Eithan and tried to wake him, but Eithan did not wake. She began kissing him and caressing him, and he groaned. This sent a tremor through her body. Eithan's eyes opened; they were red.

Wendy pulled her hands away. "Why are your eyes red? More importantly, we must get dressed. I am late!"

Reluctantly, he got dressed, not wanting to distress her. After they were dressed, they went downstairs.

"Mom!" he exclaimed. "I am going to drop off Wendy and might return a little late."

"Be careful!" Elia replied with a broad smile, fully knowing what they were doing.

They both headed out of the house and started their journey towards Wendy's house. After a long walk, they finally arrived. Wendy kissed Eithan and went inside. As Eithan was heading off, Lily pulled back the yellow curtains by the window and watched him. As Wendy entered her home, she felt happy and replayed the moments of her and Eithan in her head. Lily closed the curtains and went to Wendy, interrupting her happy thoughts. Being inquisitive, Lily asked her about the things that had happened, things that didn't concern her. Wendy scowled at her, but she didn't care. Lily, presumptuous and taking Wendy for a weakling, told her to her face that she had fallen in love with Eithan and that Wendy should break it off with him. But she was wrong.

"What? Repeat what you just said."

Lily came closer and grabbed Wendy's right hand by her wrist, squeezing and dominating. "Break it off with Eithan."

Wendy's heart thundered beneath her ribs, but she didn't move. Not this time. Not again. The painful words she swallowed for years surged to the surface, hot and unforgiving. She glared at Lily's smug face.

"As always, wanting what is not yours. Finally, you're showing your true colors. I knew that something was off about you. And for your information, he's mine, so don't you ever think about it."

Laura was on the stairs listening to the whole conversation. Wendy headed upstairs to the room, not caring about anyone around. While passing Laura, she said goodnight, not waiting or caring for a response.

"I do not need your goodnight!" Laura said to Wendy. "I am not your aunt. You are a child of a low-life, and in this house, you'll do as you're told and break up with that boy for your cousin."

Upon hearing that Wendy was a Rat, Lily thought that it was a grand opportunity to bully Wendy, but she was mistaken.

"Who do you think you are?" asked Lily in a menacing tone.

Wendy stopped, turned around, and replied, "I'm a lowlife in my own father's house. Something must be wrong with both your heads. And for your information, I will not repeat myself after today. I will not break up with Eithan because he's mine. And as for your daughter, I'm sure that there are better men out there, somewhere," she said sarcastically, with her hands apart and in doubt.

"By the way," she added, "I might have considered it if she were my cousin, but thankfully, she is not. Too bad." After declaring this, she went towards her room.

Both Wally and William, who saw the scene from a distance, were proud of her. It was time for her to stand on her own. William knew how evil and vile Elena was and was not about to let Laura have her way in his house. Upon returning to his room, William smiled. "Blood is truly thicker than water," he said under his breath. "My daughter made my day."

CHAPTER SIX

Do unto Others What You Would Have Them Do unto You! Kaboom

The next day was genuinely touching. Wally had already woken up and dressed for school, and so had the domineering shrews Elena, Laura, and her daughter Lily. Wendy was still busy readying herself in the bathroom.

When she emerged from the bathroom, her dad shouted, "Wendy, hurry up and get ready! Everyone's eating breakfast except you."

Wally joined in. "You sleepyhead, just hurry and get ready."

Wendy quickly dried off her skin and went into her room to put on clothes. Meanwhile, the doorbell rang.

"Who is it this early in the morning? Wally, get the door!" exclaimed Elena.

"All right! All right! I just wanted to eat my breakfast in peace." With an angry demeanor, he got up with a slice of toast in his hand and made an unwavering attempt to insult the person who was disturbing his breakfast. As soon as he opened the door and was about to open his mouth, he saw none other than Eithan.

He started to say "fu—" and ended up saying "fuel". "What?" asked Eithan.

"I mean, did you use fuel to get over here? It is so early in the morning, and your girlfriend is not ready yet."

Wally was so embarrassed that he made up something on the spot. However, the most embarrassed person was Eithan. He had been standing outside for more than ten minutes, juggling in his head whether to ring the doorbell or if he was too early, but he ended up ringing it anyway while he was in deep thought.

"Come inside already! What are you doing out there?" asked William. "Oh—Dad, we are coming."

"If it is not Eithan. My daughter is up in her room... and speak of the devil. Here she comes."

"Morning," Eithan said to Wendy with an elegant and heartfelt smile. Eithan was touched and was gazing at the beauty while Elena gave a half- hearted smile, which crumbled just as quickly.

"Everyone, let us eat breakfast before it gets cold," said Elena. Everyone gathered around the table and started eating.

Lily, with her overbearing and pretentious attitude, started to act meek and mild. She turned towards Eithan.

"All of us here know that you are in love with our little Wendy. What do you like about her?"

Eithan smiled, and his eyes lit up. "I love everything about her, from the way that she walks, talks, and moves, and most of all, her personality is quite enchanting. She is a bit naive, but she is as beautiful inside as she is on the outside."

After hearing these sweet words, Wendy could not contain

her radiant smile and felt embarrassed, so she hid her face with both hands. William was quite pleased, and her brother Wally tapped Eithan's shoulder. He nodded his head back and forth as he sat close to him. They knew he was telling the truth because they had their own built-in lie detector, as most supernatural beings do.

On the other hand, Elena, Laura, and her daughter's faces were wrinkled and upset, but they masked it with a smile.

"Eithan, what do you think about my lovely daughter Lily?" Laura asked. This question puzzled Eithan, but he managed to say something.

"Uhm..." Eithan began to stutter. "Is that a trick question?"

Laura laughed. "No, it's not. Lily is more charming and beautiful than Wendy, and she is also well-versed in law."

She tried her best to sound as nice as possible while laughing. Eithan bit back a scowl. Faking a smile, he said, "Quite outstanding. However, she and Wendy have totally different personalities." What Laura and Lily did not know was that Eithan was a prominent werewolf who had the ability to see through the lies and faces of people.

Laura winked at Lily. "You are late for school—time to go."

The breakfast ended in an unpleasant and sour manner, and it was all their fault. At school, Lily became popular in less than a day. She met handsome-looking guys who fell for her; however, she had no interest in any of them. Though those men were popular, her grudge against Wendy only grew because she had Eithan as her boyfriend, the most handsome guy not only in school but in town. The runner-up to him happened to be her brother, and to add to that, Michelle and Jeremy. It looked like he wanted to take a dip off the chip, meaning he wanted to join the club as one of Wendy's suitors. Just the thought of her made Lily angry. And speak of the devil—here she comes.

"Where are you going this hour, Wendy?" she said in a gentle tone, masking her honesty with other people around.

"Don't you know where I am going?" Wendy replied. "We are in the same class, Lily. I'm going to the biology lab. The professor is not fond of latecomers, so I want to get there early."

"Oh!" she shouted while covering her mouth. "I remember that Michael wanted to see you about something, but I cannot remember what it was."

Doubting her, Wendy went along with it. "Oh, really?" Wendy replied in a sarcastic tone.

"Really!"

"But there's only thirty minutes left before class begins."

"That is sufficient time. Just go and hear what he has to say, then come back quickly."

Though Wendy sensed something was up, she neglected her instincts and went anyway. On her way, she saw a figure in the corridor. It was Michael.

"Hey, did you call me?" Wendy asked.

Michael was confused. "No, why would I call you?"

"What are you talking about? Lily said that you had called me."

"I am telling you I did not. Besides, I don't even speak to her like that. Why would I tell her when I can go myself? Not to mention you have class."

"I knew it!" said Wendy, "I should have never believed her for even a second. Well, I don't believe…"

Meanwhile, as Wendy confronted Michael, Lily went to the classroom and saw Eithan and Afeisha.

"Where is Wendy?" Eithan asked.

"Wendy is in the corridor, romancing Michael," Lily replied. "What?"

Eithan quickly stormed off and headed to where they were, neglecting the class that was about to start in minutes. Afeisha kept her eyes on Lily, who was looking at her with disgust. Though she was not a supernatural being, it was a woman's instinct to sense danger and jealousy to the highest degree. It took some effort to tear her eyes away, but she did. Afeisha took her eyes off Lily and went to do her own thing, waiting for her friends.

Lily, who was presumptuous in many ways, went to the lab and started mixing chemicals. The people in the room thought that she was only practicing, but it was far from it. In fact, Lily knew exactly what she was doing. She mixed and mixed with the intention of burning Wendy and destroying her face. As time flew by, her behavior got uglier. After all the mixing, the product was a pink, slimy, yet watery chemical that no one in the class had ever seen before. Everyone was amazed, but they minded their business. Lily was quite content with herself as she looked at her potion, fantasizing about destroying Wendy's face and getting Eithan. For a second, she also thought about replacing Wendy completely. However, though she wanted her squad, she would still be fulfilled if she only had Eithan. His arms were strong, his shoulders were broad, and all she could think was how great it would be to be lying in his embrace while he kissed and cuddled her. Losing track of time, the professor came in ten minutes early and saw most of the class already seated, with some people missing.

He was surprised and happy to see that his students were managing their time properly. Not only were they seated, but one had already started mixing chemicals without causing any problems. He immediately called out the pairs who had to do an assignment together, starting with Penelope Wilson and Sophia Hastens, and placed them closer to where he sat. When he got to Eithan and Wendy, they were both missing.

"Does anyone know where Eithan and Wendy are?"

Everyone replied no, but Lily said, "Eithan went to the bathroom a few minutes ago, but I don't know about Wendy."

Afeisha jumped up defensively. "Wendy has gone to do something important. She told me that she would return before class, and if she does not, I should inform you."

Upon hearing this, the professor became intrigued about how dedicated his students were to learn. He placed them in a group because both were late. Lily stared at Wendy's friend, who didn't hesitate to scowl back at her. As time was counting down, Wendy and Eithan came running through the door.

"Hey, Eithan," said Wendy with thumping breaths. "Can't you allow me to go through the door first?"

"I was going to ask you that same question." He replied with a sarcastic smile. Both stared into each other's eyes like they were the only one's present. Everyone's eyes were on the two of them.

Immediately, the teacher cleared his throat with a gruff noise and said, "Ladies first."

Wendy went in first with style and a smile while glancing back at Eithan. Eithan felt that it was hot. Under his breath, he said, "Damn, she is making me unsettled."

Lily, who never took her eyes away, overheard and became angry. She was distracted by thoughts about all the things surrounding her. She concentrated on every thought, which intensified her hatred for Wendy even more, causing her anger to run as deep and long as the Nile.

"Class, today, there are things that we are going to do.

I want you to mix the jar on the right and the bottle on the left. Everything is already prepared."

Everyone followed the instructions that the professor had given and ended up with different results.

"Teaching is about sitting, learning, and revolting," the professor said. "It is supposed to be fun."

All the students were excited about everything the teacher said. However, when it was Lily's turn to mix, the concoction exploded, covering her face in light scratches. During the explosion, everyone was screaming, shouting, and fleeing for their lives. The professor was scared for Lily and became nervous about his teacher's license, but some of the students who were in the lab before class remembered what Lily was doing and spoke up about it before it blew out of proportion. Upon seeing Lily, Wendy felt sad, but little did she know that it was intended for her.

Lily, who was as guilty as a puppy, showed her eyes, and immediately, the professor didn't know how to respond. He asked two other girls in the class to follow her to the bathroom so that she could clean herself up. The students who carried her to the bathroom took a glimpse at her and realized that her face was okay. They wondered how that could have been possible but did not stress over the matter. Upon reaching the bathroom, Lily started cursing in the mirror and blaming Wendy once again, forgetting that the girls were beside her.

"What are you staring at? Have you not seen enough?" The tone of her voice was so scary that they thought she was not human. They ran out of the bathroom in a fright, leaving her all to herself.

Class ended early that day because of that one incident. Everyone wanted to go outside to enjoy themselves, seeing that they had time on their hands. Lily, on the other hand, was so angry that her fury could not be extinguished.

"Tonight is a full moon," she whispered under her breath. "I will see if she will be able to get away."

Passing by the female bathroom, Lily heard Wendy's and Eithan's laughing voices, along with her friends. "I will see how long they will be able to laugh," Lily said. She overheard them speaking about enjoying themselves and decided that she wanted to go with them. She used the lie that she was new in town and did not have any friends. Michael felt a little sorry for her, but everyone knew better.

"We are going to hang out at our usual spot. If you're coming, let's go!"

Following the incident, Wendy decided to be lenient with her. Thus, she tagged along.

At Feistus, everyone was having a grand time, but Lily did not forget about Wendy for a minute, so she wanted to spice things up a little.

"How about we play the Kings Game?" "What is that?" asked Michael.

"It is a game of straws where whoever gets the king gets to order two other persons to do something, and the king's orders are absolute."

"I do not like the sound of that," Wendy interjected.

"Let's try," said Michael, who was thinking about what he could do with Wendy. He was thinking about a freebie.

Afeisha, on the other hand, wanted the same thing with Michael, so she agreed as well. Eithan had some especially important people coming in, so he refused. This altered Lily's mood; her expression and character no longer fit for the game.

The game began, and Lily pleaded with her arms to her chest, wishing to pick the king's straw. The straws were scrambled, and Wendy picked straw four. Lily then picked the king's straw; Michael, straw three; Afeisha, straw two; and Eithan, who had no choice but to play, pulled straw one.

Lily then ordered that straw one and straw four should hug. When Michael saw that he was straw four and Wendy was straw one, he had a big smile on his face. He was starting to like the game even more. However, the same could not be said of Eithan and Afeisha. There was too much jealousy involved. He knew that Michael liked Wendy, and not in a friendly manner.

The straws were scrambled again, and this time, the king was Michael. The numbers were the same, but this time, Lily got straw four, and Wendy got straw three. Michael then ordered that straw three and straw one was to kiss. He hoped that the persons with the respective straws would have been Eithan and Lily, but he was in for a rude awakening.

"I am straw one," Eithan shouted. Wendy sighed with relief. She was straw three. Though it was embarrassing, they did indeed share a hot, passionate kiss, which left everyone in a trance, just staring at them. Things were going just as Lily had planned. The game was getting intense, and now it was time to get her revenge.

Eithan looked at the time. "Oh—I have to head off." "Let's end the game here," said Wendy.

"But I haven't had a turn yet," said Afeisha. "Another time," said Wendy.

Lily began setting her trap, trying to pin them against each other.

Suddenly, Sheila came into the café, along with Jeremy. "What are you doing here?"

Jeremy looked across the room to the echoed voice.

"Look who it is," said Wendy, sarcastically, to Sheila, who was staring at her. "I was on my way out."

"Be careful on your way home, Wendy. You know just as well as I do how dangerous the road can be at night."

Wendy watched her and attempted a sardonic smile. "I know,

but you know more than me, wouldn't you?"

Sheila wanted to fire back, but she went on her way, not wanting to pick a fight.

As Wendy and Eithan walked home, the world was getting darker and darker.

"Let's pick up the pace. I don't want to be in the forest at night," said Wendy.

Everyone at home—excluding Laura and Elena, who only worried about Lily and Wally—would not have been this concerned on a typical day. However, today was not a normal day. Tonight was another night of the great crimson moon.

On the other hand, Eithan's siblings were already back home. "Wendy," Eithan whispered into her left ear. "Do not worry. I'll protect you no matter what."

Wendy blushed and grabbed onto him, forgetting about the pace at which they were walking. Sheila began to put her plans into action, but this moon was like no other moon that they had ever seen. It was bigger and brighter, and the effects were fiercer. Back at home, Eithan's siblings began to wonder where he was, but they weren't too worried because they knew him well.

Michael could not understand what had just happened, but he had managed to regain his sanity. Meanwhile, back home, Wendy started to pressure her dad so she could know what was going on with the strange moon outside. This was not the weird moon she had witnessed previously. William did not want to say anything, but Wally also demanded an explanation. William had no choice but to give in.

"This type of moon is known as Mooncon Hemor. It comes from the word subconjunctival hemorrhage, which has to do with the bleeding of the eyes, but it is a little different. In this case, it is a moon that is usually a red rosewood color, but it's supposed to be a myth. This type of moon appears once every hundred years, and I guess yesterday was just that day. When it appears, it is said that people will bleed from their eyes, and it will turn red. But as for the supernatural, if they do not regain consciousness a few seconds after looking at the moon, they themselves will lose their sanity and start ripping throats. They will become unstoppable killing machines until the moon goes away."

"Is there a way to avoid such a moon?" Wendy asked.

"Yes, there is," said William. "However, because it is believed to be a myth, no one usually studies it. There is a sword by the name of Incasera. Do you know what it is?"

Wally jumps in. "Is it that old-looking sword in the hallway?"

"Yes. And that also carries its own myth. The sword Incasera has the power to cut down any creature, but what you were not told is that it protects its owner by rendering all supernatural attacks ineffective. In other words, it cancels it out."

"So, William, are you saying that by holding the sword, the moon will not affect you?" asked Elana.

"That is precisely what I'm saying, but the problem is that no one knows the owner of the sword. It must be the owner who wields it. The sword has been passed down to my family for generations, and no one has ever come to claim it. It is also said that the person who possesses the sword must have something to do with a claw and the Granchest family. That's all I know. And only two people can hold the sword. Do you want to try it? The sword reveals itself to its true owner?"

"Why not?" said Wally. "This is going to be fun. Where is the butler? I have not seen him for quite some time now."

"Now that you have mentioned it, I haven't either," said Wendy.

Laura, who was upstairs listening in on the conversation, came downstairs to join the discussion. "My daughter should be able to try the sword as well. After all, she is a Granchest." William, who did not want to get into an argument with her, scowled. Granchest was Williams's family name, not Elena's, and certainly not hers. Reluctantly, he just agreed.

"Let us all just go to the hall," he said. When they got there, the sword Incasera was nowhere to be found.

"Where is the butler?" Wally asked.

Mr. William continued from where he had left off. "The butler told me that he needed a few months off to do something concerning his family, and I gave my approval."

"So, did you see when he left?" asked Wally.

"Yes, I did, and the sword was not with him." William was growing extremely angry at the present situation. "Did any of you move the sword that was here?" Everyone said no. Because he did not want to doubt anyone, he did not pursue the matter, but he sensed something hesitant in Elena's voice. He sighed. "It is not like that person can wield the sword, anyway. In order to wield the sword, you must be powerful, and that's just the first criterion. It's also pointless when the sword's power only releases when the rightful heir wields it."

This made Laura angry. After everyone had dispersed to their rooms. Lily stood in front of the place where the sword was supposed to be, and she just stared. She then stumbled on something that she thought was never possible. By moving the statue, she could enter an opening in the wall. It was Elena's lair. And as she began looking around, she found some disturbing things as well as something she never imagined she'd see. It was, in fact, the sword. Lily grabbed the sword but did not leave any clues that she had entered the lair. She took the sword up the stairs to show her mother. When Laura gazed upon the sword, she was enthralled, but the sword did not show any signs of life while Lily was holding it. The blue, silver, and gold stayed stagnant.

"Mom, suppose the sword glows when Wally holds it," Lily said.

"That would be nice," said Laura, "But if it just happens to be Wendy or even both, I will be mad, so let's just hold on to it and hide it for a few days."

"Oh, I have good news for you. Your grandfather and the rest of the family will be coming in for a few days."

"Including Dad?" "Yes, honey."

"But why are so many of them coming?"

"The level of homicide and the disappearance of people is becoming overbearing in this town, and the government does not know what to do anymore."

"Well, that makes sense. But I will not be leaving with them when the time comes. There is someone that I want to have no matter what."

"Do not worry, honey. You'll get what's yours."

The next morning was so dreadful. After all that had happened the night before and the reports on various deaths, the children grew tired and were taking their time to do everything as if all their energy was wasted. Eithan, who made a routine to walk with Wendy to and from school, did not show up in the morning and had Wendy worried.

On their way to school, Wendy bumped into Sheila, who looked even worse than usual.

"What's her problem? She looks out of it."

Afeisha overheard Wendy as she walked in her direction. "It's not just her, but Michael seems a little weird today. And even her companions, Jeremy, and his guys. I don't know what's happening anymore."

"I hope that Michael and Eithan are fine as well," said Wendy.

As they walked into class, they discovered that two new transfer students had been added to their class.

"Good morning, students," said Mr. Sam. "Today, we have two new transfer students and one new teacher. She will be teaching you Biology." He gestured with his hands for the students to come in. "The teacher will be here later."

Two beautiful students came in and began to introduce themselves. "My name is Samantha Fishberg. It is a pleasure to meet you."

The boys in the class were all love-struck, but upon seeing

Eithan, they backed off at once. Wendy felt something that she had never felt before. She pondered on what it was, but couldn't place her finger on it. However, whatever feeling it was, it was not a good feeling.

The male transfer student then introduced himself. "My name is Franco Haynes, and it's a pleasure to meet you all." The girls were acting up, but it was not as exaggerated as when Eithan first arrived.

Mr. Sam addressed the transfer students, "Is there anyone in this class you know? I will seat you next to that person so you will be able to catch up quickly."

While Franco knew Sheila and Jeremy, he quickly said "No," but Samantha, on the other hand, said "Yes."

"Who is this person that you know?"

Samantha smirked. "The person I know is Eithan. We're quite close."

This once again made Wendy feel an unpleasant feeling, but what put the icing on the cake was when Mr. Sam told her to give her seat to Samantha, as she was sitting next to Eithan.

Franco spoke up. "Sir? Can I sit next to that charming girl who just gave up her seat?"

"Do as you wish," said Mr. Sam.

When everyone had finally been seated, Wendy's anger had simmered because she was sitting next to Afeisha and Franco.

"What's the matter with you?" said Afeisha.

"I don't know what it is, but I've started having an unpleasant feeling ever since that girl arrived."

Afeisha laughed. "That's called jealousy. You are finally feeling it. It's only right, after all. Some other chick wants to steal him away."

"If that is true, then jealousy is indeed a bitter feeling."

Overhearing their conversation, Franco began talking to Wendy, and they both laughed. Eithan, who was at the back of the room, seeing everything in plain sight, started to get jealous. His sister, whose eyes were always on him, sensed his anger and jealousy and immediately deduced that the girl at the front of the class whose seat she had taken was Wendy, his beloved girlfriend. She smirked and began planning for herself.

There was also a transfer student in Wally's class. The teacher, Mr. Primo, brought him in.

"Good morning, class. There is a new transfer student today. Introduce yourself."

"Hello, everyone. My name is Aaron Fishberg, and it is a pleasure to meet you all."

All the girls shrieked because he was indeed a beauty. He was as attractive as Eithan in every way and even cooler.

"You give off a familiar vibe," said Wally. "Is Eithan your brother?" Aaron replied in a sarcastic tone, "Of course, he is my little brother." Wally stared at him. "It looks like this class is going to be fun."

Because of the small chatter between the boys, you would

think the teacher would separate them. Instead, Primo decided to seat them next to each other. During classes, the boys got along well. They bonded over similar topics and the protectiveness of their siblings, which immediately drove them to become best friends.

The Girlfriend Meets the Siblings and the New Weird Teacher

After school, the gang came together as usual, but this time, Eithan brought Samantha, and Wally joined in, bringing along Aaron. Upon seeing Samantha with Eithan, Wendy grew upset.

"Why did you bring her along? And Wally, who is this?"

Lily loved seeing Wendy so on edge. "Can't you see that you've been replaced?"

"By whom? Though I'm not really the jealous type, I must confess that I'm starting to feel it a little."

Eithan was happy seeing Wendy the way she was. He knew that, being so naïve, she had never felt that way before. Aaron and Wally, who could not help but watch the show, were conversing with each other.

"Eithan, aren't you going to introduce us?" said Aaron.

Lily jumped in. "You know him? No wonder you are just as handsome. And I must confess you're way cooler. Maybe I should give up on Eithan and settle for you."

Aaron scowled at her comment.

"Wendy, this is my sister, Samantha," said Eithan. "We are one year apart, and that fellow whom you are looking at is my elder brother, Aaron. He's a narcissist."

"Hello, it's nice to meet you all," said Wendy. She stretched her hand to greet Samantha, but she refused, making Wendy uncomfortable. Eithan gave his sister a frown.

"It was nice to meet you, too," said Samantha. "I heard you are my brother's girlfriend. I hope it lasts and wish you luck."

Wendy replied confidently. "I don't need it. What I want, I shall have."

After Wendy shut down Samantha's unpleasant remarks, Aaron began to smile. He had developed an interest in her.

"Nice to meet you, too. And I hope that you take good care of my brother if not."

He paused for a second, and Wendy became a little afraid. Eithan reassured her that his brother has a huge complex, which is why he's so overprotective.

Upon hearing that, Wally joined the conversation. "I hope your brother can do the same because I do share your sentiment." Aaron looked up at Wally, meeting his glance.

"Is Wendy your sister?" "Yes, she is."

Samantha looked at Wally and stretched out her arm. "It is a pleasure to meet you."

However, Wally showed her the same courtesy that she had

shown his sister, and this made her excited. No one had ever turned her down before, especially because she was such a beauty, and Wally's lack of interest made her want to change that.

Michael and Afeisha had been quiet but finally decided to introduce themselves.

"Hello, I am Michael, Eithan's and Wendy's friend." "Same here, I am Afeisha."

"I'm Wendy's cousin Lily, and my target has changed. This time, I'm going for you."

Aaron watched her and pretended that he heard nothing she had said. The gang went to their usual spot to relax. They were enjoying themselves like they had never done before. Sheila came into the bar with Jeremy, and Franco tagged along.

"Why is Franco with them?" Wendy whispered. "I thought he did not know them. It seems very suspicious."

"Maybe you're overthinking it," said Michael. "It could be that they were getting along in class and wanted to go out together."

Eithan just watched, but Aaron's eyes were glued to Sheila. The way she talked, her toned skin, and her long legs all attracted him. Aaron got up from his seat and introduced himself to her. Sheila met his gaze.

"Nice to meet you. I'm Sheila."

As Sheila walked off, Aaron smirked. "I will have her."

Eithan and Samantha were completely shocked. They could not believe their ears. Their narcissistic brother, who loved only himself, had fallen in love with Sheila at first sight. Wally shook his head, knowing Sheila's true nature. He felt a connection with her when she confided in him during their date. However, it was not to the point of having feelings for her. He was just caught up in the moment. Thus, he secretly cheered Aaron on, hoping that Sheila could finally settle with a good guy. She wasn't really a bad person, but she tended to make bad decisions and to make him angry.

Lily, who beheld everything, was upset, and decided to revert to Eithan because she remembered a saying: A journey of a thousand miles starts with one step. But the path Aaron had left for her to walk was a path of lava, and she was not about to get hurt. She whispered under her breath, "A normal person would not see a beehive and put their hand in it just to obtain honey; you will get a sting."

Afeisha overheard her and asked what she was talking about. "Nothing," replied Lily.

They all had fun playing games and talking among themselves. Suddenly, in walked a tall, brown-skinned lady with an aura around her that made her seem like royalty.

A man saw her walk in and asked, "Miss, are you sure you're in the right place?"

"I am sure. I came here on business," she replied. The lady walked in the direction of Sheila, Franco, and Jeremy's table.

Aaron, who was quite perceptive, asked, "Why are Sheila and the other one afraid of that lady?"

"What are you saying?" asked Wally. "Look for yourself," said Aaron. "You are right, they are."

"But how come that Franco feller, or what's-his-name, is not scared?

He's the one who looks the most confident out of all the people there."

Wendy asked Aaron and Wally what they were up to, but they offered nothing.

"The school has been getting quite the number of transfer students lately, and it is as though something big is going to happen," said Wendy.

"Do not worry about these things," replied Eithan. "I have already promised you that no matter what happens, I will always protect you."

While they were leaving the café, the TV switched to another channel, and once again, there was breaking news. A blonde-haired female in her mid-thirties with green eyes was reporting the latest news.

"The body of a man was found floating along the gutter of Mavis Street. Authorities are saying that the deaths are becoming overwhelming, and everyone should be off the roads and streets before nine o'clock."

Once the news bulletin concluded, everyone separated. Michael decided to leave first, noting that his mom was probably worried about him. "Don't worry. I'll drop Wendy off on the way, seeing that we are both headed in the same direction."

"That is good," said Wendy. She hugged and kissed Eithan goodbye. "I'll visit you tomorrow. You should go home with your siblings. They have just returned, so use the time to catch up."

Samantha overheard and started warming up to Wendy, especially since she is Wally's sister.

Aaron, still thinking about Sheila, went home with his siblings, and they all parted ways after reaching a certain point in the forest.

While Eithan, Samantha, and Aaron were on their way home, Aaron asked him if they had recognized the woman who came into the cafe.

Eithan smirked. "I did not see any woman."

"That figure," replied Aaron. "All you have been thinking about is how to comfort your girlfriend."

"You bet I am. Why should I even spare a glimpse at another woman while I have my babe sitting in front of me?"

Aaron sighed. He could not forget the fact that ever since that lady came in, Sheila had been afraid.

Samantha said that she did not see any woman because she was busy trying to get Wally's attention.

"So, you were busy staring and trying to get his attention, and he wasn't paying attention to you," said Aaron.

Samantha began growling.

"Behave!" Aaron said. "I do not want to be mad." Samantha quickly simmered.

Meanwhile, Michael was walking back with Afeisha.

"I am thinking of giving up on Wendy," he said. "I have tried my best to get her attention, but she only sees me as her best friend. From now on, I will continue to support and protect her, but only as a friend. I see how she is when she is with Eithan, and it's the opposite of when she's with me. I should just give up. It is human nature to want what one cannot have."

Afeisha could not help but be honest. "You think I do not know how you feel? The person I like keeps looking at another girl, and she happens to be my best friend. Because I love both, all I can do is just follow along. Do you think I like doing it?"

After listening to her voice and hearing about her troubles, he felt guilty and did not know what to do. They parted on their way back. After he reached home, he went straight to his bedroom and began pondering upon what he and Afeisha had said. It started to become clear. He began seeing her in a new light, and his troubles were cast away with the realization that no matter what he did, he could not obtain those golden geese.

Wally, Lily, and Wendy had nearly reached home. Wally wondered about the strange woman he saw coming into the café. Meanwhile, Wendy was thinking about the news that she had heard.

"What are you thinking about, Lily?" asked Wally.

"We're thinking about things that are disturbing us and why. You, on the other hand, are the only person who doesn't seem bothered by any of it. You should be thinking, too. There are a lot of things going on that need to be sought out."

"Well, my grandfather, my dad, and some others are coming to help with the case, so I think we will be fine," Lily said.

"What? Your grandfather is coming? Why didn't we hear of

that?" asked Wally.

"My mom just told me last night, so I am just telling you. Besides, isn't it better that way?"

There were a lot of unsolved problems going on. While they were chatting, a bush on their path began to shake, and they all paused. Coming from behind the bush was no other than Jason, looking all beaten up.

"Are you ok?" asked Wendy.

"No, I am not. There is something that I need to tell Eithan before it's too late."

"Okay, you can tell him tomorrow. Let me take you to my place first." "That sounds good," said Jason. Moments later, he passed out.

As they arrived at the Granchest mansion, Wally jumped into action and started to treat him.

"Who is he?" asked Wally.

"You met already, but his name is Jason," said Wendy. "He is one of Eithan's best friends, along with Mandy."

"Oh, get me more clothes." Wally saw that his wounds were healing, and he immediately knew what he was.

Back in the forest, some dark, shadowed figures appeared as though they were trailing someone, but they did not find who they were looking for.

Things that Should Not Be Heard

Early the next morning, Wally knew that Jason would be healed, so he went to the guest room where he stayed. When he saw Jason, he could tell that Jason was running from something and was terrified. Jason tried to get up to show his thanks, but he was still too weak to move.

"Stay right there," said Wally. "I know what you are trying to do, but it is not necessary. After all, you're my sister's guest."

"All right," replied Jason, who was beginning to recognize that Eithan indeed had good taste in women.

"So, tell me, what were you running from in the forest? And who was chasing you?"

"I am not supposed to tell you this, but because you saved me, I'll tell you anyway. You should keep it to yourself, or you will be in great danger."

Treating the situation with levity, Wally shrugged but still listened to what he had to say.

"It was some months ago when Eithan came to confide in me about the uneasiness that he had been feeling. He told me that something is coming, and it is going to be something that we have never seen or heard." 'I cannot shake this feeling off,' he said. 'And it makes me uncomfortable.' After listening to the words that were spoken, I took some time off from school and began investigating to find out what the problem was. Eithan's instincts are always on point. But the more I investigated and found nothing, the more the situation puzzled me. I was about to give up when I found certain clues.

"Some strange people came into town yesterday, and they had a certain aura about them. A woman and a boy. But the problem lies with the boy. I overheard him commanding the woman that something must be carried out at all costs. Something in relation to a certain sword that was found, and that it must be obtained, no matter what measures must be taken. When this was said, the woman, who was obviously older, had no say. As it turns out, he is the Son of the Haynes Council."

"Haynes Council, that big corporation!" Wally exclaimed.

"Yes, that one. And it is not only a business corporation—get this, but also a corporation filled with strictly vampires and witches. And as if that wasn't bad enough, there's a hierarchy in the council, and the top is filled with elites that are coming to this town."

"No wonder they were trying to kill you," said Wally. "This is a lot of information. So, do you know when they will be here?"

"They are already here. We must be extremely careful and find the sword before they do."

"Do not worry," assured Wally. "By the way, do you happen to know the name of that sword?"

"They called it the Incasera sword."

"What!" exclaimed Wally in a high-pitched tone, which he then lowered. "I will tell you this since you gave me so much information. The sword that you just mentioned happens to be a family heirloom of ours, and the wielders of the sword must have a connection with our family. No one knows who the wielder is.

The sword chooses its owners and not the other way."

"Why did you say master's plural and not master singular?"

"Because my dad said it could be used by two," Wally remembered the woman he met at the café who had a certain aura about her. "Do you remember the woman that you saw?"

"I didn't see her properly, but I can remember their voices no problem." "All right, that's enough," said Wally, "Get some more rest, then I'll

carry you home later."

Wally went outside, and Laura was standing in front of the door. "What are you doing here?" asked Wally.

"I am just here to feed the sick child some soup so that he can get better.

Lily told me last night about the condition he was in." "Is that right?"

Before she went in, Wally turned back at Jason and blinked twice. Upon seeing it, he knew what it indicated. After Laura left the bowl of soup, she went outside and waited for him to drink it. Instead, Jason threw the bowl of soup out of the window. Wally had opened a window for him so that he could get fresh air.

Wally got ready for school. Meanwhile, Elena, who was already up, was happily preparing breakfast when the doorbell rang. She immediately stopped what she was doing and went to open the door. Upon opening the door, she saw Eithan, and her smile dropped. She left the door open for him to come inside and went back to what she was doing.

Wendy went into the guest room to visit Jason, but he was asleep when she got there. Coming down the stairs, she saw Eithan and went towards him. Eithan was happy, but he could sense that something was not right with her.

"Wendy, what is wrong?" "You need to come see this."

Eithan followed her to the guest room. She told him to open the door and go inside. He followed her instructions, but when he got inside, he beheld his weak best friend in bed. His happy face crumbled, and he dashed for him.

"What happened to him?" he asked shakily.

"I do not know. After we separated last night, we saw him in the bushes running from something."

Jason gently opened his eyes. "Eithan, is that you? I am right, it is you? Can you take me home? I feel much more comfortable and can relax at my house."

"Okay, I will…"

Eithan and Wendy lifted him up, and Wendy followed Eithan to Jason's house. As it turned out, Jason wasn't just rich; he was filthy rich. Eithan told Wendy that she should get to school before she was late because he had to attend to Jason and couldn't follow her. Wendy said she understood and wanted to stay, but he debated her until she finally gave in. The servants were shocked. They could not believe what had happened to their young master and began preparing everything for him. Looking at the servants, Wendy could tell that they were not ordinary people. Eithan went upstairs with Jason as Jason began telling him everything he had told Wally and what Wally told him. Eithan was angry with Jason for going off on his own like that, but he held his thoughts back because Jason was so weak.

Wendy was downstairs, roaming around, taking her time looking at the pictures and touring the house. A house cleaner from across the room, whose name she did not know, came up to her and began finding faults. She first looked at Wendy and asked her who she came with.

"I came with my boyfriend and his friend."

"Are you saying that you are the young head's girlfriend?" asked the servant.

"No, I am not."

"Can't be," she said, "My master does not have such poor taste."

Wendy then looked at the maid with a scornful glare. "Are you saying that I am not good enough for your master?"

"Yes."

"What's your name?"

"I am Karel." She paused for a minute as if Wendy's words were finally sinking in. "Are you saying that Eithan's your boyfriend?"

Not wanting to argue with her, Wendy just agreed. "Yes, he is." Upon hearing this, Karel grew increasingly upset.

Ever since the servant first met Eithan, she had done nothing but adored him, but he never gave her the time of day. "How did an ordinary girl like you manage to snatch someone as amazing as Eithan?"

Wendy scowled and rolled her eyes at her. This servant had overstepped, and she was beginning to burn with fury. "Now, that is none of your business, and I hope that you mind your business. You're behaving too unruly for a servant. Go and take good care of your master."

As Wendy kept stressing the word servant, Karel became angrier and angrier. Her claws started to unveil just as Eithan emerged and saw her.

"Karel! What do you think you are doing to my Wendy?"

She quickly retracted them and pasted a blinding smile onto her face. "Nothing, master Eithan."

"Go and take care of your young master upstairs."

"Yes," she replied with a bow of her head. She followed his orders.

Eithan and Wendy, though late, were still headed for school after Jason had settled in. They could still attend some classes. But Eithan could not believe what Jason had told him, especially about that sword, which had, in a matter of moments, gone from nothing to something dangerous.

"Is Jason going to be okay?" Wendy asked.

"Yes. In fact, he will be able to come back to school tomorrow. The people who were chasing him injected him with some fluids through a dart gun, and that is why he's weak. Don't worry, he'll get much better."

The couple went to their class, their minds scattered and overcome with anxiety. As soon as they arrived at class, Eithan lay his head on the desk.

The Voice that was heard

During class, Mr. Sam introduced the teacher, whom he was supposed to have introduced the day before. "Good morning, class. This is Ms. Smith. I told you previously what she is responsible for, and I hope you treat her with the respect that's due."

When Eithan set his eyes on the lady, he was surprised. It was the lady from the bar who came in with Franco and Sheila, but he could not place her face; he could only see the similarity. Observing her from head to toe, Ms. Smith started feeling like someone's eyes were on her, thoroughly examining her. She followed the stare with her eyes.

"May I help you?"

"No, you cannot," he replied with a smirk on his face. Wendy had never seen that side of him before. She intended to ask him what his problem was, but Samantha, who was sitting right beside him, spoke first.

"Are you alright? You have been uneasy for quite some time, and I don't like it."

"I am fine," replied Eithan, "It's just that she looks so familiar, but I can't remember where exactly I saw her."

"What is wrong with both my brothers? First, it was Aaron.

Now it's you."

"That's right!" Eithan shouted. "Thank you, Samantha." He held her hands within his. He remembered that Aaron had asked a strange question about the lady who had entered the bar that night.

"Excuse me, sir. I left something especially important to me with my brother, and I wish to get it."

"Why now?" asked Mr. Sam, "Class is about to begin."

After getting the teacher's permission, Eithan went to his brother's class. The students in his grade, especially the girls, could not take their eyes off him.

Their teacher, Mr. Primo, stopped when he saw Eithan at the door. "How can I help you?"

"Sir, can I borrow my brother for a minute? And Wally, too? It is for something important."

Mr. Primo stared at him for a few seconds, then decided to give in to his request. "What is your name?"

"My name is Eithan."

"Wally, someone named Eithan is calling you."

Wally got up out of his seat and headed out to meet him. Aaron began grumbling that Eithan had come to see Wally and not him, which made him uncomfortable.

"Who in here is Eithan's brother?" Mr. Primo asked. "You're also wanted."

Everyone looked at one another. Aaron was deep in his

thoughts and had not heard.

Once again, Mr. Primo asked the question. "Who in here has a brother named Eithan?" This time, it successfully woke him from his wonderland. He got up and responded, "I am."

When Aaron rose, Mr. Primo told him that his brother wanted to see him, and he quickly went. The three guys were standing together talking, and this caused a huge commotion, even though it was class time.

"Do you remember a strange lady who came into the bar with Jeremy and Sheila?" asked Eithan.

"Yes, we remember." Said both simultaneously. "What has that got to do with anything?" said Aaron.

"It turns out that woman is my biology teacher. If that was not bad enough, the guy Franco, who was with them, is also in my class.

"I guess Jason had already disclosed vital information to you, Wally, so I'll only tell Aaron."

In a couple of minutes, Eithan summarized what he had heard from Jason to Aaron. After they finished talking, Aaron began to let down his guard, hoping to catch a massive fish, but someone was not about to let that happen.

Back at home, Jason had replenished all his energy. As he thought about the secret in Wendy's house, he was brought back to when Laura gave him that drink. He shook his head. "Those people cannot be trusted, a house with many secrets. I was so uncomfortable that I couldn't even do one simple thing."

Jason, feeling like himself again, was so happy to have that behind him. Karel, one of the house cleaners attending to Jason, started to enquire about Eithan, but she stopped and uttered Wendy's name because he knew what she was going to say.

Later that afternoon, Jason felt well enough to go to the afternoon classes. When he arrived, he went straight to the principal's office to inform him about his whereabouts and that he was coming back to school. The principal, who was sitting in a comfy black leather chair with his back to him, couldn't care less. He brushed off what Jason had told him.

"I'm glad you're okay. You can go to your class, and I will inform the teachers."

Jason, who could not see the principal's face, left the principal's office in confusion. Scarcely anyone knew the principal because he hardly made an appearance during any school activities.

When Jason arrived in his classroom, he was surprised at how unfamiliar the faces he saw were. Standing there was none other than Ms. Smith, by whom he was taken. She was so beautiful that he thought the time had come for him to fall in love. He looked for his usual seat, but because he had been missing for a good amount of time, his chair had been taken by none other than Franco.

He could not help but stare at Franco because he was too familiar. "Are you okay now?" asked Eithan.

"Yes," said Jason. "I have not felt this good in a while."

Ms. Smith gave him a condescending smile, which sent a thrill down his back. Paying her no mind, he settled in.

"Now that a student has rejoined the class, I'm not going to teach anything today," said Ms. Smith. "You can divide yourselves into as many groups as you want and chat with your friends."

The whole class was happy about the new developments.

"This is the only time that I'll give you such perks, so enjoy it while you can," added Ms. Smith.

Though it seemed fun to the students, Ms. Smith had an ulterior motive for doing such a thing. She wanted to see how they bonded with each other. Franco, who was also new, had no friends, so this was the perfect opportunity to choose a clique. And coincidentally, he chose Wendy's group without hesitation, which shocked Jason.

His body may have healed, but the trauma was still there. Jason began speaking to himself. "No wonder she looked so familiar. And that voice, there's no mistake. She's the woman who was chasing me in the forest, and without a doubt, that boy was there. I can never forget that voice." Jason started to tremble.

"Are you alright?" asked Eithan.

"I am just a little giddy, but I will get over it soon. Hey, Eithan, do you remember the things that I told you?"

"Yes, I do. Why are you mentioning that right now?"

"Do you remember when I said I did not get to see their faces, but I heard their voices?"

"Yes, I remember. For Christ's sake, Jason, stop beating around the bush and just let it out."

"Guess what?"

"What!" Eithan was beginning to feel annoyed.

"I know who the owner of the voice is. The person who was chasing me in the woods was Ms. Smith, along with this Franco fella and a couple of other guys."

I guess the beating of his heart when he saw her was not love, after all, but terror. This caught him off guard. Eithan was surprised, but not to a great extent. He knew that something was off with those two, and what Jason said now confirmed his suspicion. Furthermore, Jason's hearing is superb, so there is no way that he could have made a mistake.

While the two of them were chatting, Franco walked over to where Wendy was sitting with Michael, Afeisha, and Samantha.

"Can I join this group?" he asked. "It looks more fun and interesting than the others."

Michael, who had his guard up, blatantly refused his invitation, and so did Samantha. But Wendy, who felt sorry that he had no friends, accepted him, and they all began chatting happily, but with a bit of tension.

"Why did you not join the group that Sheila and Jeremy are in?" asked Michael.

"Who is that?" replied Franco.

CHAPTER SEVEN

No More Darkness. I Choose Light

"What do you mean by 'Who is that?' We saw you come into the bar with Sheila and Jeremy the other day. Ms. Smith was also tagging along."

Franco had forgotten that those two were at the bar, so he decided to pretend that he did not know them. From a distance, Eithan and Jason could sense the heated conversation, so they decided to join them.

"Hey, what's going on?" asked Eithan.

"I asked Franco why he decided to join our group and not Sheila's and Jeremy's. Guess what his response was?"

Eithan shrugged, and Michael continued. "He asked who that was?"

"That is impossible," said Eithan, "Though my mind is occupied with a special someone—"

Wendy blushed. "It's not time for that."

Eithan continued. "I distinctly remember him entering the bar with Sheila, Jeremy, and Ms. Smith."

Franco was filled with unease. "What is this, an interrogation? I already told you I do not know who they are. That day, I was going home when I met some strangers who wanted me to join them for a drink."

"What a terrible liar," Jason said.

Franco began feigning innocence while putting on a helpless face. "All I ever wanted was to make friends with some decent-looking people, but I guess that's impossible now."

Wendy, who had no experience dealing with such people, could feel her heart melt when he began to talk. At this point, everyone was convinced that Wendy was not capable of dealing with the situation. Her heart was just too kind. However, that was just a front. In her head, she knew that something was wrong.

Franco continued his lies, trying to grasp every straw he could lay his hands-on. "I am going to the staff room. I'll be back." He took his time, gently got out of his seat, and left.

As soon as Franco was out of sight, Afeisha turned to Wendy. "How can you believe a story like that? It was obvious that he was lying!"

Wendy looked at Eithan, who stayed silent, and then started to speak. "Look, guys, I'm not the same goody-two-shoes Wendy that you once knew. Of course, I can sense that something was wrong. I am applying the method of keeping your friends close but the enemy closer."

Michael's angry face quickly changed from a frown to a smile, but Eithan's expression stayed the same.

"What's up with Eithan?"

"Nothing," he replied. "It's just that my girlfriend was being flirted with by another man, and she just smiled."

Wendy, who found that adorable, could not help but smile at him. And this time, her smile reached her eyes.

Meanwhile, Franco found Ms. Smith and informed her that he had just started plan A.

Ms. Smith could not help but be excited that their plan had started to come together. "It's all thanks to my intellect," she said.

"Don't be a narcissist," Franco replied. He suddenly remembered that when he was looking at Jason, he found something too familiar about him, but he could not quite place a finger on it. And if one thing was certain, it was that his intuition had always been on point.

"Don't worry about such idle things. Everything is in check. Just do what you must, and do not lose focus."

Franco gave her a look that said, "Stop yapping," and she immediately closed her lips. "When you and I are together alone, don't under any circumstances treat me as a student or as someone that's beneath you. Do you understand?"

"Yes."

This dragged back her memory of who was truly in charge. After telling Ms. Smith to inform the chair, Franco went back to class. When he arrived back at the classroom, Jason immediately changed the topic that they were on.

"Oh, Franco!" he exclaimed with one of his hands up, gesturing to him.

"You're back. We were just asking about heading to Rew's

Bar. Are you coming with us?"

"Yes, why not?"

"This is a good opportunity to get to know one another better."

"Why Rew's Bar and not Feistus? Didn't we go to Rew's last time?" Afeisha asked.

Wendy smiled. "Then let us go."

Michael, however, still insisted that they go to Rew's bar until the end. When they got there, everyone was happy—everyone except for Michael, because they did not go to Rew's.

Wally and Aaron were hanging out at Rew's. Aaron wanted to see if he could see Sheila and Wally, who had just gone to accompany him.

Meanwhile, back at Feistus, Samantha saw a figure in a working uniform that looked familiar and belonged to the cafe. She asked her brother if he knew the girl standing to his left, opposite the table, who had a blue cake with pink and white icing. Eithan glanced over and saw her familiar figure, but he replied to Samantha that he did not know her and that he only had eyes for Wendy. This made Samantha upset, so she just stayed silent.

After a few minutes of friendly conversation, Eithan shouted, "Oh! I remember now."

"Remember what?" asked Wendy.

"Samantha asked me if I knew the girl standing there in the uniform." "Do you?"

"Of course, I do. How can I forget? On my first day of school, I ran into her, and her books and papers fell to the ground. I helped her up, and we exchanged names. It was Ky—"

"Kylie," answered Wendy.

"Yes, that's it," replied Eithan. "I did not know that she worked here.

I'm a little surprised."

Eithan waved to Kylie and shouted her name. Upon seeing him, she came over.

"Hey, Eithan. Long time, no see."

"I have been around with my friends. Let me introduce you."

"That's all right, you don't have to. I know them. It has been quite some time, huh, Wendy?"

Wendy looked at her. "Yes."

"Oh, and Afeisha. How are you doing?" "I am fine, thank you."

Eithan looked at the girls' friendly interaction and then asked, "So, how do you three know each other?"

Kylie corrected Eithan. "Not three, but four. I also happen to know Michael too because we were all in the same grade school when we were young, and we are quite close."

"So, what happened?"

"Let us not talk about that." She turned to Eithan. "I can see that you are getting along well with your classmates. Before I forget, who are these people?"

"This is my sister Samantha, and this is our classmate Franco."

"It is nice to meet you all." She looked at Franco with a soul glare so passionate it burned the pupils of her eyes. Quickly, she dragged her eyes away and started to flirt with Eithan, which made Wendy jealous.

"Don't you have work to do?" asked Wendy.

"Of course, I do. See you around, Eithan." She hurriedly went back to her job.

Wendy glared at Eithan for a couple of minutes before she got over her anger. "Are you happy now?" she said.

"Yes. I love to see when you are a little jealous of me because I'm always like that over you."

Michael could not stand it anymore and quickly changed the conversation.

Jason then started up the abnormal conversation. "Do you believe in witches?"

Kylie, who was a short distance away, overheard their conversation and became nervous. Jason continued.

"I read a book not too long ago that I got from the school's library, and it talked about witches, vampires, werewolves, and demons. It was quite the book."

"All these things are just fiction," Afeisha said.

Wendy had come to understand that though Afeisha was her friend, she had not told her about herself. At the same time, Michael realized that he still had not told Wendy about his other form.

Michael was on edge because he knew he was not quite human, but he didn't know exactly what he was. Conversation had turned the whole room tense as if an invisible arm was strangling it. After a minute, silence crept into the room.

"What is wrong with all of you?" asked Jason. "I am just telling you about a book I found." He brought up the topic to see Franco's reaction, but instead, everyone's reaction caused him to know what had happened immediately. Everyone in the room was keeping secrets from each other.

"You need to chill out. Anyway, the book also mentions a certain sword named Incasera. Has anyone ever heard of it?"

Franco suddenly became interested. "Tell me more." "I haven't read that yet, so I don't know."

Samantha jumped in. "It is a sword of legend."

"It is said that the sword chooses its owners and not the other way around," said Afeisha.

"Owners," said Franco, who was naïve to the concept of ownership. "Yes," replied Afeisha,

"Only two people have the right to own the sword, and I do not know why. Could it be a person with a split personality or with two identities?" asked Jason.

"Could be," replied Afeisha. "After all, two separate beings cannot wield one sword. But you never know."

"How do you know all these things?" Franco asked.

"It is because I am interested in the supernatural. It happens to be a hobby of mine."

Wendy smiled. "It is getting late, so I should go now."

"Yes, we all should go and continue the conversation tomorrow." Franco left first, and the room was still tense.

"Tomorrow, I have something to tell you, Afeisha, Michael, and you too," said Wendy.

"I have something to tell you all, too."

Wendy left with Michael, who also said he had something to confess.

On their way home from the cafe, he had something to say.

While on their way home, Wendy stopped Eithan. "There's something I need to tell you," she said.

"You're just on time,'' replied Eithan. "There's something I need to tell you as well."

Wendy went first. "Do you remember when we were in the woods and those people attacked me and Sheila when you came to rescue me? I remember Jeremy saying that my blood or scent was extremely delicious and that he did not know why. After the few incidents with the moon and other strange things that have been happening around me, I asked my dad for an explanation, and as it turns out, I am a Vamolf."

Eithan became puzzled as Wendy continued. "It's a type of hybrid." "A Vamolf, that is the strangest thing I have ever heard," said Eithan.

"I'm serious, Eithan! A Vamolf is a powerful genetic combination of a werewolf and a vampire. It is indeed rare. That is why you've never heard of it. Do you believe what I am telling you?"

Eithan was silent for some minutes. "Are you telling me this because of what Jason previously said?"

"It's not only because of that. You are my boyfriend, the person I love, so you need to know. So, do you believe me?"

Eithan looked down into her eyes and saw her sincerity. "I feel guilty as well," he said. "Yes, I believe you, but there is something I also must tell you. I'm not as ordinary as you thought, either. I am a werewolf, and my friends and siblings are werewolves as well. We are from the Atlas pack."

"No wonder you were alone in the woods those nights. I found it strange that you never seemed frightened."

"Oh, so that's what you meant?" She playfully punched him in his stomach.

"What was that for?" he said.

"That was for what you said on the night we first met. So, you wanted to eat me, huh?"

"You mean that predator thing? Yes, girl, I was trying to scare you.

Besides, I fell for you that very night."

Wendy started blushing. "I fell for you the next morning," she said while covering her face.

"I know that I wasn't ordinary, especially my dad. He is what you call an Alpha," replied Wendy.

"Wally is a werewolf as well, but he does not seem too dominant," Eithan said.

"That is because he's only half," Wendy said.

"I can tell that your dad did not have it easy wooing your stepmother." "Why do you say that?"

"Hunters are not too friendly with the supernatural. It is only given that they would oppose the relationship."

"That may be true," replied Wendy. "However, my dad had it easy because it was she who wanted him and not the other way around. When my mother died, my dad had lost all hope, and she was there to comfort him. She was always there. My dad just decided to be with her so that I could get a complete home, and she already had Wally."

"So, did he love your mother that much?" "Yes."

This confused Eithan. William loved Wendy's mother. And Wally is his biological child, who is older than Wendy by some minutes, if not a year. The whole situation was strange.

"What happened to Lily?"

"I do not know. All of us headed towards the cafe, but I didn't hear her voice at all while we were there, and I didn't even notice she was missing."

"I guess she didn't make an impact on anyone because none of us missed her presence," said Eithan.

"Hey! Now's not the time to be mean, alright?" "Okay, sorry."

"I guess she went home," said Wendy.

Meanwhile, Michael and Afeisha were on their way home.

"Do you know what Wendy wanted to tell us but did not?" asked Michael.

"I don't have the faintest idea."

"Afeisha, have you ever felt like you are becoming something else that you cannot describe or that you're a part of something big you just can't explain?"

Afeisha shook her head no. "Where did all these things come from unexpectedly?"

"I do not know," replied Michael. "It's just that what Jason said back at the cafe is stuck in my mind, and I wanted to get it off my chest by speaking to you."

"I know what you mean. He did bring up such a strong topic, and those are things that I love."

"Hey, Afeisha, can I pick your brain for a second?"

Afeisha was happy because Michael started to take some interest in her. "What are your thoughts about what Jason was talking about?" he asked.

"Well, truth be told, I don't know anything. But ever since all these strange things began to happen in the town of George, I did some research, only to find out that unknown creatures live among us. For example, you have the werewolves. They are divided into three categories: the Alpha is the strongest and the leader. They have red glowing eyes.

"The omega is the weakest, yet the pack cannot survive without them. The beta follows the alpha, loyal and obedient. But what few dare speak of are the Grand alphas- terrifying, unmatched in power, rulers that even the bravest fear. And beyond them, hidden in whispers and shadows, is the legend of the Supreme Alpha. Only one is born in a generation, so rare that no mortal knows the path to its ascendancy. This Alpha is unseen, unknown, a force that exists only in fear, in stories and in the trembling hearts of those who sense its presence.

"Are there any other species apart from that?"

"Yes," said Afeisha. "There is the Uber. They're what's known as witches. These species use magic. You also have the devils, which are stronger than most species and on the same level as an Alpha. But some devils are known as the Davij. These devils are nearly as formidable as a Supreme Alpha, yet surpass even the might of a Grand Alpha, but they are said to be extinct. And lastly, you have the vampires. They are blood- sucking creatures. But there is a code that they follow. They cannot kill their kind without a cause, or something bad will happen to them. Vampires also have many levels, the strongest being Vamper. They can go without drinking blood and are as strong as a Grand Alpha, equal in strength to a Davij. However, all these things are just fiction. And as you know, there are us humans who are livestock and hunters who hunt the supernatural."

Listening to Afeisha's detailed explanation almost made

Michael's jaw drop. "Wow, Afeisha! I am impressed. You did your research thoroughly."

"Yes, I did." Afeisha's nose began swelling from the praise that Michael was giving her.

After all the talking about the supernatural, Michael had reached his destination. "Thanks for the information. You were a major help tonight."

"Anytime," replied Afeisha.

As Michael walked off, Afeisha remembered that she stumbled across a passage while she was researching. She quickly grabbed Michael by the arm.

"Have you ever heard of the term Vamolf or a moon that turns people— no, not people—the supernatural into psychos?"

Michael looked at her, dumbfounded.

"Well, I stumbled upon it. I don't want to go into detail, but you can search for it for yourself," Afeisha said, and then she quickly went inside.

Michael continued to think about what Afeisha had told him and went to do his research as soon as he got home. He typed the word Vamolf into a search engine and saw that it was a vampire half-werewolf creature that tends to be stronger than a werewolf and a vampire, depending on the parents of the individual.

As Michael finished reading about the supernatural moon's effects, he couldn't help but ponder its plausibility. After shutting down his computer, he lay on his bed, unable to sleep. Recalling the moon that had given him a headache, he questioned whether it was just a coincidence. These thoughts prompted him to search for the color rosewood online. Upon seeing its reddish hue, he was astounded, realizing that the moon's color matched. This realization deepened his intrigue. His curiosity was piqued even further by his findings about a moon called Mooncon Hemor. According to the information, this rosewood-colored moon had unusual effects on supernatural beings, causing headaches and potential loss of sanity if they stared at it for too long. The moon's impact on ordinary people was less severe, resulting in eye bleeding. Such moons were said to appear only once in a century.

Michael lay in bed, feeling the weight of exhaustion pressing down on his eyelids like a ton of bricks.

As Wendy dragged herself home, she was greeted by Lily and Wally. Wendy questioned Lily about her absence, wondering why they weren't hanging out together as planned. Lily, feeling slighted after seeing Wendy with someone else, explained that she had met Wally and Aaron at Rew's bar while Wendy was at the cafe and decided to spend time with them instead. As the evening wore on, Wendy admitted to Wally that she had something important to tell him, but she was just too tired to do so and went to bed.

The next morning, Wendy contemplated the impending conversation with her friends along with her conflicted feelings about Eithan, a wolf, and Jason, a young head. Her brother sensed her distress and inquired about it. She confided in him, discussing the complexity of the situation, preparing to confide in her friends and the challenges ahead.

Cannot Trust Your Friends Anymore

The next day was not like any other. Wendy was the first to awake, filled with anxiety about how she was going to explain things to her friends. Her brother could sense the agony she was in and asked her if she wanted to discuss what was on her mind. She told him everything, about how Eithan was a wolf and Jason a young head, and that she was prepared to tell her friends the truth and not lie to them any longer.

"That is good," said Wally. "If they are truly your friends, they will understand and stick around for sure." After saying this, Wally could not believe that Aaron, who acted the way he did, was a werewolf and not an idiot. The world is so unfair. Nevertheless, they both had something in common, and he was going to talk to him about it because of the advice he gave to his sister, whom he wanted to follow.

This morning, Eithan didn't come to pick her up, seeing that he had something to discuss with Jason and Mandy. Wendy went to school with Wally and Lily. On her way, she met Afeisha and Michael and decided to join them instead.

"Good luck!" shouted Wally. He was pulling Lily, who seemed not to want to go to school. "Good morning, guys. I hope you enjoyed your night." "Please do not speak about that. Last night for me was like hell itself," replied Michael.

"Oh my, it must have been quite the night," said Afeisha as they all giggled.

"Wendy, you said that you had something to tell me. What was it?" "Uhm… should it be right now? I do not think that now's a fun time."

"What are you talking about?" replied Afeisha. "Now is as good a time as any."

Standing next to a bench, Michael told Wendy to sit, and she complied.

She took a deep breath.

"Okay, here it goes. Let us sit down first before I start." "We're already sitting, Wendy. Stop stalling."

Wendy began telling them the secret she was keeping from them. "I am not completely human."

"What are you talking about? How can you not be human?" Afeisha asked.

"You see, I am the one you would call a Vamolf." "A Vamolf?" replied Afeisha. "Yes."

She was speechless for a second. "Vamolf, Vamolf. That is a familiar word. Where did I hear that word?"

Michael, who could not believe what he was hearing, spoke up. "That is the word that you told me last night, Afeisha. Do you have amnesia? If I am not mistaken, a Vamolf is a vampire half-wolf creature. But I have never seen you with any fangs, nor have you ever howled at a moon when you're with us. So, where did you get this ridiculous story from?"

Wendy stayed silent, but Afeisha responded to Michael. "Wendy is a realist, and she does not believe in such things, so the fact that she said it must be true. And besides, I know her long enough to tell when she's joking." Afeisha turned to Wendy.

"How long have you known that you're a Vamolf?"

"I have known for a good while now."

"So does Eithan know?" "I told him last night."

"Have you ever thought about telling us?"

"I did not want to tell you, but after listening to Jason last night, I felt so guilty that I thought I should tell you."

Afeisha could not believe what she was hearing. She became angry at the fact that Wendy did not want to tell her about the extreme changes that were happening in her life. "I thought we were friends, but I guess I was wrong since you cannot trust your friends anymore to keep an important secret like that."

"Afeisha, calm down," said Michael. "Aren't you blowing this whole thing out of proportion?"

"Do not tell me to calm down!" exclaimed Afeisha. "I am not mad about what she told me. I'm mad at myself because she didn't trust me enough to want to tell me something as important as that. I'm heading off to class now, Wendy. Give me some space so that I can think."

Wendy saw the hurt in her eyes, so she decided to give her some space to process the information. Michael was completely motionless. He did not know what to say or do because this was the first time he had ever seen Afeisha hurt, and a part of him just wanted to console her.

"What is up with you, Michael?" asked Wendy. "Didn't you say you have something to tell me? And how did you know what a Vamolf was?"

"I picked Afeisha's brain last night on our way home. Wendy, what I wanted to tell you might not sound so strange. I do not think that I'm completely human, which is weird, because my mom is human, although she never mentioned my dad. I think he wasn't completely human."

"How did you come to such a conclusion?" asked Wendy.

"It is because—" He paused for a second as he searched for the right words. "I looked up something that had happened to me a few nights ago. That night, the moon was big and red, and after I looked at it, I began to have a headache. Then I mustered the strength to pull my eyes away, and in just a few seconds, it stopped completely. I looked it up last night, trying to find clues, and what I found matches exactly what happened to me. Furthermore, I doubted it at first when the Hemor Moon appeared, but when I typed in 'rosewood', it said that it was a red color. I could not sleep because I kept thinking about it."

Wendy knew exactly what he was talking about. "I know what you're going through. I had to threaten my dad so that I could know what was going on. So, what do you think you are?" Wendy asked.

"I do not know. I know I'm not a wolf because I've looked that up, and it seems I'm not a werewolf, either. As for witches, we'll have to rule that one out. I'm not sure, but come with me this afternoon after class, and we will all visit my house. Bring Afeisha along. From today, no more secrets."

"This is the best time because Lily went back with her mom for two days. My so-called relatives will be coming to town tomorrow."

"All right then."

After entering the school gates, Michael and Wendy headed off to their classrooms. Class was a little different, as Mr. Sam smelled the tension between the girls. He could not wait, so he began teaching immediately. After school, Wendy went to Wally's class, informing him about everything that had happened and that he should grab Aaron and come home. Likewise, Michael invited Afeisha out. He did not tell her where exactly she was going, and neither did she ask, because she was thrilled to be invited out by her secret crush.

To Know Oneself

After walking for hours in what seemed like the direction to Wendy's house, Afeisha finally summoned up some courage. "Why are we walking through a forest, Michael? Be straight with me. Are we heading to Wendy's house?"

"Yes, we are," replied Michael. "I want to know who I am exactly. Wendy was hurt after listening to what you had to say, so she asked me to invite you so that her father could tell us everything. Do not worry; everything will be fine. Besides, do you remember when I was telling you that I was feeling a little off and wanted to know what it was? He is going to tell us everything." Afeisha became calm after listening to Michael explain. However, she was still a little disappointed that Michael hadn't, in fact, asked her out.

As they were walking, they saw how far Wendy had to travel every day by herself before Eithan stepped into the picture. They started to feel bad for all those times Wendy had to walk home on her own. They were both instinctively thinking about the same thing. Suddenly, Afeisha tripped on a branch, and Michael immediately caught her by her hips. This made her blush, intensifying the atmosphere.

"Uhm... we should go," said Afeisha, trying to act as if nothing had happened.

"Yes, we should."

Meanwhile, Eithan brought along Samantha, Jason, and even Mandy. Wendy, who was nervous, went home earlier than the rest, but before she did, she asked Wally to inform him about the situation. After a while, everyone gathered. The living room was quite grand, so they all decided to sit as they waited for William to arrive.

"What is that?" asked Afeisha.

"I forgot that you both have never been to my house," replied Wendy. "These things have always been in this house, and they belong to my dad. It is an inscription on a stone that is placed above a sword called Incasera. Come to think of it, it is the same sword Jason was talking about in the book. It is a family heirloom, though no one knows what it means."

"So where is it now?" asked Mandy.

"The sword? Well, it was in the house a few days ago, then it disappeared without a trace. But it is ok because the sword chooses its owner well, or at least that's what my dad says. I hope that I have given you a proper answer, but I cannot. He could have described it better. However, he is on vacation right now."

"So, you even have a butler," said Jason.

"Yes, we do, and that is because our family has been around for three generations, and we are not like your young master."

"Yes, yes, stop being sarcastic already."

William walked in. "Well, look who it is if it isn't my baby girl. Oh, and she brought her friends, and it's more than three. Well done, my baby. You've been doing well at school, after all."

"Aren't you a little paranoid, Dad? I have always had these friends." "I see," he replied.

"Now let me introduce you."

"There is no need to, said William. "I already know who they are. This girl with long black hair, brown and white skin, and black eyes is Afeisha. The handsome gentleman, with his contrasting wavy yet straight hair and green eyes, is Michael. He has a good height. The other good-looking hunk, who had short brown hair with blue eyes, is Jason. The girl with long, curly black hair, a mole above her left eye, and pale skin is Mandy. Am I right?"

"Yes, but how did you know that, Dad? It is not like I give you their exact description when I talk, do I?"

"My dear Wendy, I know all whom you interact with. It is my job to keep you safe, and your brother Wally does the same thing, doesn't he?"

"But sir, you forgot one," said Mandy.

Seeing that William did not mention Eithan, Mandy thought that he had disliked him. That would have been good for her because now she would at least stand a chance of getting Eithan's love.

"Do not worry," William assured them. "I've forgotten three. That pretty girl right there is Eithan's sister Samantha. I've already met Eithan, who happens to be my daughter's partner. He has already passed my test and Wally's, isn't that, right?" Asked William as he winked one eye at Wally's direction who laughed. Wendy blush. She couldn't believe her dad just did that.

"Yes, he has," responded Wally as he walked into the room with Aaron. "Hello there, Aaron. Nice to meet you."

"Sir, it is quite a pleasure."

"Well, let us begin. Who's first?" asked William. "I'm first. Can you tell me what exactly I am?"

"Yes, I can. But before that, let's all get our other identities out of the way, shall we? Who is first?

"I'll go first," said Mandy as she stared with a straight face. "I'm a werewolf, a Beta."

"Next will be me, Jason. I'm an Alpha werewolf." "I'm Samantha, and I'm also an Alpha werewolf. "My name is Aaron, and I'm an Alpha werewolf."

"I'm Wendy, and I'm a Vamolf, half vampire and half werewolf." Everyone who was getting the news for the first time turned to her, face filled with shock.

"Is that even possible?" asked Mandy. "The species is just too different."

"Yes, she is one," replied William. "And Wally is a half-werewolf." "So, I am surrounded by creatures?" asked Afeisha.

"Wendy decided to do this because of you, Afeisha. Furthermore, it looks like some of you do not know each other's identities, which is crucial for a lasting friendship. Your turn, Afeisha."

"I am Afeisha, and I am human." William stared at her, but he didn't say anything. He just nodded his head left to right. He knew she was human, but.

"And I am Michael. I'm not sure what I am."

"Okay, that is it. It is my turn now. I am William, Wendy's, and Wally's father, and I am a Grand werewolf, though it is rare. No wonder I sense that you are indeed strong: one more thing, Eithan. You and your brother are not just Alpha werewolves. You are close to being Grand while your brother is Supreme. However, it is best that you do not know it just yet."

Michael asked for a second time. "What am I?"

"You are supposed to know what you are," said William.

"But I do not," roared Michael. "Sometimes I'm out at night walking. I see strange things, but for some reason, I feel like it is not me but someone else."

Feeling empathetic yet happy, William said, "When you go home today, ask your mother, and she will tell you something quite interesting. Just because she does not say much doesn't mean that she knows nothing. As a matter of fact, she has most of the answers to your problems."

"Okay, but do you know my mother by chance?"

"Yes, I do. We were in the same group, but sadly, your father fell victim to—" He stopped.

"Why did you stop?"

"As I said before, your mother is in the best position to tell you." "What is going on in this town?" asked Afeisha. "A lot of strange things and strange rumors are going around."

"Not all who look human are human," said William. "And you should be afraid, especially of humans, because their hearts are more wicked than the creatures themselves, but they disguise it by covering it with a steel lid. Everything that you are thinking is true. Vampires, werewolves, witches, devils—they are all true. That is why I didn't want my daughter to go to school so far away from home. And not just that, but her naive personality wasn't fit for the world out there. However, she seemed to have changed a lot, thanks to you. Nevertheless, the most dangerous thing of them all is the moon, especially the crimson moon.

"As you know, the moon itself affects werewolves, and they either howl at the moon and transform into mindless machines or they hunt. But the crimson moon affects all supernatural creatures, whether it's werewolves, vampires, witches, or devils. Even hunters are affected by the moon, because when you go berserk, the hunters are there to put you in check, wrapped in its arms of red light. There is always the good and bad side of everything. After all, one coin has both a head and a tail. So don't watch and assume that something is what you think it is. There is always more than what meets the eye."

"Thanks, William. Oh, about those hunters you mention… who exactly are they?"

"Oh, they are—" He paused. "Let us say that they are a part

of my family. My wife's family, to be exact. They are a generation of supernatural hunters, and as Wendy told you, they will be coming tomorrow."

Samantha's face went into a slump.

"Do not worry. They will just be here to check up on George's situation," said William.

"Do you believe that hunters can be trusted?" asked Jason. "Do you want the truth?"

"Yes, I do."

"The truth is that I do not trust anyone. Not even my wife Elena. The only people I believe in are myself and, just maybe, my two children. Those hunters who are coming tomorrow are suspicious, and you should stay away from Franco Faller and Ms. Smith, the teacher. They are dangerous people."

"Why would you say that?"

"Well, the night you brought Jason back, those two were some of the people chasing him. I saw them that night, and I also happened to see you at the cafe with him."

"So, how did you know his name?"

"I am a Grand Alpha, which means that I can hear anything from a mile away, so you need to be careful. I know this is not what you wanted to hear, but that's all I have to say for now. And Michael, make sure you ask your mom. Okay, it is getting late. You should be on your way."

"One last question," said Jason. "What is the deal with the Incasera sword? And why do people want to get their hands on it?"

"Personally, I do not know, but the sword is indeed something to fear.

My father told me, the sword chooses its owner, as you already know, but the wielder must be from my lineage or have something to do with it. So, not just any person can wield it. I wonder why exactly they took the sword."

"Who was the one who forged it?" asked Aaron.

"I think it was a sorceress called Aundine, but that's all I know for now. It's getting late. You should go home now, and Afeisha, don't feel left out just because you're human. You're surrounded by amazing creatures who'll give their all to protect you, so don't sweat it."

Mr. William's words helped Afeisha feel more relaxed, and she was able to reach an understanding with Wendy about the matter.

"It looks like everything is simply fine," said Wally. Everyone went home as time was getting late.

"Aren't you glad you came?" asked Michael.

"Of course, I am," said Afeisha with a smile. "I made up with Wendy while learning that my friends are amazing people. Most of all, you're finally going to get the answer you wanted when you reach home. What's not to be happy about?"

Michael was touched by her words and smile, and his heart began to beat fast. Her smile was indeed breathtaking, but he refused to acknowledge it. He placed his hand on her head and said, "Let us go."

"In the meantime, thank you for inviting us, Wally," said Aaron. "It was worth it."

"Anytime," replied Wally, whose attention was focused on Samantha's expressionless face. "Are you okay?" he asked her.

After three minutes had passed with no response, Wally spoke once again. "I guess I am asking too much."

Wally's words fell on deaf ears. Instead of replying to him, Samantha walked towards the door to exit without sparing him a glance. Eithan was still chatting with Wendy when he kissed her and went with his brother. It was a little embarrassing because her father was present. Everyone went home thinking about the situation and what lay ahead in their lives, but Michael was undoubtedly the one who was most eager to reach home.

CHAPTER EIGHT

No More Darkness. I Choose Light

That night, as soon as Michael got home, he started waiting for his mother, who hardly ever seemed to be at home. He was determined to know what was going on, and this time, without fail, he would find out.

Meanwhile, back at the Granchest mansion, Wally wanted to know where his mother was. "Wendy! Have you seen Mom anywhere around here?"

"No, I have not. Now that you mention it, I also didn't see her earlier, which is quite odd.

"Dad! Exclaimed Wendy, "Where is Mom?"

"She is somewhere in the house," said William. "She said she had something to do, so I left her to do what she wanted."

Wally, who felt a little sad for his mother, asked his father if he really loved his mom. "Tell me the truth," he pleaded in a soft and tender voice. William asked for some water before unveiling the sad truth of their relationship. He sipped the cold water, fresh from the fridge. This cooled his throat as he seated both his children in the living room and began the tale, which was as old as time.

"Your mother and I have always been great friends, and I care for her deeply. However, as for love, my heart was given to one woman a long time ago, and when she died, my heart went along with her. Elena already knew it from the start. I warned her that the road she chose to walk would be a road of solitude, but she still chose it."

Hearing this made Wally tense, and his father recognized it.

"Wolves are creatures known for their loyalty towards one woman," said William. "Some have destined mates, and some imprints. The problem is, once you find that person, no one else can compare. Don't worry, you'll know soon. I think your sister knows the feeling. That's why I didn't drill into her boyfriend too much, because he is also a wolf that knows."

The tightness around Wally lessened. "Is the lady you love Wendy's mother?"

"Yes, I have always loved her. The five of us were indeed the best of friends. I loved her so much that I don't even believe she's dead." "You said five of us?"

"Yes, Jamain loved Serene, and there was your mom, Elena, who also loved me. Knowing her love for me, I took it upon myself to confront her at the earliest stage and told her I loved Wendine. We were together and did a lot of things. Finally, she got pregnant but died during childbirth."

"If it is like that, why am I the older child and Wendy the youngest? Or am I not your son?"

"Listen to me, son. In your life, whoever you imprint on, try to treasure and protect her, because that is something your old man couldn't do."

Wally could sense the pain in his father's voice, as if he were about to

cry.

"As I've told you before, Elena also liked me," Wally said. "I

remembered it clearly, as if it were yesterday. The five of us went out as we usually did, but there was something different on that day. I don't know how I got drunk, but I did, which is very weird, being that I have excellent alcohol tolerance and that I'm a werewolf, but I was drunk. To this day, I still cannot wrap my head around it. I woke up the next morning in bed next to Elena. That was indeed a disaster. Not knowing what or how to explain the situation to Wendine, I decided to keep it a secret, but little did I know that things can be hidden, but not for long.

"After the incident, I promised myself to keep away from alcohol and enjoy the time that I was spending with my girl. However, fate played a trick on me. Elena was a few weeks into her pregnancy and was pressured by her family to name the father of the child, but she refused. I could not allow the situation to go on any longer. I had to take responsibility. When Wendine heard it, she herself was shocked and, for that matter, also pregnant. It was a complete disaster. I had to choose between my close friend and or the woman that I loved. Maturely, I chose the woman I loved. After all, I couldn't live without her. I still don't know how I'm living without her. Nevertheless, I still saw Elena and took care of her because the fact was that she was indeed carrying my child. But nothing could compare to my girl, no matter who it was.

"The time came, and you were born. Your mother named you Wally after me. Although I don't feel that way about your mom, I loved you the second I saw you, and a few months later, your sister was born, but it was not as easy as when you were born. Wendine had some complications and died during the birth of Wendy."

William stayed silent for a moment. "Well, that is how it went." "What about the other two friends?" asked Wally.

"Oh, them. We have not been in contact for a long time, but both had a son together, and strangely enough, the father's memory was gone."

"How is it possible for a person's memory to be gone like that?" asked Wendy.

"The day after I had been drunk, I confronted him after leaving Elena, but it seemed that he did not know who I was anymore. Not only me, but Serene as well. However, she was pregnant and would later give birth to a son. My guess is he took on a different identity and started over from scratch."

"So, what happened to the woman? Did she move on?" "No, she did not. She stayed single and raised her son."

After hearing the whole story, Wally, who felt sorry for his mom, felt even more sorrow for his dad and Jamain. Something in the story didn't add up. He started feeling that something was wrong somewhere.

Elena was secretly listening to the conversation and felt remorse. She turned in the opposite direction and went inside the room.

"Oh, Dad, before I forget, tomorrow is parent-teacher conferences, so you will have to be there."

"I know. Wendy has already informed me, and your mom

must prepare for her guest, who will also be arriving tomorrow."

"Okay," said Wally as he went off to bed.

Meanwhile, in a cozy house filled with delicious, scented food, Michael was waiting for his mom, but there were no signs of her. He began to worry. He went upstairs to grab a coat before rushing out the door, only to behold his mother coming up the stairs with bags in her hand.

"Where are you going, Michael? It is quite late, you know."

"I am glad you know that," Michael replied. "Let me help you with the bags."

"I have such a handsome and gentle son." She placed her hands on his head and ruffled his hair.

"Mom, I want to ask you a few questions. Can we have a little chat?

Let us go in."

The truth about that night.

Michael and his mother went inside.

"I know what you are going to ask," said Joslyn. "It is about who you are, isn't it?"

"Yes," Michael replied. "I have been feeling and seeing a lot of weird things lately, so I went with my friend to her house, only for her dad to tell me to ask my mom."

"That's weird," Joslyn replied. "Why would he tell you that?" "I do not know why, but I'm asking to find out."

"What is the name of your friend?" asked Joslyn.

"Her name is Wendy Granchest, and her father's name is William." "I should have known it was Willy," said Joslyn.

"Mom, do you know him?"

"Yes, I do. He is one of my best friends."

"But how did he notice you? Or how did he know I was still in town? That man is really something else." Joslyn sighed. "Listen to this story, son. And in the end, you can tell me what you think."

She began. "Back when I was a college student, I had four close friends. Their names were William, Elena, Wendine, and Jamain. At that time, I also went by the name Serene. All of us were close.

"One day, we went to a place called May's Bar. It was a place where we usually spent time together. However, something happened that night. Elena joined us out, which was odd because her family was a hunter family, and they did not allow their daughter out, especially when it was late. But that day was different. William, who was great at holding his liquor, was extremely drunk, and that came off as odd to me and Jamain because we knew that, apart from being a great drinker, he was a strong werewolf. Jamain was concerned about William and decided to carry him home. Elena went with them also. I do not know what happened because I was dropped off first. However, the next day, Jamain did not remember who I was, the love of his life. I had been his girlfriend for a long time. I thought it was strange. Then, when William came, he asked Jamain why he did not take safe care of him, but Jamain didn't know who he was, either his best friend or partner in crime. I immediately concluded that Elena had done something to them."

"Why would you say that?" asked Michael.

"It was because William loved Wendine so much that he would die for her, but Elena also loved William. Nevertheless, something shocking happened a few weeks later. Elena became pregnant, and Wendine became distressed when she heard that William was responsible. She was also pregnant, and so was I, but no one knew about me. Just the two. From that moment, I have never trusted that woman, nor did I regard her as my friend. How can someone you trust do something so wicked and selfish? To make matters worse, I heard Wendine died during childbirth and William, due to his kind nature, married Elena for his son. I was so angry that I changed my name to Joslyn."

"That story indeed sounds fishy," replied Michael. "So, what exactly was Dad?"

"Oh, apart from being a stunningly handsome hunk, he was a devil, and he was a genius at math and biology."

"Wait," replied Michael, interrupting Joslyn from her reminiscing thoughts, "Did you just say he was a devil?"

"Yes, I did," answered Joslyn. "So, what does that make me?"
"It makes you a devil."

"But I thought you said my dad was dead."

"Well, I do not know where he is since he has forgotten us.

He might have started a family of his own, so I thought that was the best explanation to give. He does not know we exist."

"But Mom, why are you still single after all these years?"

"I guess somewhere in my heart I had hoped that he would return."

Michael felt the sadness in his mom, so he immediately dropped the conversation.

"Thanks Mom, I'm heading off to bed."

That night, Joslyn felt that it was time for her to forget about the past and confront William.

"Mom, before I forget, tomorrow at three is a parent and teacher conference, so it would be great if you could make it." "I will try my best," said Joslyn.

Parent-Teacher Conference

The next day was a day like no other. Elena got up early to prepare breakfast, and William was in the bedroom looking for something to wear. Wendy was thinking about introducing her parents to Eithan's, which made her a little nervous, and Wally was thinking about what Dad said the previous night. As they came down for breakfast one by one, their presence at the table brought about foul air. Everyone was sulky, except for William and Elena. Elena could not wait to see her father, uncle, and brothers coming to visit. William didn't want to see them, but was happy about attending the parent-teacher conference. That way, he could spend as little time with them as possible.

Wendy and Wally headed off to school, and so did the rest. When Mr. Sam entered the class, everyone was shocked. Mr. Sam, who wore glasses and always dressed down, was in full spirits today. He was as handsome as a statue in a royal prince painting. He was not wearing his usual big glasses that blocked his face. His bangs were placed to the side, and his chiselled, sculptured face was breathtaking. His green eyes took everyone by surprise. However, his foul mouth remained. His words were still deadly, as if bitten by a serpent.

"Hey, don't you think that he looks a little like Michael?" asked Afeisha.

"What are you talking about?" asked Wendy.

"I could not see it at first, thanks to his usual clothing and glasses, but now that he's cleaned up, there is no mistaking it."

"Well, now that you mention it, they have the same black hair and green eyes," said Wendy.

"That is what I'm saying." "But it's impossible."

"Why do you say that?" asked Afeisha.

"Because this morning, when I spoke to Michael, he told me that he was a devil. Look at Mr. Sam. Does he look like a devil? And his mannerisms and style—have you ever sensed anything inhuman about him?"

"I have not. But one thing is true." "And what is that?" asked Wendy.

"He is devilishly handsome, and his mouth is devilishly

185

mean, and that's attractive. If you ask me, I'm pretty sure he's a devil." Both girls began to laugh.

Eithan, who was sitting at the back, overheard their conversation. He could not believe that Mr. Sam was that good-looking. Apart from being handsome, there was something about his face that he did not like; something that he couldn't place, which made him annoyed.

"I know I have seen that annoying face somewhere. Where was it? I can't figure it out," said Eithan. He shook his head, hoping that his memory would provide an answer, or the disturbing thoughts would vanish.

"Class today is going to be a special day. I will not be teaching you math today. Ms. Smith and I will be present for biology classes. I was hoping you could use this free time that you have now to think about your future goals and what you would like to be in the future. We will discuss these during the conference this afternoon. Your behavior, performance, and interactions in class will all be taken into consideration. Good day."

Mr. Sam did not know why, but for some reason, he was in good spirits today. After leaving, Franco went up to Eithan and Jason, inquiring about their future goals.

"I want to be a biologist, someone who deals with genes and the human body," said Eithan.

"That's intense," said Jason. "I am going to take over the business from my dad, so my path is set in stone. What about you, Franco?"

"Oh, I am not going to be here for long, but I would like to be a president."

"Of what?" asked Wendy, who had overheard their conversation about someone's dad's company. "So, what does your dad do anyway?"

Franco felt that the questions were becoming overwhelming. "My Dad is the chairperson of the Haynes Corporation. I am not so sure as to what they do." He was lying.

"So, you are a young head like Jason, huh?"

"I guess you can say that" smirked Franco. "What about you three?" He wanted to change the topic to something else.

"Oh, I want to be a researcher, something like an archeologist, but not quite," said Afeisha. "What about you, Wendy?"

"I want to be Eithan's wife."

There was silence for a second. Hearing that, Eithan was overjoyed, though he did not show it.

"So, Wendy, are you going to throw your whole life away just to be Eithan's wife? You are pretty and smart," said Afeisha.

"I know, but I really want to be his. Besides, I'll let you know that being a wife is not an easy task. There is a lot that goes into keeping a home. And I like to write, which is something I can do in my free time."

"Let us change the subject," said Samantha. "What is your career choice, Samantha?"

"It's a secret," she replied. She did not know how or where

Wendy had the courage to say such words boldly. Under her breath, she whispered, "I also want to be Wally's wife." Eithan heard her and smiled.

After playful conversation and doing their own thing, time flew by, and it was now time for the parent-teacher conference. The parents had to stand in the back, and when their children's names were called, they would raise their hands to indicate that they were present. Luckily, all the third years were together, because the teacher knew that some parents had children in the same year but different classes.

After a few students' names were called, Franco's name was called. Ms. Smith went up to Mr. Sam, informing him that she would be his guardian. Mr. Sam then called Jason. His father was out on business, but his mom, Joanna, was present. She was a beauty to behold, with brown eyes and blonde hair. He then proceeded to call Eithan, Aaron, and Samantha. Emilia and the Author, who were present, raised their hands. People started whispering. These people were just too good-looking. More beautiful than the ones before. Mr. Primo had assigned some of his students to Mr. Sam for the conference, as he also taught them.

Wendy and Wally's names were called next. William immediately raised his hand. Mr. Sam paused for a second while staring at Mr. William. His head began to hurt a little, so he placed one of his hands on his head to lessen the pain. Next was Sheila, and her mom raised her hand. It was as if there were two Sheilas in the room, one more mature than the other. William remembered what his daughter had said that fateful night she got home. Sheila couldn't be alive, and the fact that she was could only mean one thing: she is not human. Lastly, Mr. Sam called Michael, who was in his seat but not paying attention. Once again, Mr. Sam called to see if Michael was present. This time, Michael immediately responded that he was there. At the same time, his mom rushed in.

"I am sorry I'm late," said Joslyn, who was gasping for air.

"You had sufficient time to be ready for your son's meeting," scolded Mr. Sam, who kept his head down, facing the paper. "There is no excuse. But seeing that you are tired, I will let it slide."

The children who already knew Mr. Sam's personality had informed their parents beforehand.

"That is all right," said Michael. "You're just in time."

Joslyn was so tired that her head was down, her hands on her knees, trying to catch her breath. But when she looked up, she beheld a person who looked exactly like her son. There is no way she could be mistaken for such a thing. "Is that Jamain I'm seeing right now?"

Her heart began to constrict, her eyes became glossy, and it became difficult to breathe. Michael became dumbfounded as he stared at his mom gazing at his teacher. Mr. Sam lifted his head and looked at her. Upon seeing her, Mr. Sam became restless. His head started to hurt even more, and the emptiness he felt in his chest was replaced by an ache he had not known. He requested Mr. Primo to join the class and hold the conference with Ms. Smith.

"Yes, I remembered, that was it!" exclaimed Eithan, who suddenly noticed that he was the only one talking.

"What are you talking about?" asked Wendy.

"I remember where I saw that annoyingly good-looking face,

though I am better looking."

"Stop behaving narcissistically and tell us what happened," said Afeisha.

"Do you remember this morning when Mr. Sam came in? He cleaned up quite well, but his face was still unappealing to look at. I could not place a finger on where I saw his face, but now, I do."

"You do? Then tell us where you saw his face," said Afeisha. "His face looks just like Michael's. No wonder it annoys me." "You think so too, huh, Eithan?"

"What do you mean? Is it not obvious? He's like a total replica." "I tried to tell Wendy this morning, but she didn't believe me."

Meanwhile, Michael was in his own little world, wondering how he could look so much like Mr. Sam, a man who looked ordinary just a few weeks ago. Not paying attention to the parents, William quickly took Joslyn away so as not to cause trouble.

"William, look. Isn't that Jamain?" Joslyn whispered as she broke down in tears. "He even has the same foul mouth that he always does."

Michael quickly saw that his mom had broken down and went towards her, but William was taking her away.

"What is wrong with my mom?" asked Michael. "She was very shocked. I guessed that it did shock her because it even shocked me."

"What are you talking about?" asked William. "You sound as though you have never seen that teacher before."

"Honestly speaking, this was the first time I ever saw him. He may be my teacher, but his appearance is always shabby. He wears glasses, so you would not be able to see his eyes, and his bangs cover his face. He has a mean mouth, but nevertheless, we all respect him because he is a great teacher. When I saw him today, I was in shock. It was as if I was looking at myself. I do not know if he felt the same way, though."

"Who would have thought that he was in the same place as his son?

Life is truly a mystery.

"Are you saying that man, Mr. Sam, is my father?"

"Yes, he is. That's Jamain, and you have already heard the story from your mother. I always suspected that he was Jamain, but for your mother to call him that, it must be true. They were in love. But sadly, it looks like whatever he has on him or in him has not yet subsided."

"Does that mean he still does not know us?" asked Michael.

"That is the case," said William. "I don't even think he recognizes that you look like him. A veil has been placed over his eyes. Something prevents him from knowing what he needs to. Let us carry your mother outside to get some air."

"Why not the infirmary?" replied Michael. "Were you even awaking during the conference? Mr. Sam or Jamain or your dad— whatever you choose to call him—has left to go to the infirmary, as we have triggered his headache. If we take Joslyn there now, his head will hurt even more, or he might unconsciously use his powers. Jamain is a powerful devil and should not be taken lightly."

"Okay, let us go."

Meanwhile, Mr. Sam went to the infirmary because he was sick. He lay on the bed and shut his eyes, but his headache did not stop. He began seeing image screens flashing before his eyes. In it was a picture of Eithan's father, and he called him William, and he saw Michael's mother, Joslyn.

"Why am I with that woman? Wait a minute. Isn't that the lady who arrived late this afternoon, even though she had sufficient time to get ready? Why am I with her? And we look like we were a couple? I'm calling her Serene. Is that her name? Ouch, my head hurts a lot. Let's not think any more. Go to sleep." He was talking to himself to not feel the pain anymore.

After a few minutes, his head was cool once again, and he no longer remembered the events that had taken place. Mr. Primo and Ms. Smith took over the conference and began telling the parents about the academic performance of the students. They asked the children questions about their future careers while urging the parents to not only support their choices but to be there for them. As students, they are to follow their dreams and not what their parents or individuals want them to be.

Outside, William and Michael were still attending to Joslyn. Joslyn had passed out but awoke after half an hour.

When she regained her composure, she said, "William, I have not seen you for a long time. Never mind. How have you been doing?"

"I have been doing great," said William. "And you?"

"I also have been doing great. I see that you have already met my and Jamain's son."

"Yes, I did. Ironically, he and my daughter happened to be friends just like us when we were going to school."

"Friend, huh?" said Joslyn in a soft and tender voice. She stirred the conversation in another direction. "That was Jamain today, and there is no mistaking it. I know everything about him, including his mean mouth. I see that has not changed a bit."

"Yes, it has not," said William.

"So where is Elena? I'm having a bitter time."

"She is home preparing for her family, who are coming by later." "They are coming to this town?"

"Yes," replied William.

"Why do you look worried? William, as a friend, I am going to tell you this. Beware of that family. It is troublesome."

"Why do you say that?" asked William while acting clueless.

"Do you remember seventeen years ago when we went to the bar?" "How can I forget? It was the worst day of my life."

"You were drinking with all of us and became drunk, which was odd because you are a werewolf. Jamain was worried about you and offered to take you home, but because it was late, Wendine offered to go with me and Jamain with you. Elena also went with you both. But the next day, Jamain forgot everything, including you and me, which was quite bizarre. I also heard you asking Jamain why he did not take you home, which was weird because I saw him taking you home. I do not know how you ended up with Elena, but she did something. I remember her family was a hunter family. Beware of them."

"I will," replied William.

"One more thing. I saw Elena injecting Wendine with something on the day that she was giving birth. I do not know what she injected, but I think that was what caused Wendine to stop breathing after she gave birth."

"What? How come you never told me such a thing!" exclaimed William.

"I am afraid. After all, I'm only one person."

Michael took his mom home that day, and William went back to the conference filled with anger. After the conference was over, William was still filled with hostility, but he held it in for his children's sake. "Let us go home. Our guests are waiting," he said.

"What is wrong with you, Dad? You look upset."

"Nothing," he replied. "It's just that I've had a lot of things on my mind lately, that's all."

Here They Come, The Unwanted Guests.

Upon arriving home, they saw vehicles in the yard, which could only mean one thing: the guests had arrived. William went in, greeting Cyrus, Elena, and Laura's brother, Yannick; their son, Nicholas; their brother and Laura's husband, Lionel; and Kiarra, their elder sister. One thing that stands out about the family is that you can tell they are disciplined in their training. The ladies were fit, and the guys were buff. The old man who did not want to show himself but sat at the table was named Lennox. He was their dad, as well as Wally's grandfather. A scheming and cunning old man who would stop at nothing to get what he wants.

Elena knew just how much William disliked her family, although she did not know why he hated them. To cut the tension in the room, Elena said, "Dinner is ready. Why don't we all take a seat?" Everyone took a seat around the dinner table, but the atmosphere remained tense. "Where will you all be staying?" asked Elena.

"Why can't we stay here? This is such a big house, and I am sure that William can host us," said Lennox.

"I'm sorry, but I can't," said William, who did not want to be around them. "As you know, I was hosting Laura and Lily, and my butler is not here. Furthermore, I'll be having my daughter's friends over from time to time, so I cannot host you, but you guys can stay here for the night."

"How cold," Lennox replied. "But I see your point. I do have an old house where I used to stay. Elena, you should know it because that is where you stayed when you were younger.

"You mean that house? No one has inhabited that house in a long time.

Is it even possible for people to stay there?"

"Yes, it is. I have been sending people from time to time to clean the house, so it's quite clean." He turned to Wendy. "Wendy, I have not seen you in a long time. You look just like your mother."

"Do you know my mom?"

"I did. After all, she was one of my daughter's friends. Thank you for dinner. It was delicious," said Lennox.

"Indeed, it was," said Nicholas.

"Lionel, or should I say uncle?" asked Wally.

"Lionel is fine."

"Why did you travel with Grampa and the rest of them? Don't you know why they are here?"

"Yes, in fact, I do. I am also here to investigate, but my wife and child are also here. That's why."

"That sounds reasonable." Wally could not quite put his finger on it, but something about his grandfather's words and the way he behaved was quite odd. One thing was clear, as he remembered his dad's words: No one can be trusted.

After eating dinner, everyone went to their respective rooms, contemplating the next day, but not Lennox. When Laura went back to Capes Ville, she informed him that the sword was nowhere in the house. Though he came back to investigate and settle the matter, one of the main reasons why he was in George was to obtain the sword. That unparalleled sword that chooses its owner. There is a ceremony that usually takes place on the twenty-fifth of every crimson moon. This occurrence does not usually happen. Sometimes, it takes thousands of years before it can happen. This moon is said to be more crimson than the others, and by using different equipment, astrologists have figured out that the moon will appear in just seventeen days. During this ceremony, the sword that has been lying dormant for years will be forcibly awakened, and the person who is the strongest will be chosen. Well, at least that is what he heard.

That night, when everyone was asleep, Nicholas and Lionel went out into the bushes, around and inside the house looking for the sword, but they did not find it. Wally was not asleep yet, so he went downstairs to the kitchen. He heard voices and looked outside. There they were, standing, discussing something and looking all suspicious. Wally went where he was able to overhear them. Nicholas and Lionel were discussing the sword and what Lennox wanted to do with the sword. He even overheard them talking about a conspiracy, but for fear of getting caught, Wally went back upstairs to his bedroom. Pondering what he heard, he could not go back to sleep because he wanted to know what exactly the great conspiracy was— forgetting the fact that curiosity did indeed kill the cat.

CHAPTER NINE

Things Gone Wrong

It had not been even an hour since Wally went back to sleep. However, there were other noises in the house. Forgetting that supernatural beings were a part of the Granchest house, old man Lennox went out and inspected the house, looking for the sword. He then saw an inscription: "Sword and claws must meet." But he did not know what it meant because the sword that should have been hanging above was missing. "This is such a weird house," he said. Though Lennox was a hunter, he felt that the house was just too weird and disliked it. "I'm so glad that William refused to guest me in this house because I myself would have gone crazy in this God-forsaken place."

Lily woke up and went downstairs. "Dad, is that you? Why are you up so late?"

"Oh, it is Grandpa. I'm not up late—I just heard a noise and came downstairs." That's when Lennox finally realized that if Lily could hear him, so could everyone else in the house. Wally, who came down once again, listened in on their conversation.

"Lily, do you love your grandpa?"

"Of course. Of Course, I do, and you know that."

Lennox continued. "And you know Grandpa loves you, too.

Tell me, where is the sword?"

"What sword?" asked Lily with her pretentious face. Luckily, Lennox had been pretending for a long time, so he knew when someone was doing it. "I am talking about the Incasera sword. You have been living here for a while now. Have you ever seen it?"

Lily did not want to give the sword to him and kept on denying its existence, but Lenox just pressured her even more. Finally, she said that she saw the sword.

"Where did you find it?" asked Lennox.

"I found it in Aunt Elena's room, so I took it out to examine it," replied Lily.

"Do you have it now?"

"Yes, it is in my room."

After that conversation, Lily became extremely wary of her grandpa. She could sense that something was not quite right with him. Lennox went upstairs with Lily to get the sword, but because of what had just happened, Lily did not want him inside the room.

"Wait here, Grandpa. I will go get it for you." Lily went inside the room, grabbed the sword that was indeed above her bedside stand, and gave it to Lennox.

"Thank you, Lily. I always knew that I could count on you. Do not tell anyone that you gave me the sword."

"All right," replied Lily. "And don't tell anyone it was me who had the sword."

"Well, it is a promise between us."

Wally, who was watching her and overhearing it, did not hear when Lionel and Nicholas came into the house.

"What are you doing there, kiddo? Is it not too late to get up?"

Lennox looked down at the same time and saw Wally. "What are you doing out of bed so late?"

"I was taking a walk. I felt thirsty, so I went to the kitchen to get some water. I was about to go upstairs when I saw you and Lily chatting, but I did not want to disturb you, so I decided to lie low until you finished."

"What a thoughtful boy you are. I have finished talking with Lily, so you can go to bed now."

"Okay, and good night, uncles. Tonight was quite the night."

Puzzled by what he had just said, Lennox started thinking that he had overheard his conversation with Lily, but his blank expression revealed that he was filled with doubt, and so were Lionel and Nicholas.

The next morning, everyone went downstairs for breakfast, but Lily and Wally were still asleep.

"Can someone go and wake those two up?" Elena asked.

"It is all right," said Lennox. "Those two-need sufficient sleep. They are just children."

"What are you talking about, Dad? You used to wake me and Lionel up, even our brothers, earlier than this," said Elena.

"Times have changed. Just let them sleep," Lennox replied.

"Are they tired because they were up the whole night?" asked Nicholas, not paying attention to his words.

"What do you mean by that?" asked Elena.

"When I came in with Lionel last night, Wally was chatting with our brother, and so was Lily with Dad. That is probably why they are still asleep."

"What were you talking to the kids about, Dad?"

"It is a secret," Lennox replied while gazing coldly at Nicholas. William became even more curious about what was going on in his house. He heard the racket last night but refused to get up since he did not want to raise any suspicions. After everyone had eaten their breakfast and gone to their destinations, Wally still had not come downstairs. William went up to check on him. He knocked on the door.

"Wally, are you alright? You have been here for a long time now. And knowing you, I can tell that you're already awake."

"You can come in, Dad. I am just a bit puzzled as to what happened last night."

"What's the matter, son?"

"Dad, when you said that you trust no one, was there a basis for such a claim?" asked Wally.

"Yes, there was," said William.

"No wonder you said that with such confidence. Last night, as I awoke, I saw Uncle Nicholas and Lionel outside chatting about what Grandpa intended to do and about the Incasera sword, but I did not want to get caught, so I came back upstairs, only to hear more noises. I went back down and overheard Lily and Grandpa discussing the sword once more. As it turns out, when we were looking for the sword and asking who had it, it was Mom who had the sword all along. But Lily took it from her room or lair and hid it in hers. Grampa was unusual last night."

"What do you mean by unusual?"

"Gramps was pressuring Lily to hand over the sword to him. Lily did not want to. She denied ever casting eyes on the sword. But for some reason, Grandpa could tell she was lying, so Lily had no choice but to give him the sword."

"So, it is like that," said William.

"Yes," answered Wally. "Dad, I am a little confused. Is there more to the sword than what meets the eyes or what you told us?"

"Why do you say that, Wally?"

"It is because a lot of things are revolving around that sword, and you don't seem to be concerned that Grampa has the sword."

"Wally, I am just going to tell you this, so you must keep it a secret no matter what."

"Okay, yes."

The Truth About the Sword

"The Incasera sword is just not any sword. What I told you and your friends was indeed true, as was what I told your sister, but there is another thing that I kept from you. That legendary sword is not something your father will put up in the house for display. We have visitors when I'm not around. I don't know what your mother does. And we also have a butler. Everyone is after the sword because whoever possesses the sword or becomes its owner not only has the power to slay any creature but also gains immense strength, and it is said that they gain immortality, which I think is ludicrous. However, after everything that's happened and all the supernatural that I've seen with my eyes, it's hard not to believe in something like immortality. That's why I replicated the sword and put it on display while hiding the real one."

"But how did this sword come along, Dad?"

"Long ago, there was a handsome man who fell in love with a beautiful young woman. However, they both hid their identities from the other, fearing that if they were discovered, the other would not like them anymore but would view them as monsters. They did a lot of things together. They went on dates. But they felt that to love someone genuinely, secrets should not be kept. The young man eventually decided to tell the woman the truth. It was as if their hearts were coordinated.

"They decided to meet up at night.

"'Why have you called me so late at night?'" she asked.

"'My parents would be worried, and I wanted to tell you something before we go further with our relationship.'

"'I'm guessing it couldn't wait?'

"'No, it can't.' He braced himself, then said, 'The truth is, I am a werewolf. You don't believe me, do you?' But little did he know that the woman was keeping a secret as well.

"'I do," she replied. 'I also have something to tell you. I am a vampire. I wanted to tell you, but I feared you would not want to be with me.'

"The man was happy that they could be so open, but later, he learned the harsh truth. A vampire and a werewolf together were forbidden. They tried everything they could to fight against it, but it did not work. Later, the man found a great witch named Aundine. The man went to her, pleading with her that he wanted to protect his lover, as they were in a forbidden relationship. Aundine felt sorry for the werewolf and could feel his genuine love towards the vampire woman, so she decided to forge the sword. However, for this to be done, the witch told him that he needed some of her blood. He did as he was told, and he got her blood with her permission. The witch then asked for two of his claws, and he gave them to her.

"She spent seven whole days crafting the sword. It became her best masterpiece, as her powers went into the sword with every strike. After seven days, she went to deliver the sword, but it was already too late. Some werewolves who were against them attacked the house of the vampire woman and killed her. In retaliation for their lost daughter, they also attacked the man and killed him. When Aundine got to the man's house, he was already dead. She was filled with sorrow and decided to give the woman the sword, but she also was already dead. Since both died, she tried to destroy it but couldn't. Aundine grieved and decided that she would never make a sword so powerful for anyone ever again.

"She then began her search for a person she considered worthy of possessing the sword, but found no one, until one day, when she was sitting in a bar, and she saw your great-grandfather. After taking a long look at him and into the future, she saw something and gave him the sword, explaining to him all that had happened. She knew he was also a werewolf and told him that he should keep the sword safe from people who would want to abuse it until it chooses its owners. That is why the sword has always been in this family."

"Dad, do you have any idea what she saw in Grandpa's future?"

"I do not know, but whatever she saw, it had to be someone capable of using the sword in his lineage. That's all I know. Wally, no more questions, and don't tell anyone about the sword giving immortality. It's time to get out of bed. You are already late for school."

"Okay, Dad, and thanks for telling me the truth." William smiled. "No problem."

Wally hurried to school. He was pleased that his dad could confide in him about such things. Being distracted by his thoughts, he forgot about those around him and just kept on walking. He knocked into someone and quickly came back to reality.

"Are you alright?"

"I'm sorry, I was not paying attention. Oh, it's Kylie Primo."
"Do you know me?" she asked.

"I do. I am Wally. Have you forgotten? I'm Wendy's big brother."

"It's nice to meet you. And remember to take your head out of the clouds when walking. It's not safe for those around you."

Wally began smiling. "That's true, I guess I should. Let me help you with those. I noticed that you are always in the library. Why is that?"

"Oh, that is because I'm the library assistant," answered Kylie. "Is that even fun?" asked Wally.

"For me, it is. I get to read a lot of books on different things, even though they can be quite confusing at times."

"Do they have any books on supernatural in the library?"

"Yes, they do, and I think you should come to the library when you have free time, you and your friends, seeing that you are all interested in the same things."

"Okay, I will be off." Wally wondered why she would say such things, but he was already late for class.

After that encounter with Kylie, Wally could not help but wonder why she would say something like that. "We are all interested in the same things." He quickly went to class, but Kylie went back to the library. In the afternoon that day, Wally met Wendy while he was going to the cafeteria, along with Eithan and Samantha, who were in the same class.

"Hey, guys. I wanted to tell you something. Kylie said, 'If you are interested in learning about the supernatural, then go to the library."

"Okay," Samantha replied, staring at him intensely, which made him feel uncomfortable.

"How did Kylie know that we're interested in supernatural?" asked Aaron. "She must have overheard it when you were talking."

"Do not be ridiculous!" exclaimed Eithan. "I remember when we were introduced. At that time, the discussion had not yet been touched. Furthermore, after we introduced ourselves, she went on her way. The conversation about the supernatural was brought up, and she was nowhere in sight, so there's no possible way she would know."

"Aren't you blowing this out of proportion, Eithan? She heard us when she was attending to the other customers."

"Why are you defending her, Wendy?"

"I am not. It's just that you're saying that she was so far away from us, and we were talking discreetly so that no other table or people could hear us. This means that she is a psychic or a stalker." After jesting with Eithan, she stopped and became serious. "I have known Kylie for a long time. If she says something, then we should consider it. Besides, it doesn't hurt to try the library. And maybe Kylie is another supernatural in the shadows, who knows.

After a few minutes of thinking about what she had said, she realized she had given strength to Eithan's point. She looked at him, and Eithan just watched her and patted her head.

"Let us go for lunch. We will talk about this later," Eithan said. "Are you joining us, Wally?"

"No, I will be heading to the library now to do some research."

Wally left the two of them and went to the library, where he met Kylie once again.

"Hey, Kylie. I am here to read some books."

So, do you want all the books on the supernatural?" asked Kylie.

"Yes, that would be nice. While we're at it, how did you know that my friends are interested in such things?" asked Wally.

"It is a secret that I'm not revealing." Kylie went to the place where the supernatural books were and grabbed them one by one to give to him.

Surprisingly, there were only three books.

"Uhm, Kylie?" said Wally. "I saw you going all over the library grabbing books, and I am quite sure that you know this library like the back of your hand, so why are there only three supernatural books? And what are you going to do with all those books?"

"To answer your questions, I don't know why there are only these three books in the library. Maybe because people think it's just fiction, and it would be a waste of time to have too much of it in the library. However, these other books are the books that I'm about to read." She pointed at the pile of books on her desk.

"Oh," replied Wally. "Can I pick your brain for a minute?"

"Of course, you can, but I would also like to read, so you will need to be quick."

"Ok, let us see. First, I'd like you to tell me all you know about a sword called Incasera."

"Why would you think that I know such a sword?"

"First, when I opened these books just to scan through, I saw your name on all of them. This means that you borrowed the books to read, which leads to you having some knowledge and a curiosity to learn about the supernatural. Not to mention the way that you talk, it is like you have some secret."

"What are you talking about? Anyway, stop trying to pick my brain with your uncertain remarks; they make me feel uncomfortable."

"And why is that, my dear Kylie?" Wally began smirking while teasing her, and this threw her off her feet.

"Fine, I will tell you what you want to know. First, I borrowed the books because I wanted to know about the strange things happening in this town that no one seems to be investigating or bothering to care about. After reading the book, I noticed that certain things that have been happening in this town seem to add up. As for that sword, it is not mentioned in detail, but from the knowledge that has been passed down to me by my mother, I know that that sword was initially forged to protect lovers who were in a forbidden relationship.

"One of the greatest witches who ever lived was touched by their love and requested the man for the blood of his lover and his claws. In the hands of the wrong person, it can do great harm, but no need to worry about that because the sword has a mind of its own and chooses its owners."

"So, can the sword be forced under any ritual to become the weapon of another?"

"Good question, Wally, but I'm not sure. If someone forces you to do something that you don't want to do, what would you do?"

"Well, I would be upset, and I'd probably retaliate in some way or another," replied Wally.

Kylie continued. "Well, the sword will probably find its own retaliation.

After all, it does have a mind of its own." "Well, that does make sense."

"There are two people who can wield the sword, since it was a sword forged for lovers."

"A sword for lovers. Lovers... lovers... lovers... Wait a minute! Could that be the keyword?"

"What are you talking about?" asked Kylie.

You said, "It was a sword forged to protect one's lover." Could it be that the sword is waiting for the lovers to reincarnate?"

"What do you mean by that?" asked Kylie.

"Think about it. The sword has a relationship with the Granchest family because it has been in that family for years but has remained dormant. It is because the previous owner, who used his claws, was a werewolf. So, the question is, if he were a werewolf, then his girlfriend must be a vampire. After all, that's what forbidden love is."

"Do you think so?"

"Yes, that is true, and if what I was told by my father is correct, then the wielder is a Granchest werewolf and a vampire. However, something is still missing from this story, and I feel that it is closer than what we are looking for."

Kylie forgot that she had chosen her own books to read and was engrossed in Wally's conclusions.

"Hey, Wally, can I trust you?"

"Of course, you can. Do you want something?"

"No, it's nothing. I will be heading to class to do some thinking on my own. You can stay if you want."

Meanwhile, Eithan, Wendy, and the whole clique were on their way to the library, excluding Lily and Franco, who were busy. When they walked in, they saw Wally deeply engrossed in reading. He did not hear them when they entered, nor when they sat.

"Hey, bro!" Wendy exclaimed, but to no avail. Once more, she called "Wally!" He turned around, and there they all were.

"Please do not shout. This is a library." He whispered, his voice calm but firm. She rolled her eyes, clearly unimpressed and swallowing a retort. He arched an eyebrow, just enough to dare her, and immediately, she fell silent, though a smirk lingered on her lips.

"Are you alright?" asked Aaron.

"Yes, I am. I was just concentrating on this book. I've received both good and bad news. Tell me which one you want to hear first."

"Can we at least hear the good news first? I'm sick of hearing the bad news first," said Jason.

"Alright. I have gotten more information on the Incasera sword, and I think that it will help us out a lot. The bad news is that no one can be trusted, not in my family. I have this feeling that my grandfather, whom I overheard late at night speaking to Lily, demanding that she tell him where the sword is, is going to use it for some evil purpose."

"Wait a minute, why would Grandpa ask Lily for the sword? And how does he even know about the sword?"

"As it turns out, Lily found the sword in some room that my mother hid it in and kept it all this time. Now the sword is in Grandpa's hand, and I have overheard some ritual that is going to take place."

"Oh my!" exclaimed Wendy. Jason just nodded his head.

"Why are you shaking your head as if you're in denial?" asked Eithan.

"I knew those people could not be trusted from the first day that I met them."

"Do you know something that we do not?"

Jason continued. "I was worried about Eithan, so I went to your house to look for him, but no one was home. I went inside, and there were a lot of creepy-looking statues and other weird things in it, but what struck me the most was the hidden room."

"What hidden room!" Wally and Wendy said simultaneously.

"Well, I guess that you did not know your house had another room, which must be where Lily found the sword. What I saw in that room made me afraid. Your mother is up to something, and whatever it is, it's not good. As for Lily and her mother, I do not trust them either, not for a second. Lily's mother, Laura, offered me something to drink while you were out so that I could get better, but I threw it away. I do like you, Wendy, and Wally. I also like your father. But everyone else in your household cannot be trusted."

Wally sighed. After Jason had informed them about the things that had happened in their home, Wendy received it as a shock, but not Wally, for he knew the things that had taken place in their home and was not about to comment.

"I have already shared the good and shocking news," said Wally. "Now it's time to explain." "Firstly, I heard good news from Kylie. Though there are not a lot of supernatural books available, valuable information can still be found in three of them."

"Wait, let's hear the explanation of the good news first," Samantha cuts in, her voice sharp with impatience.

The conversation twisted like a frayed wire, snapping back and forth between Wally's news and the unraveling situation at home. The tension in the room thickened, words colliding and overlapping, meaning getting lost in the mess.

Samantha, despite her insistence on hearing the truth, couldn't seem to stop herself from interrupting again and again. Her need for answers clashed with her inability to listen, and it was wearing thin. Wally's patience cracked.

"Can you at least wait your turn?" he snapped, his tone low and laced with warning. Immediately, Samantha grew silent, her lips pressed together and fire dimming from her eyes.

Wally smirked, cold, tired, and distant. Not because he found the situation amusing, but because it was the only armour he had left. A shield forged in frustration. Then, he spoke, his voice steady once again.

"After picking Kylie's brain, it turns out that the sword Incasera has two owners. I have concluded that the two owners of the sword are a werewolf and a vampire.

"And how did you get to that conclusion?" asked Aaron.

"From what I have gathered from Kylie, the sword is a sword that protects. It was a forbidden love between a male werewolf and a female vampire that brought about the birth of the sword. A powerful witch named Grenadine was moved by their deep love and forged the sword. I have also gathered from my father that they were extremely powerful, both the vampire and the werewolf, but they were killed unexpectedly."

"When the witch Grenadine went to deliver the sword, they were already dead. Then, soon after, she saw my ancestor and knew that one of us in our family would be able to wield the sword, so she gave it to him, telling him the origins of it. My dad only told me a day ago."

"So, how exactly was the sword ever forged?" said Afeisha.

"His sword was forged from the fangs of the wolf and the blood of the vampire, and if it fell into the wrong hands, then it would be a catastrophe."

"So, has anyone ever seen the sword?" asked Michael. "Wally, Wendy?" "The sword was hanging in their house all the time," said Wendy. "The sword is blue." Wally stayed silent. "Is it true, Wally?"

Wally hesitated for a moment, then said, "Yes." Wendy knew when Wally was lying and did not want to rouse any suspicion.

"So, we don't have to worry about it falling into the wrong hands because the sword chooses its owner," said Jason.

"And that brings us to the bad news!" exclaimed Wally. "Apart from the sword being in my grandfather's hands, he is going to perform a ritual to subdue the sword. I will try to get more details, but whatever it is, it isn't good.

"Why do you say that?" asked Afeisha.

"If you force the sword to do something that it does not want, it can go rampant. Remember, it has a mind of its own. It is like succumbing to a human being, bending them to do your will. Of course, they will lash out. And the sword is not an ordinary sword, so you can picture the casualties. And the authorities in this town cannot do anything about it because they themselves don't know what's going on. Come to think of it, today is the seventh day, but the classes must stay back for the concert that the upper class will be putting on. They have called the police to secure the entrance, and Officer Paul will be there because it is an important event."

"Where did you overhear such a thing? asked Samantha."

"I overheard one of the teachers talking about it." "So why did they choose tonight of all nights?" "I do not know. They just did."

After the gathering in the library, everyone went back to class. Mr. Sam informed the students that there would be a concert that would be held in the afternoon, and every student was required to attend.

Never tired of seeing Mr. Sam clean up, Wendy asked him, "Do you have a girlfriend?"

"No, Wendy, I do not. And I have no intention of dating anyone." Wanting to tease him, she asked, "Are you gay?"

The whole classroom watched her, but it was as if only she and Sam were in their own world, blotting everyone out, excluding Eithan.

"Of course, I am not. It's just that I—I what? It's none of your business, so stop questioning your teacher."

Ever since Mr. Sam cleaned up, it took a while before they could settle into their newly transformed selves. But as for Michael, they kept asking if Mr. Sam was not his father.

The Curtain's Lifted; They Really Do Exist

Later that evening, when school was over, the students were told to assemble in the hall for the concert. Time had already passed, and it was night. The concert had started, and the students on the stage were playing various instruments, including the piano, the flute, the cello, and the violin. It was an amazing concert. The instructor was none other than Mr. Primo.

Surprisingly, Kylie was also part of the band. She played the violin with such grace that she captivated Franco. Franco's eyes could not come off her. It was as if he were lost in some world or trapped. Yes, trapped is the word— trapped in a formidable cage that was hard to break out.

Lily, who was also there, did not understand the beauty of such music because she had never been to such concerts. She looked across the room, laid her eyes on Franco, and went up to him.

"Hey, Franco, have you seen the others?"

Franco paid her no mind. Once again, she shouted at him, but he gave her the same response, which was no response. She decided to use a different tactic. She waved both of her hands in his line of vision, but that still did not work. She became so mad and fuming that she slapped him, and a moment before the slap connected, the music stopped. Everyone heard the slap and looked in that direction.

"Aww..." he shouted. "W–w–why did you do that?" asked Franco with a stutter.

"I am sorry," cried Lily. "I have been trying to get your attention for about an hour now. Do you know how many things I have tried, but to no avail? It is like you were caught by an enchanter."

"What are you talking about? The concert was just so amazing that it touched me."

"Oh, it touched you all right," replied Lily sarcastically. "I wanted to ask you where the others were."

"I do not know where they are. I've been separated from them for quite a while due to some business. Another song is about to be played, so you'll have to go on your own."

"Okay, have fun with what you are doing. I will get going."

Lily was in a panic, but Franco failed to see it. She went on her way, searching for anyone she knew to inform them about what she had seen. Finally, in the lonely corridor of the school, she saw Michael's back. She went up to take a closer look, and there he was, staring at a shadow that looked like a big dog with claws as big as a grown man's finger. Michael started running. He grabbed Lily by the hand, and they both started running. Immediately, the figure from the shadows emerged from the dark and began running after them. To escape, he dragged her into a classroom, covered her mouth, and hid behind a desk. The figure outside came by the door and then disappeared.

"What was that?" asked Lily.

"It was something inhuman," replied Michael. "So why were you standing there staring at it?"

"I knew that it was there, but that is not what I was looking at. Have you forgotten—or do you not know the strange rumors about this town? On the seventh day, which is today, George's moon turns red. It is the crimson moon. There are a lot of strange things that happen on this day. That's why businesses tend to close early. But tonight, there is a concert. And because nothing has been happening recently, everyone seems to have forgotten. But tonight, they will see for themselves what is hidden in the dark."

"I have never seen you talk this much, Michael."

"Well, there is a first time for everything. Oh—before I forget. I was going to tell you all that I saw a couple of figures moving fast. I was born into a family of hunters, so I know. What I saw were vampires, and they were at the school. It is like the moon made them crazy. They do not have a sense of danger anymore, and they are just killing for the sake of it. Well, the concert should be done by now, let us go."

Michael and Lily went to look for the others, and eventually, they both wound up by the concert hall. They were a little too late because the beasts had already made their appearance on the stage, and so did the human-like creatures in the crowd.

A student started screaming, and there it was, clamping into the neck of the child, draining him of all the blood he had. The child's heart began to stop, and he suddenly went still.

"Monster!" another student exclaimed. But this time, it was on the stage, ripping a student apart. Every person on the stage dropped whatever instrument they were holding and began to run towards the exit. They were running for their lives. In the middle of the catastrophe was Officer Paul.

Officer Paul is a proud man, and he opposes anything that violates the law. He is upright and brave. Mr. Primo, who was also on the stage instructing the choir, also headed for the door. The exit was small, but the students squeezed through, nonetheless. Mr. Primo and two other teachers who were fleeing through the exits with the students saw Officer Paul running not behind but in front of the students, heading for safety.

Mr. Primo started shouting at once. "Officer Paul! Officer Paul!" Officer Paul turned around and saw Primo calling him. "Not now, Mr. Primo! Safety first, safety first."

He repeated himself and showed no signs of stopping, and neither did Mr. Primo. The students all went to Mr. Sam's classroom, as that classroom was the biggest. Some went to the library, which was also grand. But that did not stop the creature from looking around the school. When they finally got away, there was still one person on the concert stage who was too frightened to move.

Wally, Eithan, Afeisha, Wendy, and Michael did not rush out with the students because if the beast were to attack, they would also be hurt. When everything was clear, they all stood up and looked at each other.

"It seems like we all had the same idea," said Wendy. "We did."

When they turned around, they beheld a showdown. Lily and Franco stood up and looked in the same direction. Standing on the concert stage was Kylie and the big, fully transformed werewolf. But what was surprising was that the werewolf made no attempt to gobble her up, and it did not get too close. Finally, the werewolf moved, but it could not get closer, no matter how hard it tried. Kylie, who was afraid, turned into a completely different person.

The wolf itself felt fear, and for the first time, Kylie felt great using her powers. As soon as she turned around, she saw them.

"Witch!" Wally quickly exclaimed. "And do not try to hide it anymore!

I figured you were something, but this—this is absurd." She shook her head in denial, then confessed.

"The truth is, I am a witch. Do you remember the story I told you about the sword and the witch who was deeply touched? That is my ancestor."

Lily and Franco were confused.

221

Not completely trusting them, Samantha quickly changed the topic. "The beast is still around, and we have some human-like creatures as well. What are we going to do?"

"I do not know, but we must do something, that's for sure."

The Unusual Moon and the Excessive Siblings

Wendy and Ethan were still in the forest, romancing their way out, and the moon was taking its time with its appearance from behind an existing cloud. It was the only cloud in the sky, which seemed a little strange, but no one noticed it except for Michael and, of course, Lily.

Lily had already split from the couple back at the cafe and was on the way home, but she took a different path from the couple. Back at home, once again, Wally wanted to go out to look for them. Although he trusted Eithan completely, he had a vague idea of what was going to happen, and he was ignorant of Eithan's other form.

"Dad, I am going out to find Wendy."

"What are you talking about, Wally? Stay in the house! She will be home soon!" screamed Elena.

"What are you saying, Mom?"

"You know as well as I do that tonight is not exactly a night when one should be roaming outside.

"Yes, I know that. But all I am saying is that she will return in time." Wally looked at his mother, unable to conceal his determination.

"Why are you giving me that face? I said you're not going out to look for her."

William overheard her. "What's the matter?" he asked. Wally told his dad about the situation.

"It's okay," said William. "I don't want my daughter or my son to be out of the house, especially tonight. I can feel something very ominous is about to happen tonight, but I just can't place my finger on it."

Wally looked at his dad's worried face. "Has this type of thing ever happened before?"

"No! And that is what has me so upset tonight."

Meanwhile, Wendy and Eithan were taking their time exiting the forest and decided to take a little detour before going home. They took the route they walked on the night they first met, stopping next to a tree with a big stone, sitting there hugging each other and in their own little world.

"I wish that we didn't have to part like this," said Wendy.

"Soon, we will be able to stay together always, and nothing will be able to tear us apart," said Eithan.

Wendy smiled, took Eithan's hand, placed it around her neck, and cuddled closer in his arms. Then she gazed up at the sky and beheld it. There was a single white cloud in the sky with something looking like a rosewood color coming out from behind it. When she saw the moon, she quickly threw off Eithan's hand and stood upright.

Eithan felt unpleasant about the shrug. "What's the problem?" he asked her.

"Look at that—the sky. Doesn't it look strange to you? It's the first time I've seen something like that.

Eithan's mind, which was filled with Wendy, immediately looked up at the moon and, with fear, said, "Wendy, let's get you home. It's not safe anymore."

"What's not safe?" replied Wendy. "The whole town. It's not safe."

At home, William told Wally to stay inside while he went to get Wendy.

"What about my daughter, Lily?" asked Laura, who knew what was going on.

William sighed. "Don't worry, I'll try to see if I can find her, too." "Don't try. Make sure you find her," said Laura.

In the forest, Wendy demanded that Eithan tell her what was happening, but Eithan still refused, which upset her. Her trust in him started to slip.

"When you get home, you should ask your father about it," said Eithan.

Wendy, who was curious, remembered what curiosity does to a man, and she immediately gave in. They held hands and ran towards their house. On the way, they saw some bushes moving. They were on guard, but as they stood, William emerged from the bushes.

"Dad? What are you doing here?"

"I am here to get you," he replied. "Let's go home for now." He then looked at Eithan. "Thank you for bringing my daughter home. And you need to get home as soon as possible."

Eithan gave his thanks and went on his way, full speed towards his house. William enquired about Lily from Wendy, seeing that they were all out together, but Wendy replied that she did not know where Lily was. Suddenly, Lily came out of the bushes on the other side.

"Lily, what are you doing there?" "I lost my way," said Lily.

William told the girls that they should all go home, seeing that they were close to their homes. When he stepped out of the house, he had gazed at the sky, and he knew for sure this time that being outside was indeed dangerous. When they finally stepped foot inside their house, and Eithan had reached home, along with Michael and Afeisha, the moon completely came out from behind the white cloud, which did not change color. At the same time, Sheila and Jeremy were still in town at the cafe. Sheila happens to be related to the cafe owner, and he gave her permission to lock up.

The cafe was the only thing in town that was open at that hour, and people were enjoying themselves inside, forgetting that it was the seventh day. They were drinking and partying to their heart's content, not knowing that wine "Bites like a snake and poisons like a viper." They had no temperance.

Meanwhile, Aaron, Eithan's elder brother, and Samantha, who was the same age as him, were overwhelmed by seeing Eithan, as they had not seen him in a long time. Aaron went up to

Eithan and patted his head.

"You have grown, little bro. It's been some time."

Eithan was also fond of his big brother. "I have, and I am not a little kid anymore."

Aaron laughed. "No, you're not. Have you gotten yourself a girlfriend now?"

"Yes, I have."

Aaron laughed. "That is good."

Upon hearing this sentence, Samantha was quite displeased, as she was also fond of Eithan. "So, when are we going to meet her?" she asked.

"Soon!" Eithan said in an overexcited tone. "Mom and Dad have already met her, and they liked her. Do not worry, you will meet her soon, and I know that you'll also like her."

Both Samantha and Aaron, who were obviously not too happy with the situation, agreed.

Back at the bar, Sheila decided it was time to close and that the people should go home. When the customers walked out, some drunk and some sober, they looked up at the sky and started running as if they were crazy. But what was even worse was that their eyes became just as red as the moon.

Sheila, Jeremy, and their crew began bleeding from their eyes, and they began ripping people's throats and sucking blood, as though their sanity was gone. They broke into houses, and a huge blood bath happened that night.

Michael, who had nothing to do and was already home, thought about what was happening at the café. He hugged Wendy with tender and soft skin before opening the front door and looking up at the sky for one second, immediately closing the door. His eyes began hurting, and they turned red.

CHAPTER TEN

The Moon Is Getting Stronger, And So Is the Beast's Identity

After a discussion that left Lily and Franco in the dark, Eithan decided that he was going to follow the beast to investigate. To him, the beast was so familiar that the mere thought of it disgusted him, and there was only one person who could evoke such emotions within him. Eithan headed off to where the beast was, not only to find out the uncertainty behind the familiar beast, but also because his claws were also showing. The moon was so strong, forcing a change upon the supernatural.

For the first time in Michael's life, he began feeling different. He already knew what he was, but he had never felt such power. The power within him lay dormant, but the moon behaved aggressively.

"Let us just go," said Afeisha, who was perfectly fine but overcome with fear. She wanted to leave immediately.

"Afeisha has a point. We are all affected by some unknown entity or third party, and it's making us become something that we don't want," said Michael.

"What are you talking about, Michael? I'm perfectly fine," said Lily.

Franco, on the other hand, was becoming bloodthirsty, and

his fangs were already out. He sank them into his lips to prevent anyone from seeing, but Michael could tell he was in severe pain, and he grinned.

"You may be alright," said Samantha. "But look at Wally and at me, and especially Franco—he looks like he's dying there."

After Samantha said that Franco could not hold it anymore and slipped out. The speed at which he departed was so fast that everyone thought he had disappeared.

"Hey, guys! Don't you forget something?" exclaimed Wally. "The beast and vampires are still out there hurting people, and Eithan and Franco are missing."

"Let's go to the library," said Kylie.

"I know you love to read, but this is not the time for the library."

"No," replied Kylie. "A lot of students ran outside, and the two biggest rooms in the school, apart from the basement, were Ms. Smith's classroom and the library. My guess is that's where they went, and the beast and the vampires will be heading there as well."

"Okay, that is a solid point," said Aaron. "So, this is the plan, Lilly. Do you know how to defend yourself?"

"Yes, I am from a family of hunters."

"Okay. Because if not, you would have just been a heavy load, and we can't afford dead weight right now. Afeisha, you will go with Michael."

"I do not think that's safe. She should go with Wendy."

"Alright." Disappointed by Michael's response, Afeisha went with Wendy.

"Cheer up," said Wendy. "I know I am not Michael, but I'm capable of protecting you."

"Okay, Samantha, you are strong, but if you cannot handle it, you know how to signal me. Okay, everyone, our job is to protect the students until the moon goes down. Today is the seventh day, but if you feel like you cannot control it, the situation will be to retreat."

"Okay." Samantha was lost as to what Aaron was talking about. Control it? She thought. She was lost in her own thoughts about him, unable to keep up.

Meanwhile, Eithan was chasing the beast. Though he did not turn into a beast, his claws and fangs were out.

"Hey, wait up," said Eithan, "Where are you going?"

The beast paid no attention to what was said, nor did he mind him. Though the beast's mind was clouded by the moon, he could sense that Eithan was one of his kind, although he was unable to recognize him. Realizing that the beast had no intention of stopping, Eithan decided to use his brain. A full change was not an option, seeing that he feared that his mind would be clouded like a beast and that things would turn out even more disastrously. He decided that it was time to act before such a beast with a killer instinct re-entered the school. There was only one thing left to do, and that was to bring him back to his senses. He ran faster than he had ever run but to no avail. He then stumbled upon a big log of wood and threw it at the beast.

It did not hurt the beast, but it did feel some slight pain from its impact. Immediately, the beast stopped and turned to him.

"What is the matter?" said Eithan. "Did the little bitty log hit you? Did you feel pain?"

Though the beast's mind was indeed foggy, after hearing Eithan's taunts, he could not quite put his finger on why he was so upset at Eithan's childish attacks or why he hated him so much, but one thing was clear: his drive and hunger to annihilate him were still intact. The beast charged at Eithan at full speed, and the moon became an energy drink for him. He tossed his claws at Eithan but was unable to injure him. The fight between them took about five minutes. Then, when the right time came, and the beast thrust his two arms at Eithan to pound him into the ground, Eithan caught his arms. The beast was surprised at the amount of strength he still had, and immediately, Eithan roared fiercely directly to his face. The beast became scared and still. He was forcibly returned to his human form. Eithan waited patiently for him to open his eyes, and when he finally did, he spoke.

"Where am I?"

"I knew it was you, Zayn. No wonder I felt that familiar aura that you emitted."

"Yeah—yes, I can hardly remember what happened, but seeing you here, I now know why I wanted to destroy you so badly. Anyway, what is going on? And why does my head still hurt?"

"It is probably because of the moon. It is making a lot of supernatural, including you, go crazy. I am just barely managing to hold on."

"Is that so? The proud and arrogant Eithan finally admits to something he has trouble defeating. And to think that something is a moon."

"I hate you right now, so it's no wonder we do not get along. I have other stuff to do." Eithan cleaned himself up.

"All right," replied Zayn. "And as embarrassed as it may sound, thank you for returning me to my senses."

"It is no problem. After all, I am your Alpha." "Can you stop being sarcastic for once? Just go." "That is what I was about to do."

The Moon Goes Down, Help from A Strange Woman

Eithan headed off to where the rest of the party were. Meanwhile, everyone assembled in the library. The roar that was previously heard, the echoes of the roar, made them even more afraid. Suddenly, there was a knock on the library door, which threw everyone on edge. Immediately, the knocking stopped, and a huge commotion echoed outside as if there was a great war, but no one dared to open it and look. Fear was instilled in everyone, and some were searching for means to escape the library.

"Do not panic!" screamed the police officer. "We will be alright as soon as the moon goes down. We will have to sleep in the library."

"How do you know that?" asked one of the students.

"It is just my instinct telling me to stay until the moon goes down."

"It was that same instinct that told you to protect yourself and leave us to die," another student said."

"I don't even know why you are a police officer, nor why you are here. A police officer is to protect and preserve the lives of others, but instead, you protected yourself and made some of us die. Not only that, but you were rushing ahead of us to safety, and we placed our trust in you."

The other students began mumbling.

Mr. Paul spoke his mind as the situation became dire. "Listen to me. Before I became a police officer, as you say, I was first a human. Do you expect me to go up against something inhuman? And furthermore, you said you placed your trust in me. Let me tell you this: put your trust in God because only he can get us out of this mess. I came to this school to protect you, but fighting supernatural creatures was not on the list. So yes, I ran for safety, and I hope that you know that staying alive means that you can live to fight another day."

After listening to what Mr. Paul said, the uneasiness in the room and the unsettling of the students stopped, but the noise outside the door continued. In the hallway, there was a fight between another werewolf and a vampire. There was a third knocking on the door, but once again, no one dared to open it.

Outside the door was a vampire. It realized that no one was going to open the door, so it decided to get rid of the door entirely, but then a werewolf showed up and they immediately began to fight. The fight was so intense that it broke a couple of the classroom doors, but not the library door. Eventually, Aaron, Lily, and Wally ran into the fight. Trying to subdue the beast, each person fought with all they had, but they still did not prevail.

The beast had the better of them.

Lily was dumbfounded at the strength of the beast and seeing everyone acting crazy. "What is going on?" she said. "Everyone is out of their minds. It's like a festival of madness." She then turned to Wally, who did not have much to say.

Aaron jumped in. "Retreat is the best strategy."

Aaron grabbed Lily and Wally, and the rest had no choice but to retreat. As they went out, a strange woman came, and she subdued the beast effortlessly, which made them question their abilities. Witnessing this gave Wendy a sense of Deja vu. She walked toward the woman slowly. She could feel the warmth and familiarity of the woman down to her bones. Aaron quickly grabbed Wendy's hand.

"Are you alright?" asked Aaron. "Y–yes, I am."

"Who was that strange woman, and why did she help us?" "No clue who she is, but I can tell that she is quite strong." "One thing is for sure: that is not human."

"Well, the good thing is the moon is going down, and we are saved." The beast headed towards the school grounds, making a quick escape. "Are you alright?"

"Yes, I am. I mean—we are."

"Okay, good. You look like you had it rough. Why don't you all join the other students?"

"We will," replied Lily. "But first, tell us how you subdued the beasts." "No problem. I subdued them because I was stronger. You should go now."

The lady walked off after telling them that they should go to where the other students were and that they should be careful. After her touching advice, Wendy could feel a warm and tender feeling coming from her, so she asked.

"What's your name?"

"Why do you want to know my name?"

"I want your name, obviously, because you are our savior," she said.

The lady paused for a minute before answering. "Wendine."

After hearing her name, Wendy could not put a name to the feeling she suddenly felt, but she began to weep bitterly.

"Why do you cry?" asked Aaron.

At the same time, Eithan came in. "What is the matter?"

"I do not know!" he exclaimed. "Tears had just started falling down her cheeks."

"It is nothing, Eithan. I don't know why these tears are rolling down my face, but for some reason, my heart felt a gush of happiness when I saw that woman."

"What woman are you talking about?"

"There was a woman who suddenly came in, and she helped us fight rather than ask for our help. It is best to say that she defeated them on her own without needing assistance from any of us."

"Let us leave, it's already late."

After the noise from outside became quiet, Mr. Primo took it upon himself to open the door and look outside. He saw a strange Lady in the hallway and asked her if everything had gone back to normal.

"Yes," she replied. The students were filled with joy, and they hurried home with another police officer after Chief Paul called a transport to carry them home. After the students got home safely, Officer Paul went back to the station with a clouded mind. Unable to comprehend what he saw; he went through files of previous victims and witnesses. He remembered the strange rumors that he had heard about the town from the residents themselves and from various witnesses, but he paid no mind. Because of what he had just witnessed, he had no choice but to look for something that would be of greater force in counteracting such abominable beings.

Field Trip, Memories Returned, and Bonds Strengthened

After the incident that took place that night, everyone seemed to be on edge, so the principal decided that there would be a trip for the classes that were involved in the incident. However, the parents of each child would have to be present as well. Wendy relayed the message to her parents. However, because of the guests at the house, Elena decided that William should go with the kids and that Lilian should also go with Lily. However, Lilian declined the offer and told William that he should represent the three of them, seeing that they are all cousins. William agreed to the ridiculous demand placed on him. However, he only agreed to such a reason because he knew that certain people would be there.

Confused as to why William agreed without saying anything, Elena had much to do in her laboratory and did not want to be disturbed while her dad and brothers went to the police station to speak with Mr. Paul. Everyone was already packed for the field trip, and they had to meet up at school.

As everyone gathered at the school grounds, Mr. Primo stood next to Wendine as they took in the scene.

"Why is the principal not here?"

Mr. Primo started addressing the crowd. "The principal has some serious issues to deal with, especially regarding some students who didn't make it. He decided to hold a special event for them and give them a field trip to ease their minds of the horrors they had witnessed. We will be going to Labuda. There will be a few teachers and police on this trip to ensure the safety of everyone. Furthermore, since our destination is expensive, the school will cover the cost. One more thing: I will introduce you to a new teacher who will be joining us on this trip."

"Good morning, students. It is a pleasure to meet you. My name is Wendine, and I will be joining you on this trip."

The students were astonished at how beautiful the teacher looked, but the person who was even more shocked was none other than William. Seeing his sweetheart up there, the woman he had longed for all these years, standing up there in the flesh. He wanted to shout out to her, but he didn't want to draw attention to himself. He held it in, painfully.

Mr. Sam was also shocked, as his memories came flooding back to him.

He held his head as if he were in pain but made no sound.

Everyone went on the bus. Parents sat with each other, the students stayed together, and the same went for the teachers. Only the police officers were placed at distinct locations on the bus.

Mr. Jamain looked at William. "Isn't that your daughter's mom, our Wendine, who we thought died years ago? Why is she still living?"

"I don't know, said William. "But on this trip, I'm going to find out what happened. I have been living like a soulless doll all these years, like an empty shell, just because I thought she was gone. But to realize that she was alive and did not come to look for me? I'm filled with mixed feelings right now."

"Do not worry, Willy. There is bound to be a reasonable explanation as to why she didn't try to contact us."

After listening to Jamain's comforting words, William could sense burning stares from two directions. When he looked, he saw Mr. Sam staring at him. Then he noticed Wendine was also staring at him. He wanted to get up and go over there, but it was best to wait until everyone had gotten off the bus.

After riding for hours, Labuda was finally in sight. The students shouted for joy because the long ride was enough to give them a headache. Getting off the bus, the students were instructed to go to the rooms assigned to them. Parents, teachers, and police would room together, and students were by themselves, grouped together with roommates. After going to their rooms, they were then to regather.

William was dilly-dallying outside, looking at the place. Though he was wealthy, it was his first time visiting such a place. As he arrived at his room and opened the door, he saw none other than Mr. Sam unpacking. He was shocked to find out that he was his roommate. But what was even more surprising was what Mr. Sam said.

"What took you so long, William? I thought that you weren't going to show up. I see you never change."

"What do you remember about who I am?"

"What are you talking about, William? How can I forget who you are when you are my best friend?"

Speechless, William went into the room and started to unpack. "Jamain, do you know that you have a son? I do."

"You do?"

William paused. "He looked just like you."

"Wow, I know that I am not the greatest father. After all, I was not present for his birth. He must be mad to know that his good-for-nothing father is present in his life."

"I do not think he is mad. His mom explained the situation to him."

"Speaking of the situation, has his mom moved on?" "Moved on where?" asked William.

"Stop kidding me. You know what I mean."

"Do not worry about Joslyn. She has always loved you—you and only you—so you do not have to worry. I see that you retained your original memories as well as the memories of the past.

"Yes, I did. And I must say that I am a heck of a good

teacher."

"Yes, you are," said William sarcastically. "So, tell me. How did you do it? How did you retain your memories?"

"I do not know exactly, but when I saw Wendine on the stage and heard that we were coming to Labuda, my head started hurting, and before I knew it, memory screens started flashing before my eyes."

"Well, all in all, I'm glad you're back."

"Thank you," replied Jamain. Now, I can find the underlying cause of what happened years ago."

"Do not worry, I will tell you. But can we discuss that matter later? We must gather for an announcement."

Both left the room and headed for the announcement. Everyone was already present when they got there. William grabbed Jamain and told him that he should only reveal the latest developments to people he trusts, and to pretend to be the same for the rest. Jamain quickly agreed, knowing that things were not as they seemed.

Mr. Primo started speaking. "This trip is to relieve the stress of the incident and schoolwork. Parents and teachers: have fun."

After the brief declaration, everyone went their own ways. Jamain went to look for his beloved Joslyn, but she was nowhere to be found. Instead, he met up with Michael. He could not believe his eyes. The kid looked exactly like him.

"Hi, it's nice to meet you again," he muttered. "I think it's the first time meeting you like this. I hope you'll forgive me."

241

Michael was puzzled. "What are you talking about?" "You do know that I'm your father, right?"

Michael was bewildered by what was said. He replied in shock. "So, your memories have returned. You know who I am?"

"Of course, I do. You are my son. I'm sorry I couldn't remember, or I wasn't there for you. Please forgive me..." Jamain became overcome with emotions, hugged his son, and wept bitterly. He was emotional, but he went in and hugged him again. Deep down, he missed a father figure in his life. "It's a secret that I got my memory back. You are not to tell anyone about this because it can be dangerous.

"Okay," Michael replied. "Where is your mom?"

"Here she comes. I will give both of you space to talk." "You have all grown up."

"Yes, I have, and I will be needing you to teach me certain things." "No problem," he replied as he ran off.

Meanwhile, Joslyn was looking for her son to cheer him up about meeting his forgetful father, but as she walked along the path, she saw both chatting and could not help but watch. Suddenly, he jumped onto him and hugged him. Seeing this made her emotional. She pretended that she was looking for him so as not to create suspicion. When Jamain saw her coming towards him, he remembered things from the past. The woman he loved the most ran towards him, looking beautiful. When she got closer to him, he immediately hugged her without a second thought. He thought about embracing her, and his body acted before he knew it.

"Uhm, Jamain, are you alright?" "Yes, I am, my sweet

Joslyn."

"That is what you used to call me. Have your memories returned?"

"Yes, they have, and I missed you a lot. All these lonely years without you and my son. The world is indeed a wicked place."

Joslyn was filled with joy and kissed him passionately, as if she were starving for his affection. She finally got it, like a hungry dog that finally got the bone. "I missed you, too, baby. I missed you. Life was hard without you, but now you're back, and I am happy." She embraced him while moaning vigorously.

Jamain began to feel lustful, having not embraced her in a long time. He immediately put her down and calmed himself so as not to draw attention to himself. She teased him, but what he didn't know was that she was feeling it too.

"So, tell me, Jamain. How did you regain your memories?"

"When I saw Wendine on the stage back at the school and that we were going to Labuda, my head started hurting, and that is when I began to remember. I stared at William on the bus, and we just happened to be roommates."

"So, does William know that you got your memories back?"

"Yes, he does—only him, you, and our son. I would like it if you could keep it a secret. In the dark, events are happening that you don't know exist, but I will explain it all to you another time."

"Alright. So, what should we do now?" asked Joslyn.

"We are here for fun, so let us have some, shall we? Let's go to my room."

"What about William?"

"William has gone to look for Wendine, so we have room for ourselves." Joslyn kissed Jamain.

"Let us make up for the time that we missed, shall we?" said Jamain. Joslyn laughed first.

Michael was staring at them because he had not gone too far out of sight. I have never seen Mom this genuinely happy before. I hope it stays this way, he thought. Then he turned back around and went off to do his own thing.

Meanwhile, William was looking for Wendine, but he could not find her. She was also looking for him but did not see him either. However, she did meet two other people.

"Hey, what are you up to?" said Wendy.

"Nothing much. Just looking for you," replied Eithan.

"Oh. I am here now. Let us go have some fun. All our friends are here." Eithan grabbed Wendy by the waist and whispered to her. "On this trip, I want to spend more time with you."

"No problem, I want the same. Let us go."

Wendine could not believe her eyes. Her daughter had grown up so big that she got herself a handsome boy. Just seeing how intimate those two were made her want to find William even more. Finally, she saw William from a distance, questioning Mr. Primo. Then she saw Primo point in her direction. William turned around and saw her. For the first time, he knew his heart was not dead but alive. He walked in her direction. As he approached closer, Wendine began to put up her guard, knowing how fearsome he could be.

Michael was filled with mixed emotions. "It has been too long, Wendine," he said.

"Yes, it has," she replied as she fought back the urge to jump into his arms.

"I know you already know what I'm about to ask, but I'll ask anyway. Where have you been all these years? Why haven't you tried to contact me?"

"Why would I do that?" asked Wendine, "Are you not married now to one of our closest friends? And you have a son with her. How can I intrude on your family?"

William's heart dampened. "You know that you are the only one I love.

I have and always will."

"But that is impossible now because you are married. And to answer your question, I have not been up for long, but I know it has something to do with Elena's father, and I am not entirely sure. My mind is clouded when there's clarity."

"Jamain's memory has also returned, so I am guessing that something big is going to happen."

"I guess so. Was that all the reason you were looking for me?"

"No, you look beautiful, Wendine. You always have and you always will."

Wendine began to blush. "It seems you have not changed. Always the smooth talker, I see."

"Only for you," said William.

The tense air surrounding both began to dissipate, and something else began to take over. A strong aroma filled with love that was concealed for too long. William was feeling it, and so was Wendine. Coincidently, Wendine had a room for herself, and she lured William away to the room. On their way, Eithan spotted Wendine.

"Hey, Wendy, isn't that your dad and the new teacher? Where are they going?"

"I do not know," replied Wendy. "Let's tag along."

With their minds filled with lust, William and Wendy, who were two strong supernatural beings, were unable to sense that Eithan and Wendy were following them.

"Hey, Wendy, is this the right thing to do?"

"Yes. After all, that woman feels familiar, and my dad is a married man who has no heart for cheating. Why would he be attracted to her? Something is fishy. Not even my stepmother can cause such behavior.

"Okay, but if it is not what we think, we will leave." "All right."

Both Eithan and Wendy followed them, and they stopped at Wendine's room. Wendy placed her ear to the door.

"If there is any cheating, I will immediately break down this door. How could my dad cheat? I know he does not love anyone besides me and Wally, but still." Wendy began hearing noises from inside the room and heard her dad spouting cheesy lines—

something a teenager in their heart would do. This made her feel disgusted. She knew immediately what was taking place inside.

On the other hand, Eithan was there taking in everything, and it looked like he could not wait to listen more.

"What the hell are you doing?" replied Wendy. "We're here to watch them, not to be strung along."

"Alright, but I want to make sure that what you're doing is the right thing."

"What are you saying, Ethan? This is wrong."

"|It may be wrong, but when you see your dad that happy and excited, are you sure you want to ruin it?"

For a second, Wendy hesitated, but she concluded that it was wrong and told Eithan to put himself in her shoes.

"It's impossible," Eithan said. "My dad loves my mom too much. Besides, have you ever heard the term imprinting? When a wolf imprints on a person, it can only be that person for the rest of their life."

"Well, if it is like that, then that means that my dad imprinted on Elena, even though he did not love her."

"You are wrong. A wolf can only imprint on who he loves."

"Well–well–would not that mean he imprinted on my mom? Why is he doing that with her? Didn't you say that women give you a special feeling?"

"Listen closely to see what it is. I think they are conversing before they get to the good part."

"All right, I will."

Once again, Wendy and Eithan put their ears to the door. Inside, they heard William talking.

"Have you seen your daughter, Wendine?" "Yes, I have."

"Well, she looks as beautiful as you."

"I also noticed she has her own boyfriend now," said Wendine. "You mean Eithan?"

"Is that the name of the handsome youth?" "Yes, it is."

"Well, he is quite the catch. I am happy for her. I met her during the incident, but I still cannot tell her I'm her mother. I don't want her to get deeper involved in this mess, and I also don't know what's going on or why I woke up from my slumber."

"Enough of that. Now's not the time for that. Let's enjoy ourselves."

William and Wendine started having sex, and Eithan and Wendy could not walk away fast enough. They did not want to hear any more of the sounds and moans protruding from the bedroom. Eithan could feel that Wendy was beyond surprised to hear and listen to her father let go of himself with so much vigour.

CHAPTER ELEVEN

You Are a Disease, Both You and Your Mother

E lena went to the kitchen and took away Wendy's plate as she was eating. It was her third round of eating braised pork with stew, fish, rice, and wine. It was indeed a feast. Filled with anger, she told Wendy that she should stop eating her food, as it was not made for her. Wendy became sullen. She was sad at the words that came from Elena's lips but was even more disappointed that she could not eat the delicacy that was before her.

"Why can't I eat the food?" she asked Elena. "My father has lost his appetite, and you have also lost it. I made sure to leave food for Wally. So, what's the problem?"

"The problem, you ask. I'll tell you what the problem is. You and your mother are set on ruining my life. You are a disease, and not to mention your mother. She stole the love of my life, and now that she is dead, she still can't allow me to be with him."

Wendy became shocked at Elena's view of her after all these years. Meanwhile, Wally stood outside the door. He heard every word that was said by his mother to Wendy, not to mention William, who heard her loud and clear thanks to his supernatural hearing.

"Wh–what are you saying? Now I see. That is the reason you've been treating me like this all these years. I've noticed it, but I keep telling myself that it was a lie. You're just tough on me because you want the best for me. I never really imagined that you hated me to this extent. Only my dad and my brother Wally, along with my mom, are my true family, since you seem not to like me. Let me ask you a question. Who did my dad meet and fall in love with first? You or my mom?"

Elena stayed silent for a minute. "Let me tell you a story. Your dad met me first. We fell in love and did everything together until your mother came along. She pretended to be my friend while aiming for my boyfriend. She was successful in seducing him, and you were the result. It baffles me   how much he loves you when he knows that your mom is a man snatcher."

After listening to what Elena said, Wendy almost believed her, but luckily for her, she had heard how much her dad loved her mom. Knowing this made her think that flaws were within Elena's story.

"What, you don't believe me anymore? Let me ask you. Who is older, you or Wally?"

"Wally." said Wendy.

"Then that's all the proof you need."

Elena talked with so much confidence that Wendy began to doubt herself. William couldn't take the words lashed out at his precious daughter and he appeared on the staircase.

"Elena!" he exclaimed. "What nonsense are you spewing to my daughter? I do not care what you usually say, but when you slander my love like that, I won't let it stand."

"Wh–what are you talking about, honey?"

"Don't 'honey' me. I overheard every word that was said by you from the very beginning. I have told you once, and I'll tell you again. I do not love you that way. To me, you are an important friend, as well as Wally's precious mother, but I will not allow you to tell my children lies. They deserve to know the truth. Wally! You can come inside now. I know you are out there, standing and listening to the conversation."

Wally opened the door slowly and came in with a look that was not pleasing to the eyes. "Dad, you're as sharp as ever. Anyway, I also overheard everything from scratch, and I must say, it wasn't very pleasant.

William continued. "I have always been an honest man to my children and to you, so I will not start lying now."

Though Wally already knew the story, William said it in front of everyone once more. "Listen carefully. Because, after this time, I will not be repeating it. When I was younger, I met a beautiful girl whose name was Wendine. She was and will always be the love of my life, and she is Wendy's mother. I had my friends Jamain and Joslyn with me, and we all got along well. Later, Joslyn met Elena and introduced her to us, and we all got along. Not knowing that Elena developed secret feelings for me, I enjoyed myself with my girl and our friends, but her feelings grew deeper. She wanted me for herself, even if it meant destroying the friendships that took a long time to build, and I do not know why. She found out about my identity. I didn't know how that happened, but I later found out she was a hunter. The truth is, I do not want to say what despicable method she used to conceive Wally, but Wally is my son, and I love him very much. Later, Wendine was also pregnant, and she gave birth to Wendy and died.

Elena, I really do not want to hurt you or make you look despicable in front of the children, but please don't sully my children's ears with lies."

"H–how did you know?" asked Elena.

"I have always known that something was wrong somewhere. Do you not know the attributes of a wolf? When we imprint on a person, it does not change, so loving you was impossible from the start, being that I had already imprinted on someone else. Do you understand now? It is because Wendine died, and my love for my son made me keep my mouth shut while you were saying all those hurtful things to my daughter. I will not tolerate it. Understand?"

Preparation: The Moon is Near

"I hear you." Full of fear, she agreed on the spot without a reply. Elena looked hurt. She looked for her son to defend her, but he did not. He was there from the start and knew the whole situation, so there was no way that his mother could have fed him lies, even if she had not talked. She wanted him to defend her, but he refused.

As hurt as she looked, Elena remained silent. Wendy felt sad and sorry for her after hearing her father's stern words to her. He did not beat around the bush and told her off as it was. Wendy knew how it felt to be in love, not to mention when the man you loved was not reciprocating your feelings. She imagined Eithan and her in that situation and quickly dropped the topic.

Wendy went back to the kitchen to reclaim the food her so-called mother had taken from her, and once more began to eat joyfully. William went back to his room, feeling even worse than before. But the one who felt the worst was Wally. He eagerly wanted his family to be happy, even though he knew that his father did not love his mom. "How can you expect such happiness?" he said to himself softly. "It is falling, yet it's so hard to catch. It's so near yet hard to grab." He began saying things to himself and then quickly left for his bedroom.

After everyone departed, Elena was left standing alone. She was too embarrassed to confront her son, wondering why he didn't stand up for her. She couldn't go to the kitchen because she knew that she had lost the battle between her and Wendy, not to mention that the girl in question was joyfully eating the food she had taken away. And she couldn't go to the room because she couldn't face him after spouting all those lies.

What was left was to go outside for some fresh air and think to herself. Despite what happened, she still blamed Wendy and her mother for her misfortunes and had no intention of stopping until her life was filled with misery. Elena was filled with her thoughts. She paid no mind to her surroundings, nor did she pay any attention to where she was going. Clearing her head was important, so she walked wherever her feet carried her. Surprisingly enough, she ran into Eithan, who was on his way over to her house, and yet she still did not respond.

"Are you alright?" he asked.

No answer came his way. He asked once more. "Mrs. Elena, are you alright?"

Once again, she gave no response. Eithan then realized that

Elena was so occupied with something on her mind that she paid him no attention at all. He decided to leave her and not disturb her journey. He continued through the forest until he reached Wendy's house.

Knock-Knock. There was someone outside the door.

"Wally, could you get to the door?" asked Wendy. "Wally! Why is he not answering?" She knew her dad was in the room and did not want to bother him. Nevertheless, getting up to open the door became tiring for Wendy. There was so much delicious food to eat and leaving it to answer the door would have been a kill. Outside the door stood Eithan for some minutes. Wendy was still inside, contemplating whether she should get up to open the door.

Eithan knocked once more. "Hello, is anybody home? It's me, Eithan. When she realized it was her beloved left stranded outside the door, she quickly got up and went towards the door to open it.

"Hey, Eithan," she said in a bewitching voice. "Sorry for not coming to the door on time. I was busy eating in the kitchen."

"That is okay. So, may I come in? It's no problem." Wendy took Eithan to the kitchen to partake in what she was eating.

"Delicious," he said. "Who prepared this meal?"

"It was my stepmom who prepared it to welcome my father."

"Well, I can see that you all were having a feast. Look at all those empty plates, not to mention that you're still eating."

Wendy began to blush. "When we got home, my dad lost his appetite, and so did Wally. My stepmom went for a walk, so

I'm alone." "So, you're telling me that you alone are eating all of this. "Yes," she responded.

"It's as if you're eating for you and two others."

Both laughed and gave no deep thought to what was said, not knowing that there was more to it than just eating.

"Now that you mention it, on my way here, I saw Elena. She was—what should I say—absent-minded. I greeted her twice, but she did not. She was in deep thought, or something happened that made her behave that way."

"It is a long story, but I hope she gets a grip soon. She insulted me and told me a story that was a complete lie about my mom and dad and her relationship. My dad overheard it and pulled her socks up, which resulted in the way she was when you met her."

"I never expected that to happen," said Eithan. "But I hope that everything turns out well for your brother and your family. It is not good to fight." Eithan tried to comfort her with fitting words but was a little upset deep down.

Meanwhile, Elena was still walking, and before she knew it, her legs carried her off to her old house. There, she met her brothers but not her dad. He was somewhere looking for mischief, as usual.

Plans in Action: Trust No One

"Why do you look like that, Elena?" said Lionel.

"This is just how I look after investing half of my life in

unrequited love. He will never love me, no matter what I do. This is what I get for loving another person's man." She quickly broke into tears after expressing everything that was in her heart.

After crying for some time, her heart felt lighter, and it was as if a heavy load was lifted off her shoulders. She looked brand new.

"Listen here, Elena. I am not much of a love expert, but there's one thing I do know. We are hunters, and we are not supposed to be weak, but we love to bring any strong man to their knees when it is reciprocated. William is a handsome, strong man and an Alpha werewolf. He had already imprinted on his lover, not to mention his love for her. It is overwhelming. I do not think I could have still been hung up on a dead woman all these years, but he was, and that's where we differ. I love you as my dear sister, so I am telling you this. William has never loved you and will never love you, so give up. I know that you did something unbelievable. How could you be pregnant with Wally when William didn't give you the time of day? Please, for your sake, please give up."

After listening to her father's consoling words, she returned home.

Eithan had already left.

The next morning, everyone awoke. Breakfast was already prepared, and she did her usual routine, calling them to breakfast. When they walked into the kitchen, they noticed the air surrounding Elena had become warm. She was different from yesterday, as if she were a completely different person. However, William knew. He could sense that she recognized something important, so he sat and ate what she made. After they ate and went on their way to school, William told Elena that he was going to spend the day out.

"Can we talk now that the children have gone to school?" asked Elena. "No problem," said William, "I'm all ears."

"I have re-evaluated myself and realized that I have been loving a man who doesn't love me for the past years. Even though I do not like your daughter because she reminds me of her mom, I am still the mother of your son, and despite all things, I still love you. Please, William, give me a chance. This is me asking earnestly, seeing that the woman you love is no more."

"Listen to me, Elena. And this is me earnestly speaking. Once again, I cannot give you a chance because I do not love you. My heart has always belonged to Wendine and only her. You have been forcing yourself on me, but it is never going to work. I am sure there is a guy out there for you. I remember back then, there was a guy called Cory Welding who was very much in love with you. What I am doing to you is exactly what you did to him. Yes, you are the mother of my son, Wally, but do not forget, I did not make love to you. You and your father were the ones who drugged me and did that. One more thing. My lover is not dead, and she has never died. I do not know why you hate my daughter, but she is precious to me, and so is her mom. Wally is also dear to me. Elena, please give yourself a chance and move on with your life. Otherwise, you'll always remain unhappy."

"So, you knew what we did all along?"

"Of course, I knew," said William. "I have always been suspicious, and you have just confirmed it."

Elena once again broke down in tears. She got an outright rejection and left the house for her father, and this time, she met him at home.

"Is it unusual for you to come to visit me, Elena?"

"Yes, it is, Dad. Not to mention, you are part of the reason I'm in this state. If only we had not moved here, if only you didn't push me to love that man, I wouldn't have felt so much love for him, I wouldn't have hurt my friends, and I would have been happier than I am now."

"Calm down, Elena. Let's go to the kitchen to talk."

She quietly went into the kitchen with her dad, and both sat around the table.

"The sword is a potent and valuable tool that can be useful for a lot of things," said Lennox. "It should not be placed in the hands of anyone apart from our family. With the sword, we can work wonders. Are you even listening to me, Elena?"

Elena got up out of her seat.

"Where are you going?" said Lennox.

"I'm going to the kitchen for some water. Every time we have a conversation, it is always about the sword. The sword, sword, sword. Hey, Dad. Is the sword that important to you?"

"Yes, it is. Harnessing the power of the sword can even give one immortality."

"Let me state it differently. In your heart, Dad, does the sword weigh more or is it more valuable than your own daughter?"

"You want the truth, so let me tell you the truth. The value of my flesh and blood—my daughter, sons, and grandchildren—pales in comparison to the sword."

Elena broke down in tears and quickly stretched her hand, picked up a sharp, middle-sized dagger, and pointed it at her father. "Now I see. We were at your disposal, so you used us and threw us away when you wanted to. What kind of father are you?" She steamed once more. It was obvious that she had lost it. She charged at him without any hesitation and swung the dagger, wishing to pierce him and cut him into pieces.

"Are you crazy, Elena? I am your father."

"My father is all right. It is that sarcasm I am hearing."

Once again, she started displaying her skills as a hunter and pierced his skin.

"Do not make me angry at you, Elena. Children should listen to their parents, which is what they are for."

"You've got to be kidding me. Parents need to keep their desires to themselves and keep out of their children's love lives."

Both daughter and father fought for three hours. Hearing the noise from outside, Lionel rushed in.

"Why are both of you fighting like this?" Lionel said. "Do you not know that you will be heard?" He paused after getting a good look at the situation. "W–w–why do you look like that?"

"Stay out of this, Lionel, or I will cut you down. Do not side with this man. He wants to sacrifice us for his plans. Are you okay with that? Let me tell you, the sword he is searching for is more important to him than his own children, and he will not blink to kill us in an instant to achieve his means."

"She is lying. After being corrupted by her husband, she

came here and started going berserk, trying to harm me."

Without a second thought, Lionel immediately believed what his father was saying but still held hope for what she said. He knew that Elena's love had become an obsession, and she had lingering problems with Dad because of what had previously happened.

"Elena? I think it's time that you went home," said Lionel. "It's getting late, and I don't want to see you out late at night because your family will be worried."

"Okay, brother, but please tell your dad to stay away from me and don't show up at my house ever again. He's not welcome. I don't want him gambling with my children's lives."

Are you alright, Mom?" said Wendy. Even though she knew Elena hated her, she was still the woman who had raised her all these years.

"Why do you ask?" Elena replied.

"There is something different about you, and I can't understand what it is like. You were a bird tied to a tree, worrying about when you would be released. After you're released, your wings have become strong, and now, you're soaring through the sky."

"Yes, mom. Dad and I have also noticed this," said Wally.

Elena smiled, and for the first time, it was a smile worth seeing. She was genuinely happy, and they saw it. Elena always thought that no one cared for her, but now she noticed that everything was in her head. They realized the slightest difference and wanted to know what was happening to her.

Eithan also agreed because he had seen her two days ago, and she was indeed looking preoccupied with worries. After airing everything out on the table, everyone ate and went to their respective beds except for Eithan and William. William gave Eithan the gusset room next to Wendy's room because he considered him family and someone that he trusted. He also realized that nothing that he could do was going to keep Eithan's hands off Wendy, because he had been there and done the same thing with Wendy's mother. So, he went with the flow.

Now Lennox was in cahoots with Officer Paul. Ever since Lennox came by the station, he had been filling his head with stories about wolves, witches, demons, and much more. This made Officer Paul skeptical about the whole situation. Ever since that night, he had been trying to find out what that monster is. The tearing of human flesh is like a knife slicing butter. Everything was beginning to make sense. Officer Paul began to believe Lennox, but he was still a man who lived by his motto when the odds were against him: "Survive today to fight tomorrow."

After receiving such an important call from Elena, Lionel went to tell his other brother and his uncle. And just when he was about to inform his dad, he overheard him muttering to himself about how dangerous tonight's moon was. Nevertheless, there was something he had to obtain tonight, and that was not about to stop him from getting his hands on it.

Lennox summoned Lionel, Nicholas, and Yannick to come to the sitting room. Karel had already returned with Laura, Lily, and her husband because they knew that something ominous was brewing, and they did not want anything to happen to their daughter. When they gathered, Lionel told them that tonight was the night that they would go hunting. He explained that creatures of the night would be going on a rampage. Mixing truth with fiction was always Lennox's style, but things didn't go as planned. Everyone already knew the truth, thanks to Elena, who was not about to leave.

"Dad, as much as I would like to oblige, I have to say that I'm not feeling too well," said Lionel. "I have been feeling under the weather."

"You did say the beasts will be on a rampage, and I'm not strong enough to face such a foe," said Nicholas as he walked off towards his room.

Yannick wanted to go out to hunt, but Lionel gave him a stern look. "Father, I don't know what it is you want outside, but tonight is not the night." After saying this, he also went off to his room and dragged along Yannick.

Feeling depressed, Lennox became angry. Lionel was becoming more like his sister, rebellious and defiant, and this was starting to get in the way of his plans. Lennox concluded that the only one he could use was Yannick. He was gullible and quick to do anything he asked for recognition. The failed attempt to retrieve one of the main keys to his plan pierced him in the heart like an arrow.

Meanwhile, at the Granchest mansion, Wendy was in her room, her thoughts constantly on Eithan being in the next room. Her nervousness increased, and she began to feel uneasy. Her thoughts began to go haywire, forgetting that Eithan was a full-bred Alpha wolf. Eithan heard her thoughts. He knew what she was thinking, and he was becoming uneasy. It was bad enough that the moon was making him queasy. Eithan snapped. He got up out of his bed, opened the door, and knocked on Wendy's door. It only took three footsteps, which William heard, but he tried his best to block it out. Wally was also facing a rough night. He was trying to control himself. As the door opened, Wendy saw Eithan waiting for her in the hallway and jumped into his arms.

Growling at her, his sanity snapped, and so did the door behind them. He took her to bed and let his animal instincts loose on her. He threw her on the bed and ripped her clothes off. She was quick to rip his off as well. He placed his hands around her neck and began kissing her and caressing her body. He sucked on her breast and fondled them, intrigued by the softness of her voluptuous bosom. She pressed his head against them, and he began thrusting his member between her legs, slipping it in, causing her to orgasm repeatedly. She rode him like a bicycle and had sex in different positions, having lost herself to instincts. It was a hot and wet night of passion that lasted for two hours. They fell asleep in each other's arms. Accustomed to waking up early, Eithan returned to his room and kissed her before he left.

Truth of the Grand Library

The next day, the group of friends gathered. They all went off towards Jason's house. When they got there, Jason took them to the grand library. But surprisingly, it wasn't in the house. It was in another location. It was white and exceptionally small—too small for the word grand.

"Are you kidding me? How can you call this a grand library, Jason?" said Franco. "It looks smaller than my doghouse." Michael and Jeremy smiled.

"Let us just go inside."

As they got inside, Wendy said, "Are you pulling my toes right now?"

Eithan, who had entered it for the first time, was shocked. The inside of the library contrasted with the outside. Inside, the library was filled with knowledge never seen before, and it *was* grand. Ancient words were written on the walls, like runes. Franco took back his words while Jason puffed his head high. They all began searching for any clues they could find to know about the situation they were in, but they found nothing. Kylie translated the ancient writing but still had no clues. What she translated was

"A child born with legendary powers will shake the world and defeat It."

The translation was cut short and did not make sense. They searched and searched for hours, but still had no further clues. While continuing to check the walls, Kylie saw a red marking on the wall, which was strange because it did not look like the others. She quickly alerted the guys.

"Hey, come look at this!" she exclaimed.

Everyone gathered, even book geek Eithan, who seemed to be stuck in one of the books. It was surprising that he heard her voice for the first time, being that he was so deeply absorbed by what he was reading. After they got to the wall, they all wondered what the red markings were about. Even Jason became dumbfounded at what he saw. He didn't visit the library often because it was not something that anyone could casually enter. He had to plead with his parents for the entire day just to get a go-ahead.

Curious about what the red markings were, Kylie followed the markings and came upon a lighted red dot. She pressed the dot, which turned out to be a button surrounded by a palm, but that did not work.

"Come here, Eithan." She asked him to try to reassure her that she was right. Eithan pressed the button, but it still did not work. For a moment, Kylie thought that the button needed an Alpha wolf strong enough to press it down, but to her surprise, it still did not work.

"Let Jason try!" exclaimed Mandy. "After all, the library belongs to his family.

"Good point, Mandy. I see that you're not all that useless," smirked Samantha.

Mandy sucked her teeth. She always felt that Samantha had something against her, but she could never really figure out what. Jason proceeded to open the door. He placed his right palm on the button, but nothing happened. Everyone became puzzled as they were out of options.

"Try the other hand, Jason," said Kylie.

This time, he tried his left hand on the button, and surprisingly, it worked. The wall was filled with red markings, and before their eyes the wall twisted and spun around. They became astounded. There was another library found inside the grand library, but astonishingly enough, there was something about this one that felt odd and out of place. The vibe it gave off was like nothing that they'd seen before, and it was right.

Curious as they were, they began checking out the books. The books they found all had connections with the supernatural world and much more. Creatures that they thought did not exist existed within these books. Any abnormality that could not be seen, heard, or even spoken of was found within this library. Luckily for Kylie, she found a book that explained the current situation they were in, and it was called The Curse of a Crimson Moon. When she saw the book, she tried to flip through it, but neither the page nor the book cover turned. As she looked around, she saw that not only was she facing this problem, but everyone who was with her had the same problem. Everyone but Jason. Eithan released it first, because he was the first to try to open a book, followed by Kylie.

Watching Jason read the book as if nothing was wrong, Kylie called out to him.

"Jason, can you come here for a minute?" Jason came over, and so did the others.

"We can't read the books in the library," said Eithan.

"Now that I think about it, the other books were also hard to open," said Jeremy.

"We do not have to worry about such trivial stuff," said Michael. "Even though we got in, there is at least one person among us who can open and read the books."

Kylie quickly agreed with Michael. "Jason, this book, The Curse of a Crimson Moon, was found on the fifth shelf, and it is the book we've been looking for. Jason took the book from Kylie's hand and began to read. The book spoke about the effects of a crimson full moon and on the supernatural. It spoke about everything that they had come across so far. And most importantly, Jason read about the ritual with the Incasera sword, which happens during a certain crimson moon every thousand years. It was impossible to read the whole book, as it contained thousands of pages.

"Now that I think about it, all the books in this library are quite big," said Wendy.

After they finished exploring, they departed the library and went to their respective homes to do what they had to do. A little more knowledgeable than before they came.

The Bloodline of Jason's Family

That very evening, when Jason's parents got home around dinnertime, they were chatting happily.

"Did you enjoy yourself at the grand library today?" Jason's mother asked.

"So, you were at the library with your friends," said Grandpa.

Jason looked at his mother. "Yes, I enjoyed." Then he looked to his grandfather. "Yes, I was at the library today.

"Hey, Dad, I was wondering why the grand library is called the grand library. I was surprised when I first went inside, seeing that the outside was small, and the inside was unusually big. I don't think that's why it's called the grand library, right?"

His dad laughed. "You're right, son. This library has been passed down in our family for generations, and that's what it has been called. If you want to know why it's called that, you should ask your grandfather."

He turned towards his grandfather, but for some reason, there was a moment of silence that crept across the room. Then his grandfather began to speak.

"What your dad said is correct. The library has been passed down in this family for generations, and you are also right. It is not called the grand library because the inside is big, but because there is another library present inside the already big library. This library holds forbidden knowledge that should not be made public. Thus, only a family member can open it. That's what I heard from my father anyway."

Jason became intrigued. "I knew it. Ever since I saw the library inside with those big books, I knew that that was the reason it was called the grand library."

"What!" exclaimed his grandfather. "You mean you've entered the other library with those kids?"

"Yes, we did enter the library because there was something we were searching for that was not present in the first library. When one of my friends was looking around, she stumbled upon red markings that looked like runes, and by following them, we saw a red lighted button. After pressing it so many times, it did not open. One of my friends suggested that I press it, but it still didn't budge because I was using my right hand. When I tried my left hand, it worked. The second library gave off a mysterious air, and I was the only one who could open and read from the books."

Hearing this made his grandfather's day; what he assumed to be a legend turned out to be true.

"This is something that should be recorded in history books," said Dad who couldn't believe what he was hearing.

"Who knew that such a thing could happen to my son in just a day?" said Grandpa. "Who was this friend of yours who found the library? Is she a witch or something?"

"Yes, she is. Why do you ask?"

"I figured as much. Listen to me, boy. Make sure that you don't enter that part of the library carelessly. And if you do, make sure that you carry no one in. Witches are thirsty for knowledge, but more than that, there will be people—especially supernatural people—who will kill for a chance to enter that library. And when they do, it's not only you that will be in danger but us as well, because only our family lineage can open and read those books."

After listening to what his grandfather was saying, he realized how dangerous the situation was. He told his grandfather about the current situation they were in, but he already knew.

Leaving Jason's house, Kylie could not help but wonder about the library that no one else could open. She pondered over it. She also realized that the library is called a grand library because of its size and the massive books.

Wendy also went home and gave the news to her father. She told him what happened. William was amazed at what Wendy said. He already knew about the existence of the library, but he did not know where it was. He also told Wendy that she should not, under any circumstances, reveal this to anybody. Pondering on what her dad said, she decided to take his advice to heart. Wendy went to her room, still feeling distressed and bothered about what was going on.

Two weeks had passed since that day, but Wendy was still not feeling well. Every little thing she smelled made her feel queasy, and she wanted to vomit. Her complexion had changed. She had started to look pale. William noticed the change, and so did Wally, but they said nothing.

She did not want to go to school. And when she did go, especially when she was around Michael and Afeisha, she began to show unusual signs, which made them think the impossible had happened.

On a Wednesday, Wendine came to school and saw her daughter looking sick. With a sincere heart, she went up to her and asked, "Are you alright, my child?"

Wendy, knowing that she was her mother, decided to put her trust in her. "These days, I have been feeling sick. I throw up what I eat, even at the slightest smell of food, not to mention my senses are very keen."

"Wendy!" exclaimed Wendine. "These are all signs pointing to pregnancy. Are you pregnant?"

Wendy herself was in shock. "I-I don't think so."

"Let me ask you a question. "When did you start feeling like this?" "It was two weeks ago."

"Since it was two weeks ago, when did you sleep with Eithan?"

Wendy became embarrassed. "It was on the night of the full moon that we lost all sanity, and one thing led to another."

"My child, there is no doubt about it. You have become pregnant."

Hearing this, Eithan became shocked, fainted, and ended

up in the nurse's office.

CHAPTER TWELVE

Receiving The Shock of a Lifetime, Eithan's Choice

After feeling the shock of a lifetime, Eithan regained his consciousness. He was about to become a father at such an early age, and he did not have the experience to take care of a child. But the mere thought of having one with the woman he loved filled him with excitement in many ways, with a hint of nervousness. Eithan knew he had to tell Mr. William about their current circumstance, but Wendy refused. She wanted to be the one to break the news to him while bearing all the blame.

"How can I let you do that!" exclaimed Eithan. He had forgotten that they were in the infirmary. Hearing the nonsense that spewed from her lips infuriated him even more. "Wendy," he said. "I think it's about time that you close that mouth. I may not have any experience in all this, but there's one thing that I'm certain of, and that is that I have always taken responsibility for everything I do. And this time, I intend to do so. Do you want to shoulder the burden by yourself, making me look incapable?"

Wendy was shocked. This was the first time she saw Eithan mad, and she became scared. But in fact, this was the first time that Eithan had gotten angry. Only the person he loved could have dragged out such emotion that he himself did not think he had. He quickly regained his composure and went outside.

As Eithan went out to blow off his steam, Wendy was inside the room feeling hot and bothered. What Eithan said struck a chord with her, and she felt happy. The man that she loved said the words that she wanted to hear, and even became mad just from listening to her selfish wishes.

"Girls are such complicated beings to understand," she said while slapping her cheeks and smiling.

Meanwhile, Eithan was still outside, trying to find a reasonable excuse for getting mad, but he could not think of a solid one. Time passed, and Eithan went home by himself, trying to produce a good explanation to give to his parents, but nothing seemed to click. He decided to break the news to them just as it was given to him. Earlier, he took the time to tell Jason about what was going on and the reason for Wendy's behaviour. Jason was shocked. He could not believe that Eithan was going to become a father at such a young and tender age. Not to mention, his becoming a Godfather so early was quite intriguing.

As Eithan got closer to the door, he became increasingly nervous, but there was nothing that could be done. Eithan went up to the porch and second-guessed himself on whether to tell his parents. He was constantly changing his mind. He was about to go inside when someone opened the door after seeing a shadow linger in front of the door for an unusual number of minutes.

"Oh, it is you," Eithan said to Samantha.

"Why are you lingering in front of the door like that? It has been about thirty minutes. Everyone has already gathered to eat, but you haven't come yet."

Eithan went inside. Before he went to his room, he sat around the table with his family and ate.

"Mom, Dad, I'll be heading over to the Granchest house soon. But before that, I want to discuss something with you. Aaron, it is best for you to stay here, too, because what I am about to say will impact our family."

Tension began to fill the air, and the nervous aura that Eithan exuded began to surround them as if they were bathing in it.

"Wendy is—" He paused.

"Wendy is what?" asked Aaron. "Can you please come out with it and not leave us in the dark like that? I've never seen you so nervous before, and it's eating away at your conscience, so tell us the problem already."

"Wendy is pregnant with my first child."

"Wh–What! Are you out of your mind!" screamed Aaron. "You will be having a child in mere months at such an early age— and before me."

Samantha was so shocked out of her mind that she froze up, becoming unable to utter any words—positive or negative.

"Aren't you complaining about the wrong things here, Aaron?" said their father, who was coming towards them. He continued. "I can't be angry at you because I know that it's within a young man's nature. Well, a beast will do those types of things, especially with the woman you've imprinted on. However, I cannot deny that I'm shaken, but what has happened cannot be changed. I suggest you explain the situation to William. I know he is the understanding type, but he's quite protective of his daughter."

His mother also agreed with his father. Eithan was happy to know how understanding his parents were and headed off to Wendy's house right away. After reaching her house, she opened the door and welcomed him inside. Wally looked at him, grabbed his shirt by the neck, and punched him in the face. It turned out that Wendy had broken the news to them earlier than expected.

Lying on the floor, Wendy ran towards Eithan and asked Wally if he did that.

"Are you seriously asking me right now? You are pregnant at such an age, and it's his fault."

"Come on, big brother. You knew for a fact that he was my boyfriend, and something like this was going to happen sooner or later."

Wally could not believe what he was hearing. It was as if she had been brainwashed.

"Say something, Dad!" Exclaimed Wally.

William looked at his daughter, then at Eithan. "I already knew. I was waiting for Wendy, or rather, Eithan, to explain things to me since he is a man, and he did come. Furthermore, my daughter seemed to be madly in love with him, and he was going to take responsibility, right?"

"Y-yes, I intend to," said Eithan.

"Well, the matter is solved. I was prepared for this the moment you said you were going to stay over. I knew something like this would happen because everyone was trying their hardest to control their urges. Even you, Wally."

Wally was guilty and could not say anything.

"Thus, Eithan found Wendy, who was his perfect outlet, so, what can I say?"

Hearing these words uttered from her father's lips made her feel embarrassed yet happy, but neither Elena nor Wally gave in. They were still upset about the situation. William, on the other hand, was ecstatic about having his first grandchild, but if it were someone else who had gotten his daughter pregnant, he would have ripped them apart. Although he tried to play it cool, when he first found out, he wanted to rip his head off, but he wouldn't let them know.

The Way Forward, the Thousand-Year Crimson Moon

After the big commotion, they all settled down. Wally and Elena concluded that a child was about to be born, and there was nothing that could be done about the situation.

"I know I can be overbearing and overprotective sometimes, but you need to understand that raising a child is not a walk in the park."

"I know Wally, which is why this child is going to have his or her grandparents, parents, and uncle to help look after him or her," said Wendy.

Everyone was touched by what she said and prided ~~pried~~ no further. After everything that happened, Eithan spent some minutes with Wendy, and then he went back home to tell his mom the good news.

Meanwhile, Lennox was as bustling as ever. He manipulated Officer Paul, gathering the necessary information to achieve his grand goal. Having his plan thwarted by his daughter was a minor setback for him. He already had what he wanted, and there were just three things left to obtain. The strange inscription required a special child, a crystallized necklace, the staff of a grand witch, and a grave worthy of the dead.

The keys were bizarre, but there was a reason all these items were needed. After engaging in endless research, Lennox was at a dead end. The thousand-year moon was in two days, and he was missing the things necessary for it to become a success. Lennox constructed a brilliant plan. Now that he was affiliated with the police, he could use Officer Paul to secure a way into his grandchildren's school. For some reason, his intuition was telling him that what he was looking for would be found in the school. His intuition was just as strong and on point as any woman, and he was not about to ignore it.

Following that, Lennox went to visit Officer Paul at the station, as usual. When Officer Paul saw him, he went out to greet Lennox. To him, Lennox was a terrifying human being. He was so cruel that the thought of getting on his bad side struck fear into his heart. Paul's philosophy was and remains the same: whether it be monsters or Lennox, "Save himself and live to fight tomorrow." His cowardly nature was what elevated him to his current position and earned him the respect that he had built up over the years.

"I want a favor from you," said Lennox. "I want to work at the school where the monster attacked you all during the concert. Would that be, okay?"

"That will be no problem, but is there a reason you want to work there?"

Lennox hesitated. "Remember, I am a hunter. My grandchildren— three of them—go to that school, and it is my duty as a grandfather to protect my children. However, I want to go undercover."

Officer Paul knew deep down that Mr. Lennox was not the affectionate person he portrayed himself to be, but he did not want to pry any further. He granted Lennox's request. Lennox thought that Officer Paul was a sword he could wield as he saw fit, but little did he know that Officer Paul had his own intentions and knew that he was planning something excessive. His aura gave him away, and fortunately for Officer Paul, he had developed an ability from all his cowardice to sense and, if possible, avoid danger.

The very next day, as Lennox and Wendy headed off to school, Wendy was thinking about the future. She knew deep down that her belly would show sooner or later, and that was something she could not do even if she wanted to. Minutes before class started, Wendy saw her two best friends and walked up to them to talk.

"Why are we here in an abandoned classroom?" said Afeisha. "There is something that I must tell you," answered Wendy. "We also have something to tell you. Right, Michael?"

"You go first," Wendy said.

"Afeisha and I have taken our relationship to another level beyond friendship. We have started dating, and I think it is only fair that we tell you."

"Y–yes," said Afeisha while she blushed and looked

embarrassed.

Wendy was shocked at what Michael said. "So, all the time we were friends, both of you had a crush on each other and didn't tell me. Not to mention, you were secretly dating behind my back. I should feel betrayed, but I'm glad that you told me."

There was a sense of relief in Afeisha's sighs as she let them out one after the other.

"You mentioned that you have something important to tell us?"

"Yes, I was going to tell you that I'm pregnant. It happened on the night of the crimson moon when Eithan stayed over at our house." Wendy continued to blabber but heard no sound but the sound of her voice.

She looked at Michael and Afeisha, only to see their amazed yet speechless faces with ridiculous expressions. Finally, they started talking.

"Have you told Eithan yet?"

"Yes, I did. My stepmom, mom, dad, and Wally also know, along with Eithan's parents."

"Is there a reason you're being repetitive?" asked Michael. "And just when was I being repetitive?" asked Wendy.

"I know you, and you have never been repetitive before."

Wendy began speaking in her mind. Michael is both handsome and inquisitive as well as alert. He noticed the little hint that I placed in my words. I cannot let him know that I have my real Mom, right? I promised Dad.

"Don't read too much into the situation, Wendy. It's just as I said. Let us go to class, and we'll talk later." Michael knew he was still in the dark, but he did not want her to feel uncomfortable, so he stopped.

While going to their class, they saw a janitor in the school for the first time. There was something familiar about the janitor, but Wendy did not know what it was. Fortuitously, Wally had already met the janitor and deduced after speaking to him that he was, in fact, Lennox. What threw him off guard was what someone of his calibre was doing at school as a janitor.

One by one, Lennox met Wendy's friends without knowing who they were. Beforehand, he met Kylie. His intuition, as usual, was pricking at him, urging him to acknowledge her as something he needed. Next, he met Michael and Afeisha. He was shocked upon seeing him.

"How is he still so young?" he said to himself. "I really must be getting old. How can he be that young? We fed him something to mess up his head, so that cannot be. He must be another child."

When he glanced at Afeisha, he knew she was not what he was looking for, but there was still something about her that he couldn't put his finger on. He also met Eithan's friends. The weird and the strange, the smart and the dumb, he met them all.

"This is really a special place," said Lennox.

During lunchtime, Wendy told Kylie and the others about her pregnancy. The day was favorable for Lennox because he was in the right place at the right time. He overheard about the pregnancy and knew what she was all along. That gave him the idea that his so-called granddaughter Wendy was one of the keys. That made two keys, but he didn't know that he had already found all the keys. By listening to and following the children, Lennox learned of the existence of the grand library, but information on who and how to get there was omitted.

I have found all the keys to Jason's abduction.

"Guys, don't you think that we are being watched and analyzed? I have been feeling like someone has been eyeing me today, but I do not know who it is."

Their conversation quickly changed, and Lennox moved away. Determined as he was, he continued to roam the school. Near the teachers' lounge, he overheard two teachers speaking about a student. This student had been missing classes as well as entire school days lately, and they wanted to visit his house to speak to his parents. Concurrently, William was perturbed. He had never felt so anxious before. Ever since that day of the last moon, he had heightened his awareness to match the anxiousness he felt.

"His family is no ordinary family," said one of the teachers. "So, you cannot just go up and enter as you wish."

"Then I'll hire a bodyguard."

"You do not have to do that. There is a janitor working at the school who can accompany you."

"What! You want a janitor to follow me to a nobleman's house? If something happens to me, what is he going to do? Mop the floor?"

"You don't know this. Only a few teachers know. But he was sent by Officer Paul as a security guard. However, he is an outstanding man who chose to work as a janitor for our safety. The boy's house is not near, so that is why I'm sending protection to you."

After their discussion, they appointed Lennox to escort the teacher, whose name was Ms. Simmons, to Jason's house. Happy to accept the proposal, Lennox remembered hearing that name. Reflecting on his thoughts, it occurred to him. He was the boy who was walking with Wendy's boyfriend earlier, but they separated. The boyfriend went to class and took him to the roof. It was like everything was just falling into his lap.

Not long after he agreed, Wendine passed by and chatted with a teacher. Lennox again recognized her with a glance. He knew because he had used his daughter to plot against her, and for what?

"That useless girl couldn't even accomplish one task," he muttered. "The heavens must have blessed me. Now the keys are coming to me one after another."

Lennox did not know that it goes both ways. Wendine also recognized him. Though she pretended not to, seeing him had raised signs of concern. The conniving old man, whom she still thought was conspiring with his children, was too devious to leave unchecked. Without uttering a single word to him, she went by, and Lennox smirked.

Later, Lennox did as he was told. He followed the teacher to Jason's house. His parents were not home, and neither were his grandparents. Ms. Simmons rang the doorbell. Once more, they rang again, and this time, someone opened the door. It was none other than Jason himself.

"Are your parents' home?" asked Ms. Simmons. "No, they are not," responded Jason in a cold voice. "When will they return?" she continued.

"I don't know?" he replied.

Lennox saw that Simmons' way of getting through to Jason was not going to work. Furthermore, he had his plans when he decided to accompany her and was not about to let her get in the way.

"Your name is Jason, right?" asked Lennox. "Why don't you invite us in for some tea? After all, your teacher and I have trodden all this way to meet you."

Jason fixed his eyes on the old man before him. "I can let Ms. Simmons in because I know her, but who are you, Mister? You talk big, but I have no intention of letting some strange old man into my home."

Lennox did not expect Jason's guard to be so impenetrable because he had the teacher with him, but he had not played all his hands yet. There was still a card to be played.

"My name is Lennox, and I am Wendy's and Wally's grandfather. In fact, you could say that I'm your friend Eithan's in-law."

Hearing these words filled with confidence, it was clear to him that Lennox was telling the truth. But there was still something about the old man that he could not put his hands on. Nevertheless, he let both in. When they walked inside, Ms. Simmons began asking questions, but Jason only answered the questions he wanted to. Eventually, she ran out of questions, and tension filled the air.

Lennox had no problem cutting the tension. "I heard about a library.

Do you know anything about it?"

"What are you asking, Mr. Lennox?" said Ms. Simmons.

Lennox gave her a stern look, and she immediately stopped talking.

Jason became on edge. "What are you talking about? What library?"

Lennox came forward. "I'm talking about the grand library. I overheard your friends speaking about it earlier."

"I-I don't know anything about any grand library," said Jason sternly.

He began to wonder why an old man like this would want to know about the library. He instinctively remembered that Eithan once told him that, apart from Wally and William, no other person in Wendy's family could be trusted. Not only that, but his grandfather warned him about the existence of the library and how it was known to the bad people.

Jason immediately got up from the couch, asked for an excuse, and went to his room. He took his computer and video called Eithan. He began to tell Eithan what was going on at his house. Eithan connected with the others, and all of them began to chat. Even Wally was included. When the information about their grandfather being at his house was relayed, Wendy and Wally warned Jason not to tell him about the grand library and to get out of the house.

"He is dangerous."

"He was at school today acting like a Janitor, and that got me confused," said Wally.

"What!" exclaimed Wendy.

"Get out of the house!" shouted Eithan to Jason.

Confident in his wolf abilities, Jason said that he could handle it.

"Are you dumb?" said Wally. "He is no ordinary being. He's experienced, veteran hu—" Wally's chat cut off, and so did Wendy's. Only Eithan and the others were left.

"What was he about to say?"

"Jason, I know that you are a strong wolf, but I'm telling you, you need to vacate the house," said Kylie. "That man is a hunter, an exceptional one, and what he wants is not just the location of the library but information on something which should not be given, and you are the key."

Jason became tense, but it was already too late. Lennox and Ms. Simmons had been waiting for him for quite some time, but he did not return. Lennox had already guessed what he was doing and knocked out Ms. Simmons. He snuck upstairs and started listening to the conversation between him and Kylie on the computer. Lennox then snuck up behind Jason and gave him two injections. One was a truth serum, and the other was a drug that rendered the supernatural useless for some minutes. He then turned off the computer and tied it up. There was one thing he knew: that what he was looking for could be found in Jason.

Access to the Grand Library; Preparation for the Big Day Ahead

Minutes later, Jason awoke. He found himself tied to a piece of furniture. When he looked around, his teacher was nowhere to be found; only a man stood hovering over him with an arrow in his hand. One look at it, and he knew instantly that it was not an ordinary bow and arrow. The man was so adept at what he was doing that surrendering peacefully was the only option ahead.

"I see you're awake," said Lennox, "Now let us try again. What do you know about the grand library?"

Jason stumbled. "I-I do not—It's a library that is found within our family," Jason shocked himself. He wanted to say he did not know, but for some reason, he told him the truth.

"Oh, I see you're still resisting," muttered Lennox. "But don't waste your time. I have fed you a truth serum, so whatever I ask you, you'll have no choice but to tell me the truth."

Jason became frustrated at his uselessness.

Once more, Lennox asked. "How do I get to the grand library? And does it provide all information on the supernatural?"

"Yes," replied Jason.

"Once more, do you know anything about keys needed for a

specific sword, the Incasera sword?"

"No," he responded.

However, Lennox changed his tactic. "Do you know of any powerful witches with a staff?

"Yes. Wendy's friend, Kylie, is a powerful witch whose grandmother was Grenadine."

Lennox began to laugh. He knew who that was from all the tailing he did at school. He asked two more questions. "How do I enter the grand library? And do you know anything about a crystallized necklace?"

"To get to the grand library, you need me to open the way for you. And as for a crystallized necklace, I don't know."

Lennox was pleased with what he heard, so he made Jason stand, pointed his bow and arrow at him, and made him lead the way to the grand library. The effects of the truth serum had begun to leave his system.

Meanwhile, the gang—Wally, Eithan, Kylie, Michael, and Afeisha— all headed towards Jason's house. Eithan and Wally forbid Wendy from coming because they did not want to put stress on her body in case any fighting had to happen.

Jason and Lennox arrived at the library. "This is the grand library," said Jason.

Lennox could tell that, though the outside was small, and the inside was indeed grand, a grand library with supernatural information would not be so easy to enter.

Once more, he asked, "Is this really the grand library?" Jason said, "Yes," a second time.

Lennox gawked at him. He knew he was lying. At once, he raised his bow and arrow and shot him in the leg.

"Aaah!" he screamed. He was in excruciating pain. "What did you just shoot me with?" he asked while holding his foot, trying to take out the arrow.

"The young ones think that they can outsmart us old folks. However, it's way too early to outsmart a hunter like me. This arrow is made with a special type of silver and mixed with something that is quite effective against wolves. If you do not show me the way to the library, the next arrow will be piercing your shoulder."

After experiencing such pain, Jason did not think he could take another. If he continued to delay, the old man would eventually kill him. Jason immediately went to where the marking was and took Lennox with him.

Lennox was stunned at the marking on the wall and was able to make out more of its writings than Kylie. He read it in his mind.

"Another Vamolf will bear a powerful Vamolf child, and this child will be the saviour of the supernatural world. The child will own the mighty sword, the Incasera, and it will transform in its hands."

Lennox could not make out the other markings, but he knew what it meant and who it was. Jason pressed the red button, leading Lennox into the true library that held all knowledge.

"Now, this is what I'm talking about."

Lennox tied Jason up again so that he would not be able to flee, and he began looking for the books he wanted. He found three books: Swords, The Crimson Moons, and the Book of Sacrifice. They were exactly what he needed. Lennox then took the books to the front. First, he opened the Book of Sacrifice. He tried turning the pages, but for some reason, he could not open the book.

"Why can't I open the book?" asked Lennox.

"You cannot open the books because only the person you tied up can open them and read the books in this library," said Jason while he laughed.

Lennox untied Jason and gave him the book to open. He was confident enough in his abilities to untie him completely. Lennox told him to look for immortality. Jason got up and opened the book for him. He began flipping through the pages until he came upon a way to obtain immortality. Jason began reading and looking at the pictures. What Lennox saw on the pages were blank pages, one after the other. Jason began.

"To obtain immortality, the five keys must be placed on a grave worthy of the dead. The grave will be used as an altar for a thousand-year-old crimson moon, which has the power to do the impossible. To achieve this, you need the keys, which are a crystal necklace, a gift worthy of the dead, a powerful witch staff, a Vamolf's child, and lastly, the Incasera sword inscription.

"The child will be laid in on the grave wearing the crystal necklace. The sword will be standing at the top of the grave where the child is placed, and the staff in the hand. When the moonlight begins to shine, the sword will glow, which signals that it is time to read the inscription and pierce the child. The one holding the sword will then get the powers from the keys, making him immortal."

Hearing this reading made Lennox laugh loudly and evilly. Lennox told Jason to pick up the book, Swords. He then told him to look for the information on the Incasera sword. Jason began flipping through the pages, and he found it.

"The Incasera sword is a fierce and powerful sword, able to cut down any supernatural being. It chooses its owner and not the other way around. The sword has been passed down to the branch's family for generations and can manipulate the mind of a welder if it is wielded not by its true owner. It is a sword to protect. A grand and powerful witch carved the sword from an Alpha's fang to protect an Alpha vampire that he loved, and so the sword could only be wielded by two."

That was the end of the Incasera sword section. Lennox was disappointed because he already knew that piece of information. Upon reading the books, Jason realized what Lennox was trying to do, and he also concluded that the information on the sword was scattered throughout the books in the library, and he was not about to tell him that. Lennox told him to open The Crimson Moons. He told him to look for information on the thousand-year crimson moon.

Jason opened the book, and what he saw was surprising. There were a lot of different moons. The one that occurs every seventh day is the unusual moon. There was the thousand-year moon and many more moons. He now understood why Kylie had previously told them that they were not to come out of their house, no matter what. Jason began reading.

"The thousand-year crimson moon, as its name depicts, happens every thousand years. This is a powerful moon that has the power to heighten the raw instincts of supernatural beings, but at the same time, it is a moon used for various rituals. It is a double-edged sword."

While Jason was still busy reading for Lennox, Eithan and the others arrived at Jason's house, but it was empty.

CHAPTER THIRTEEN

All The Keys, The Missing Persons

When they got there, the place was empty. Jason was nowhere to be found. Kylie, a quick thinker, spoke first.

"Let's go to the grand library. Maybe your grandfather wanted to obtain information, so he stalked us at school, and now he wants the information that we lack."

They headed to the grand library, as they already knew the route. When they got there, it was empty. They knew that they could not enter the grand library even if they tried, so they prepared shelves for an ambush by standing at different points. They waited and waited, but nothing happened. Suddenly, the door opened, and Jason and Lennox emerged.

"Thanks for your assistance," said Lennox. "Now I no longer need you. Others having access to this library will become a pain soon, so here is my farewell gift to you."

Lennox grabbed his last arrow and shot Jason, aiming for his heart. Jason dodged it just in time, but it did graze his hands. Jason took out his claws and looked at him, ready to tear him to shreds. Lennox was well prepared because he had sensed that five persons hiding behind Jason. Lennox became a little serious. He took not only his bow but also hidden knives and daggers. They may be kids, but for Lennox, no one was going to get in the way of his plans. Not his daughters, not his grandsons, and certainly not some strangers he barely even knew.

Jason rushed towards Lennox, but he threw daggers at him, which caused him to retreat. Michael, who was not in total control of his demon powers, knew that an ambush would not work on Lennox, so he shouted for them to attack him simultaneously. Everyone dispatched and charged toward Lennox, with Wally leading. With no remorse for his grandson, Lennox pierced Wally with an arrow to his leg, used darts on Michael, and dodged Kylie's spell. Doing that gave Eithan the opportunity to wound him, but that did not stop him from catching Kylie. Using spells gave her away so easily that they were the ones who fell into his trap.

When Lennox got what he wanted, he retreated. Baffled by what had just happened, everyone was astonished. Even six of them could not defeat a human, or better yet a decisive one. Not to mention, the old man kidnapped Kylie. Eithan was the only uninjured member of the group. He had no choice but to bandage up the injured and pull the arrow out of Wally's leg. Jason immediately conveyed to them what had happened.

Eithan immediately went to the Granchest house, carrying Wally with him, to show and tell William what had taken place. Of course, when they arrived there, Elena was home. She also received the news and saw what had happened to her son. Elena had already cut ties with her dad and knew that the only thing left for her to do now was fight against him. She also wanted to tell her brother, Lionel, what he did. She shut herself in her laboratory inside the house.

Inside that laboratory, Elena was making potions and experimenting with things that she would need; things that could work on the supernatural as well as humans. Ever since the day she had disowned her dad, she had been looking for ways to bring him down. She always wondered where her dad got the strength he possessed, because it was not human, but of a monster.

Meanwhile, Michael contacted Franco, and he told him about Kylie's kidnapping and Lennox's intentions. Franco had fallen in love with Kylie. She also knew that he was a vampire, and his father was scheming for something, but she still loved him. Hearing this news made Franco angry. He could no longer trust his dad. Everything was becoming so complicated because of a sword that had the power to grant immortality.

Lennox went home and carried Kylie with him. He locked her up in his secret basement so none of his sons would ask him any questions. Afterwards, he went inside his room, reached for a first aid kit on top of his cupboard, and began treating himself. As it turns out, he was not able to evade Kylie's magic spell completely and was hurt to some extent, but those markings healed on their own. What stayed was the injury given by the wolf Eithan.

It was late in the evening, and Officer Paul came to his house. He did not want to, but he had no choice. His task was to accompany Ms. Simmons to Jason's house, but Ms. Simmons never made it back home. When he visited Jason's house, he could tell that the boy was injured, but he did not pry too far because his gut told him that it had something to do with Lennox.

Lennox opened the door. He saw Officer Paul standing in front of the door and was annoyed. He was not in the mood to be visited by anyone, especially a cowardly man like Officer Paul. Having no intention to indulge in his questioning, he promptly said, "If you are wondering what happened to Lady Simmons, then I don't know. I followed her as instructed, but his parents were not home, so we retreated. Is that good enough for you?"

Officer Paul beamed at him. He knew that he was lying because he looked injured, and that did not explain why Jason also looked hurt.

"Listen, Lennox! I know that I can be a coward most of the time, but you must remember that you got the job because my reputation was on the line. I will not have you or anyone tarnish what I tried so hard to build."

Lennox was amazed. He didn't know whether to clap or laugh. Officer Paul was not only a coward but a man who valued his reputation even if he had to confront danger. His determination touched Lennox.

"Lady Simmons is behind a large orange tree that leads to Jason's house. After I knocked her out, I did not want to carry her, so I just left her there. She is supposed to already be awake by now."

Listen to Lennox, there was no room for words. Officer Paul was wondering if Lennox was really listening to the words uttered from his lips. In front of an officer, he brazenly said he knocked out a woman and stashed her behind a tree. He could not believe or stand him any longer.

"Listen, Lennox!" he shouted sternly, "I do not want you to come down by the station anymore. In fact, I don't want you anywhere near me because I will arrest you."

Lennox gave him an evil grin and shut his door.

"He's really an evil man," whispered Officer Paul while calling an order for his fellow police officers to patrol the forest to look for Ms. Simmons.

When they found Ms. Simmons, she was not behind the tree but at the entrance of the forest, with her memories distorted. Lennox did something to her that made her unable even to remember her name, where she lived, what she did, or why she was standing in front of the forest. Guilt pierced Officer Paul because he knew who had put her in that condition. Officer Paul went to the hospital and took her bills with assurance from the doctor that she would get better. After a long and stressful day filled with worries, Officer Paul was finally about to get some sleep when he received a call. A child by the name of Kylie had gone missing. Night had already come, and she was still not home.

In the meantime, Eithan and Wally were still conversing with William. They were telling him that Wendy being pregnant was a key that Lennox needed for his grand plan. The three stayed up, making plans on how to protect Wendy from the devious Lennox while Elena, who was in the laboratory, was cooking up ways to murder him. The thought of that old fox harming her son was something she could not stand.

The Crimson Moon: Who is Lennox Really

Early the next day, everyone woke up feeling uneasy. Kylie's parents were especially concerned about their missing daughter. Officer Paul was restless. Now, he had to look for Kylie and do regular checkups on Ms. Simmons. Inviting Lennox into his life was one of the mistakes that he painfully regretted. Eithan, Wally, and William persuaded Wendy to stay home from school that day. Jason, Michael, and Afeisha headed to Kylie's house first thing in the morning before they went to school. When they got there, they met Franco, who looked extremely tired; Jeremy, who was as active as usual; and Sheila, who did not give a hoot about what was taking place.

"What are you doing here?" asked Afeisha,

"Oh, come on," said Franco, "If it was Michael who was kidnapped, I'm sure you'd be at his house the next morning."

At once, Afeisha realized that to Franco, Kylie meant the world to him, and immediately, she held her peace. Franco went up to knock on the door, but the door opened before he could knock.

"Why have your children come this early in the morning?" said Kylie's father, Mr. Primo.

Her worried mother, Alison, also came out and saw them. She began to cry because she realized that caring friends surrounded her daughter, and her eyes were fixated on Franco.

Although she was a witch, the strong powers of her great-grandmother skipped her generation and went to her daughter. Even so, she knew without a doubt what the students were but pretended not to. She could tell that among her daughter's friends, Franco was more worried about her, as if something precious had been taken from him. Without delay, she realized that her daughter had been acting strangely lately. Could this young man be the reason? She smiled.

"I'll leave my daughter in your capable hands."

Franco, who heard her thoughts, smiled, and said, "Thank you."

It was not a common thing for a vampire to be with a witch, but because of modern times, races have been intermixing, and Franco knew this was a form of blessing from her mother.

"Does your daughter have a staff which she uses to manifest her powers?" Jason asked.

"Why do you want to know?" asked Alison. "Even if you are her friend, I cannot just give you something as important as a witch's staff. After all, giving someone a witch's stuff is like giving away their life."

"Well, she has already been taken away, and so will her staff," said Jason. "The person who kidnapped her did so because she was a powerful witch, and all witches have a staff. Lennox, the man who kidnapped her, is seeking immortality, and her staff is one of the keys she needs."

Alison could not believe what she was hearing. She knew immediately that it had something to do with the cursed sword. Dumbfounded at what they were talking about, Mr. Primo urged the children to return to school. But before that, Alison made known to them that the staff was with Kylie, and it always is.

"She has been using her magic through her enchantments, but her staff is the belt she wears. Have you ever thought that her belt was a little weird? I gave it to her on her birthday, but she has never noticed it. To put it briefly, if she is under extreme stress, the light on her belt will start to shine a certain color, and if she takes it off, it will take the shape of a staff."

"So, what you are saying is all the keys—except the sword, of course— are in that old cougar's house?"

"Yes," replied Alison. "I'm sorry I couldn't be of use."

"It's alright," said Afeisha, "It's not like he knows that the belt she is wearing is actually the staff?"

"That may be true," replied Alison. "However, if a person is sensitive to the aura or sees the belt with their supernatural eyes, they will know instinctively. Fortunately for us, this Lennox feller is human."

"Don't celebrate yet," replied Jason, "Don't forget that neither of us could take him down. Not even with Kylie, whose magic is so omnipotent. Eventually, he will realize that what he is looking for is already in the palm of my hands."

"Thanks for your time," said Michael. "We should go to school now."

They headed off to school, discussing recent events about what was happening. What got them on edge was why Lennox was so desperate to collect the keys.

"It's not like anyone knows when there is going to be a thousand years of crimson moon, right?" said Sheila.

Jeremy began thinking. "Suppose the reason why he is so desperate is that he knows when the thousand-year crimson moon is going to occur, and it's very close—maybe even tonight?"

As selfish as Jeremy is, his Intelligence Quotient is remarkably high. Franco was not about to dismiss the claims that he made because what he said was logical.

Pondering on what Jeremy said, Franco looked at Jason. "When you guys were fighting against Lennox, was there anything that seemed off to you?"

"Now that you mention it, when he came to our house the first time, he demanded to know about the grand library. When we finally got there, he wanted to know about the keys desperately, as if he was running out of time."

"If what you said is true, then Jeremy's logic was correct. Tonight's the crimson moon. We need to find the sword quickly."

The Time Has Come; All Keys are in Place.

Subsequently, William went to visit Wendine to update her on the situation ahead. Wendine was out of school for the day, so they made plans to meet up. William had left Wendy at home by herself because he knew that Elena was home and she was well cared for, not to mention that he had not seen Wendine for quite some time, so he was excited. Curious as to what William was up to, Elena also left the house minutes after he did.

William didn't notice that he was being followed because of his excitement about meeting Wendine, and he paid dearly for it. Elena saw him meet up with a woman. She knew that his heart was not hers and had accepted that fact, but it was still hard for her to watch. Elena began walking away, feeling depressed, until she heard William call the name of the woman. It was Wendine.

Elena was shocked. "Wh–what is going on? W–Wendine! But she died!

How is this even possible?"

Once again, she went even closer to get a better look at the woman. It was, without a doubt, Wendine. Although she was mad about Wendine, a feeling of relief hovered over her.

While William was at Wendine's house enjoying some adult fun, someone dropped by the Granchest mansion for a visit. As the doorbell rang, Wendy thought it would be Elena, but to her surprise, it was none other than Lennox.

"Aren't you going to let your sweet grandfather in?" asked Lennox. "Not in a million years," said Wendy. "And you're not my grandfather.

Which grandfather in their right mind would try to kill their children and grandchildren?"

"You're forgetting something. It was my grandson who tried to injure me. I just defended myself, and he got himself hurt in the process."

Lennox walked into the house as if he were a welcome guest. "I see you are home by yourself. That's not being clever. After all, you must take care of my great-grandchild properly. But not to worry, I am here."

Lennox rendered Wendy useless. For some reason, Wendy could not use her powers properly because of the pregnancy.

Lennox immediately knocked her out and began looking for the sword. He knew that if there was a place where the sword could be hidden, it was in the Granchest manor. He hurriedly looked for the sword before William returned. William can be quite the monster when he is upset, and at Lennox's current strength, defeating William would be an arduous task to achieve. Lennox continued to search and search, but to no avail. He could not find the sword, no matter what he did.

Lennox stopped searching for a while. He began to take deep breaths, placing himself in the shoes of William. "If I were a wolf, a protector of the Incasera sword, where would I hide it?" He began thinking and thinking. Suddenly, it hit him. The sword had never left the house. It was so obvious that searching for it became ridiculous.

After he retrieved it, he began laughing sinisterly. Without a second thought, he took Wendy and went home to prepare for the moon to come.

After the lovemaking session at Wendine's house, William started to feel uneasy. Something was beginning to bug him, so for the first time in a long time, he took her home with him. He told her that he had a feeling that the moon was closer than they thought.

When they arrived at the house, William met Elena standing in front of the door, facing them but not moving. He thought the reason for her unmoving state was that she saw Wendine, but little did he know that it was because of something greater. William and Wendine inched closer.

"Hello, Elena. I haven't seen you for a long time. Especially with what you and your father did to Jamain and William."

As sorrowful as Elena looked, she could feel the hostility within her voice, so she said nothing.

"Listen, Elena," said William. "Wendine didn't die. She is alive, so you don't have to feel guilty anymore." Elena still did not speak. William immediately noticed that something was wrong.

He rushed into the house, with Wendine following behind. He began to search for his one precious daughter, but she was nowhere to be found. Filled with anger, William turned and howled as loudly as he could. It was remarkable that all the birds and animals within a 5.5-meter radius began to panic. It echoed so loudly that people thought it was a bad omen.

When Eithan heard the roar, he knew that there was just one man powerful enough to let out such a roar, and that was William. Listening to the painful roar, he left school and headed towards the Granchest mansion. Fear came over him that something had happened to Wendy and his unborn child.

Jason, who was with him and gave him the latest update about the thousand-year moon being tonight, went along with him to Wendy's house. Wally was also busy, but he went home the minute he heard the cry. William had lost his sanity. He immediately went towards Elena.

"Where is my baby girl?"

It was the first time she saw William angry to the extent that he was going to kill her.

"I don't know?" she said.

William immediately lost it. He grabbed her by the throat and lifted her off the ground. Elena closed her eyes in preparation for death, but Wendine grabbed William's hand and told him to let her go. William also growled at Wendine for a minute, then he came back to his senses.

"Why did you let my daughter out of your sight?"

"It's not like I wanted to leave her. But when I saw you going out, I got curious and followed. That is when I saw you and Wendine enjoying yourselves. When I got back, she was already gone. How can you blame me, William? This is such a critical time, and you left your only daughter, whom you deemed precious, to have fun?"

William could not believe it. What Elena said hit a mark because it was true.

Eithan and Wally reached home.

"Why is the new teacher in my house?"

Wendine looked at Wally. She could see some of William and Elena's features in him.

"So, I guess you are Wally," said Wendine. She then looked at Elena with disgust and hatred. She wanted her children to be William's and all his to be hers, but Elena got in the middle. However deep down, she knew it wasn't Wally's fault.

The Last Key: The Night Has Come

"This teacher that you see here is named Wendine," said William. "What! Wendine... do you mean Wendine, Wendy's mother?" said Wally.

"Yes," said William. "You catch on quickly."

Eithan, who did not care for their family reunion, noticed that Wendy was missing. "Where is Wendy?"

"Lennox has taken her, both," said William.

"What do you mean by both? Are you talking about Wendy and her unborn child?"

"No, I'm referring to Wendy, who is caring for her unborn child, and the Incasera sword. Lennox has gotten his hands on it."

Eithan's knees began to weaken as he drooped to the ground, fighting for the breath caught in his throat. Like melted iron, the weight of the truth flattens him.

He clutched his chest. The silence he felt wasn't just pain. In fact, it was the echo of her name screamed and unanswered. It wasn't just panic he felt but failure. He dug his claws into the ground, trying to claw back time, but he couldn't. Overwhelmed by grief, pain, and rage, he huffed, "She was mine to protect."

Eithan briefly paused while he collected himself.

"We need to produce a plan," he said. "We cannot allow Wendy to become Lennox's key for immortality."

Meanwhile, Lennox had already returned to his home. Because he was home by himself, he went through the front door carrying Wendy on his shoulders and the sword in his left hand. The door in the basement began to creak. Without delay, Kylie knew that Lennox was coming, but she did not know what to do. Escaping had become too much for her because Lennox bound her with some strange ropes and rendered her unable to speak. The door finally opened, and Kylie began to feel scared. The wicked old man was not human.

When the door finally opened, what Kylie saw was shocking. Lennox brought in Wendy, who was in a sleepful state, but she knew better. Lennox had knocked out Wendy and brought her for one of the keys. There was no way that Wally would allow her sister to go with the old man after he was injured and tried to kill him. Filled with panic, Kylie began to tremble. She was so scared. After Lennox put down Wendy gently, he bound her with the same ropes he used to bind Kylie. He then picked up Kylie.

"Where is the staff?" Lennox demanded.

"I-I don't know what you are talking about," said Kylie.

"Are you trying to fool?' said Lennox, "Are you not a witch?" "Yes, I am."

"The last time I checked, all witches have a staff."

"I'm different!" said Kylie. "I have never had one before."

"Well, I guess I should just use you as the staff. After all, there is no time to find your mother."

A strange emotion she had never felt came over her. She was filled with anger and hatred. Suddenly, her belt began to glow. Lennox had never paid attention to something as useless as one belt, but when he laid his eyes on the glowing belt, he knew what it was and tried taking it off her.

As he tried taking it off, his hands began to burn. Someone other than the owner of the staff couldn't take it off or wield a witch's staff. Lennox then tossed Kylie to the ground and demanded that she take off the belt. Kylie was puzzled. Why would Lennox want her to take off her belt? As smart as she was, she could not even tell that what she was wearing was what he wanted.

"Why do you want my belt?" she asked. "This was given to me by my mother on my birthday, and I cannot hand it over to strangers. It means a lot to me."

Lennox glared at her. "This is not a request nor a negotiation. It's an order. I don't want to lay my hands on a lady, especially a young and brazen girl like you, so take off the belt."

Kylie began taking the belt off. The glowing light started forming the head of the staff, resembling a crozier. She then fell to her knees. All this while, she was self-conscious about not owning a staff, and all along, it was with her.

Lennox took the staff, erased her memory, and sent her away. She was no longer of any use to him. He wanted to kill her at once, but he did not.

Late in the evening, Kylie returned home as if nothing had happened. She knocked on the door, and her mother opened it. She was filled with joy and happiness to see her daughter alive and well. She remembered what Jason had said earlier, so she looked at her daughter's pants loop, but the belt was missing. She began crying. Her daughter must have gone through a lot.

Franco, who had been given their number earlier, called to check on her and see if she had any news.

"My daughter has returned home, but her staff has gone missing," said Alison.

Hearing Alison utter such words, Franco knew what had happened. She was no longer of use, so he let her go, erasing all her memories of the accident while keeping everything else intact. When Franco heard the news, he headed over by himself, first informing Jason and Eithan. When he called Eithan, he could hear the sadness in his tone.

"Has something happened to Wendy?" asked Franco.

"Yes, in fact. Lennox captured Wendy to be used as a key." Franco felt a wave of sadness because he knew what it was like. He did not know what to do when Kylie was gone.

"There is a mixture of good news and shocking news," said Franco. "Kylie has returned home, but Lennox has gotten his hands on her staff."

"If what we thought is going to happen, then Lennox has in his hands all the keys needed to obtain immortality, because he also has in his hands the Incasera sword," said Eithan.

"Let us plan quickly because night is going to fall soon." Franco and the others headed to the Granchest house.

Lennox was home listening to every conversation that Franco was having. He knew that with his son's new friends, he would obtain what he needed. He gave Franco, whom he kept on a tight leash, a yard. He allowed him to do what he wanted. Because in the end, there could only be one winner, and that was him. After spending so much time in the Granchest mansion, he did not have a clue how to obtain the sword. Not to mention, the sword that was on display was a mere fake. As he was thinking, he began to second-guess himself.

"Who said it was a fake? I have never heard William or Elena say it was a fake. Could it be? That was the real thing. I'm such a fool. Nevertheless, I will leave that old guy to do everything for me, and in the end, I will be victorious.

CHAPTER FOURTEEN

The Rising of The Moon, All the Keys Assembling

Jason, Franco, and the others gathered at Wally's house. When they got there, they saw their teacher and became confused.

"Why are you here?" said Michael.

Wendine smiled, "I'm here to help rescue my daughter." Everyone was confused.

"Who is your daughter?" "Wendy, of course."

"But I thought she said that her mother died. Now that I remember it, I remember she said that her dad, mom, stepmom, and brother knew she was pregnant. I confronted her, but she denied all allegations. So, this was what she meant. Stupid Wendy! Doesn't she know she can trust us? If she found her mother, why didn't she just say so rather than keep us in the dark?"

"That may be my fault," said William. "When we returned from the trip, I told her to keep it a secret. Today was the day that everyone besides me and Wendy found out."

"Not exactly," said Eithan. "I already knew that she was her mother. We were tailing you the whole time on the trip, but you did not notice us. We even went to that room and overheard your conversation and other things."

Wendine began to blush from embarrassment, and so did William, to think his daughter saw him like that. After they got that out of the way, they began waiting for another person to arrive. A few minutes had passed, but they saw no one.

"Are you sure that the other person is coming? After all, time is not on our side," said Franco.

Seconds later, Jamain arrived. "Sorry for the wait, guys. Now let us discuss our plans."

"Why is teacher Sam here?" asked Franco.

"Let us get all the questions done and over so we can get on with the plans," said Jeremy.

William answered Franco's question. "Jamain, better known as teacher Sam, is my best friend from high school as well as Michael's father. When we were in high school, Lennox did something to him through his daughter Elena, causing him to have a severe memory disorder. The headaches he has been having after seeing Michael and us at the parent-teacher meeting began to wear off, bringing back his memories.

"Who wants to talk more? We will do that later, but for now, we need to plan. Does anyone know where Lennox will be at this time tonight?"

Silence filled the room. Everyone became anxious. Even though they made solid plans, it will be useless if they are not where the enemy is.

"One of the keys was a worthy grave of the dead, right?" said Eithan. "He has the staff, the sword that has the inscription installed in it, and the child and Wendy are keys, so that makes four keys. There are still two keys missing: a crystal necklace and the grave worthy of the dead. Does anyone know anything about a crystal necklace and a worthy grave?"

They all began thinking hard. Suddenly, Wendine remembered. She had a crystal necklace that she gave to Wendy when she was a baby. She turned to William.

"Does Wendy wear an azure crystal necklace?"

"Yes," said Elena. She wears it every day and doesn't take it off because it reminds her that she had a mother."

"That necklace has been passed down in my family for generations. When she is in real danger, like a life-or-death situation, it will protect her in its own way."

"That explains it," said Jeremy. "When I met her for the first time, I could tell that something was wrong. I could not bite her. That meant the necklace, which had been suppressing her abilities, had revealed that she was a Vamolf. Vampires are not allowed to bite other vampires, but from time to time they break the law."

"Then that means the only thing left is the grave worthy of the dead. "Where can we find a grave worthy of the dead?" William began to think. It suddenly hit him. "Could it be the place where Wendine was buried?"

"How could that be, Dad? It is indeed a worthy grave for a powerful vampire woman, like Wendine, but she is no longer dead."

"I guess you're right, but where can we find such a worthy grave?" "Dad! Could it be—Mom, your family had been hunters for generations.

So, tell me, is there anyone in your family who has a grave worthy enough to be used for such a grand sacrifice?"

Elena began to think. "Of course, my mom has a worthy grave, and a couple of others in our family. It is not unusual for families to have worthy graves. I remember that man telling me something about a grave when speaking about the sword. He said everything lies with the beginning of the Incasera sword."

"The beginning of the Incasera sword," Wally began pondering. He remembered the story his father had told him about how the sword came to be. Upon pondering, nothing came to mind. Eithan began to pace back and forth. He then took his writing hand, which formed a fist, and slammed it into his left palm.

"Got it!" Wally shouted. "A grave worthy of the dead!"

"What is it?" said Jason. The night had finally fallen, and Wally found the clue he needed to commence their plan.

Who is Worthy of that Grave? Plans Made into Actions

"Dad! he said once again. "Do you remember the story you told me about how the Incasera sword came to be?"

"Yes, of course I know. The grave that is worthy of the dead belongs to your great-great-grandfather. How do you know that? If you're wrong, we will be in big trouble."

"Think about it, Dad. Mom said that her grandfather told her that everything began with the sword. Was it not your great-grandfather who fell in love with a vampire and broke his fang to make a sword that would protect her, disobeying his clan? What is more worthy than an act of love?"

"So, tell us: where was he buried?" asked Franco.

"He was buried in our ancestral home. A place where the moon meets the soul. They say this was because long ago, people believed that the moonlight would guide the souls to heaven. If you think about it, wolves transform with the moon, so it is only logical that they will need the moon for the afterlife as well."

When William finally finished speaking, he realized just how worthy the grave truly was. They all made their plans and headed out. Because of their lengthy discussions, time was no longer on their side, and where they were going was not close by.

Lennox was already present at the Granchest Ancestors Hall, making his preparations. First, he looked for the name of the man who used his fangs to create the sword. When he found him, he placed Wendy, whom he had knocked unconscious, to lie on the gravestone.

He already knew she was wearing a crystal necklace, so he took out a necklace that was underneath her garments and placed it on the top of her chest. He took the staff and placed it in her hands, waiting for the thousand- year crimson moon to reveal itself from under the dark clouds that screened it in the sky.

Patiently, he was waiting upon a moon that was so close but looked distant. Finally, peeking from under the clouds was what revealed itself to be a clear, white moon. To him, it looked like any ordinary moon. Suddenly, the whiteness of the moon began to fade, and it started to be painted in red, as if it were getting dyed.

Piece by piece, it began to look even redder than before. It was, without a doubt, the moon he was looking for.

When he saw the moon being dyed, he started laughing. His ambition began to take form. As he prepared for the emission of light from the moon, William arrived on the scene and began fighting him.

Everyone had left to pursue Lennox except for Afeisha, who went to get more useful information about the situation they were facing. During the battle, William found that he was becoming stronger and stronger. He quickly realized that the moon was like a double-edged sword. What threw him off guard was that Lennox, who was a human being, was also getting stronger and matching the ability of an Alpha wolf.

The fighting between the two became relentless and merciless. The more they fought, the stronger Lennox seemed to become. Wally and Jason went toward the grave where Wendy was and began untying her. Lennox was also intelligent. He knew that if he had just placed the unconscious Wendy in the grave and assembled the keys, she would wake up soon and destroy his plans. Instead, he placed her on the grave with the keys and took a special kind of rope with two stakes and hammered them into the ground on opposite sides. He also took precautions in case there were any interruptions.

As Wally and Franco tried to take out the iron stakes hammered into the ground, they noticed that Michael, Sheila, Jeremy, and the others were not with them. Lennox had set various traps around the graveyard while waiting patiently for the moon. He was the head of their hunting organization and brought in reinforcement, which fought off Jeremy and the others. It was a bloody battle, and no one was about to give in. Deep down,

Lennox knew that those who he had called in would have been his sacrificial pawns to buy him time. Though they were human, they were without a doubt strong. But because of the moon, those with supernatural traits overpowered them, although it took some time for it to happen.

"What in the world are you?" asked William. "We've been fighting for this long, and I still can't scratch you."

Lennox began to laugh hysterically. "You are indeed strong," said Lennox. "But it will take more than that to beat me. Let's get serious."

Wendine and Jamain joined in the fight, but the three of them were still not enough.

As they continued to battle without paying attention to the sky above, the moon became completely red. It showed a great brightness, which dyed the sky its color. Everyone present felt that something was amiss, and they all looked up. They beheld the thousand-year crimson moon, which was deemed to be a fiction. What was most shocking was that a beam of light from the moon suddenly engulfed Wendy and the keys as she recovered consciousness.

Wendy began to scream. The moon was giving strength to her and the baby, and the sword, which was placed at her head, came off the ground and began to hover over her in the air.

"What is going on?" said Lennox. "This was not what I read. Maybe it's just part of the ceremony." Something fell off Lennox. "Maybe that brat read me the wrong things."

"What's that sound?" said Wendine.

"It is coming from the sword. The sword is howling. It's as if it's crying out," said Michael.

Lennox immediately rushed towards Wendy. He blasted Wally and Franco out of the way and quickly took hold of the Incasera sword. Power began to flow into him. He mistakenly took it for the beginning of the ritual process for immortality.

"Tell me what exactly you are," said William. "From the way you blasted Franco and Wally like they were pieces of paper floating in thin air, you definitely can't be human."

Lennox smirked. "It's about time I show you people my true form."

The sword stopped howling, and Lennox emitted a fearsome aura. "I nearly died some years ago. Being a hunter used to be such an honorable job, but when I nearly died, I realized something important. Why should I waste my life on people who do not know I exist? Why should I protect them for no thanks at all? Just discrimination. Have you ever watched a movie with heroes? They go all out, even sacrificing their lives for citizens, and when they fail, what do those people do? They curse and discriminate against them, even referring to them as freaks. A hunter's job is like that, so I decided I was not going to die for anyone but myself. I want real power, and that is where the Incasera sword comes in. I want immortality to rule."

After he spoke these words, he burst out of his human flesh. What stood before their eyes was unknown to them.

"This is my truth," said Lennox.

"Wh–what is that?" Asked Wendine. "Is it even possible for a being like that to exist?"

Everyone was shocked out of their minds. What was before them was a two-legged creature with wings on its back. Its two legs were not feet but those of a wolf. It was sharp, and it had the same amount of head as it did feet. Its arms were well built, and it held the Incasera sword. All traces of humanity were gone from Lennox. No one could have recognized how it is that he came to look for that, but they wondered.

"This is going to be auspicious," said Jamain. "It was disadvantageous enough that he was already strong. Now he has the strength of the sword backing him, as well as the moon empowering him. We really are outmatched."

Minutes later, Elena, who had finished her experiment, came to the battlefield. What she saw was beyond her imagination. She saw her father, or what was left of him. She had some thoughts on how he came to be that way, but she kept them to herself. She knew it was through some experiment.

Lennox began to use the sword. With a swing, a huge hole was made within the earth. Jamain, Wendy, and William charged toward the enemy and began to fight once again. The more they fought, the more they realized how strong he really was. Franco and Wally were tied up fighting against other hunters ever since the light incident.

Eithan rushed towards Wendy, who was once again unconscious after the light was retracted and took her out of the grave. Franco and Wally had successfully removed the iron stakes from the ground. Eithan took her to a safer place away from the battle.

She was finally in his arms. His past failure weaves a thread of dread into a fabric of hope. He cradled her in his arms like a baby, brushing strands away from her pale face. Eithan whispered her name into her ear, as if to wake her, not paying attention to the battle going on around them. Though the battle raged, in that moment, she was all that mattered to him. He didn't want to leave her again, though he had to. Eithan pressed a kiss to her forehead before returning to the battlefield to face Lennox.

On his way back, he noticed some strange men observing the fight. The men were dressed in blue. They weren't Lennox hunters and certainly weren't on their side. Who were these men? The thoughts ran through his mind, but there was no time to stop and talk.

When Eithan had gotten close to where the primary fight was taking place, he saw that his companions were on the defensive, but Elena was at a distance with her gun, gearing to shoot.

"What is she trying to do? Does she think that a puny bullet is going to hurt that thing? She's crazy."

Eithan joined the battle. Lennox, who wanted to test out his newly found power, decided to use the Incasera sword, but it did not work. In his hands, the Incasera sword was like a useless piece of metal. Filled with rage, Lennox mounted the sword into the ground. His intention to massacre everyone grew—especially Jason, whom he thought gave him erroneous information.

What he did not know was that he was indeed given the right information, but the ritual was not complete. It cannot be called a sacrifice if there was no sacrifice. When the sword was hovering over Wendy, he did not pierce her. Instead, overcome with greed, he took the howling sword, thinking he would obtain immortality that way.

He charged desperately towards William and his companions and completely decimated them. He was so blinded by hatred that he did not even care whether he lost his life, but he was confident that he wouldn't.

Elena, who was waiting for an appropriate time to shoot the creature, shot at it but missed. The drug she developed was a drug that can render anyone—even a supernatural being—useless by reverting them to their original state. She had only enough time to make three, and one had already been used. Failing to pierce Lennox, her location was given away, and Lennox headed for her.

Lennox was knocking Elena around, and she began spitting blood. As he held her in the air, about to snap her neck, she took out the drug she had in her pocket and injected him with it.

He began to go berserk. He threw Elena onto a nearby wall, which cracked a few of her ribs. As they watched Lennox go hysterical, he started to get smaller and smaller. He reverted to being the human he once was.

"What is happening to me, you Vixen? I cursed the day I gave birth to you. Why do you always have to ruin my plans?"

"It was my mom who gave birth to me," Elena said while spewing blood. "I am tired of your manipulation. And you even dare to hurt my son! Attack him, William!"

Wendine gazed at her. She did not like the way she called William, but she knew that now wasn't the time for jealousy.

"Now that you have reverted to being human, we are going to kick your sorry—"

"My sorry what?" said Lennox. I may have reverted to being

a human, but I still have the power within me. My useless daughter hurriedly made the drug she injected me with."

Once again, Lennox took up the sword and began fighting. The hunter troupe that Lennox had brought in were all dead. He was the only one standing, and he was exhausted. Fighting against many opponents at the same time was sapping his strength now that he was human. "You know what?" He said exhaustedly.

"Every time the Billsman's treaty was mentioned, my mood soured." He remembered the day it was signed. A fragile pack between humans, hunters and supernatural. The hunters were not to hunt the supernatural unless the supernatural became a danger to themselves and others. Though he signed the treaty because of William, to him it was a betrayal.

Instead, he thought-

Why should they thrive while we wither?

"We are but dust,'' he whispered bitterly. "Fading like flowers that bloom in the morning, only to die with the setting sun. One gust from nature and we're nothing."

Though born a proud hunter, for the first time Lennox felt no power- only mortality. "Sooner or later," he muttered, "my thread will be cut. I'll become another old man waiting at Death's door."

Lennox gritted his teeth, rage simmering beneath resignation.

Then, an idea came to him. "What if I can use the vampires, the wolves, the shifters to enhance myself?" This idea pounded in his mind time after time, even when he tried to stifle it, it would not die. Eventually, the idea became a living, breathing soul.

Lennox began hunting in secret. Only the unsuspecting, the unawaken. He studied their blood and their gifts. As if he were a mad man, he searched for the impossible, immortality.

That's when he met Simon. He couldn't overpower him, not with the power Simon held. However, Simon had a small weakness, his affection for his daughter Elena.

And Lennox was good at manipulating loyalty.

He planned with Simon the search for the Incasera sword. Promising to share the power and gifts of immortality.

One by one he abandoned the hunter's code. Power, blood, and ambition consuming his every desire, his every being. He would not accept the fate life have given him. Instead, he would break it.

When Lennox became vulnerable and weak, he left himself open and was attacked from behind. However, he managed to get away, but not without paying a hefty price. What he had left was a few seconds, but he managed to see the person who had attacked him.

"You scoundrel, I thought we had a deal," he said. Then he dropped to the ground and died.

"This situation has become even more unpleasant," said Eithan.

"Why is the principal here? And why did he kill Lennox?" said Michael. "He is our principal, but he was a butler until recently. What is happening?"

"Why are you here, Dad?"

"The principal is your dad?" shouted Wally. Things were getting increasingly out of hand.

"Questions and more questions. Stop bombarding me with meaningless questions," he said. "I will just tell you. My real name is Simon. Do you remember me, William?"

"I know you as my butler who served me all these years," said William. "Anything other than that, I do not know. You have so many identities. How am I supposed to know?"

"I remember you," said Jamain. "When we were in high school, you were the guy that was obsessed with Elena, but she didn't give you the time of day."

"Elena had a handsome guy obsessing over her, and she rejected him?" said Wendine. "That means she wanted to ruin my relationship with William all along. She pretended to be my friend but was not."

Elena was nearly unconscious. "I'm sorry, Wendine," she said. "I did love William, even now. I appreciated Simon's love. I did not want to come between you and William, because you were both important to me, but my dad manipulated me. For everything I did, I apologize." Elena lost consciousness and fell to the floor. Wally hurried over to his mother. No matter what she did, she was still his mother.

Simon looked at Elena. Although he had an inkling of feelings for her, he watched as she pathetically dropped to the ground, and his thoughts were simply that he wasted his time. He then turned to William.

"I always hated you ever since Elena rejected me and began wagging her tail after a guy like you. What was so inferior about me and superior about you? I do not know. Being your butler, I served you well because I did not want you to be suspicious. Looking for that sword was quite a pain. Who knew that the real sword was in front of me all along? When I realized that it was of no use staying with you, I immediately retired and returned to my original position, reverting to the principal I had been.

"My foolish son was to carry out some missions by investigating his new friends, but I guess he got too friendly. He began withholding information from me, so I bugged him. Oh, yes. I know all about the grand library, his girlfriend, and much more. I formed a deal with Lennox, who was hungry and thirsty for power, and I predicted everything."

William was disgusted. He could not stand listening to Simon any longer. William and the others geared towards Simon, but Simon took up the Incasera sword, pointed it at them, and yelled, "Attack!" When he did this, men who were dressed in blue emerged from the darkness. They were, without a doubt, vampires as well as Simon's troops.

As they were fighting, Franco cried out.

"Dad! Why are you doing this?"

Simon laughed. "Isn't it simple? It's because of power. Why else would anyone be doing such things if it isn't to obtain immortality? There comes a time when everyone will die, and when they do, they will disappear. But if one wants to live comfortably and long, there are only three things that they need: immortality, money, and power. It wouldn't make sense to obtain immortality and be penniless. You'd suffer forever. If you obtain immortality but you're weak, you'll be pushed around and live your life in constant fear. You need all three."

After saying this, he called out to his son to join him. Franco had never disobeyed his father before, but he hesitated for the first time in his life. Following him would result in him betraying his friends and the love of his life and ignoring him would cause him to lose the only father he had. Franco became like a chained animal.

Kylie Shows Up to the Battle, Afeisha's Secret.

Lost in thought of what to do, Franco stood still in the middle of the battlefield while others were fighting all around him. Suddenly, Kylie entered the battlefield. She regained her memories by using a forbidden technique that only her mother knew. Lennox miscalculated that her mother would have been able to restore her memory, but Simon did. He wanted Kylie to come to the battlefield so that he could kill her himself.

He preconceived that his son would hesitate because he had now found love. When she entered the battlefield, she immediately saw Franco crouching on the ground. She then shouted his name, only to realize that Franco had not heard her. Kylie then went towards Franco, bypassing all the attacks made by Simon's army with her resurrected powers. She dragged Franco from the midst of the fight and tried snapping him out of it, but it did not work. She had never seen him so weak, so fragile, as if he were about to break.

Having no time to waste, she went towards where her staff was. The moon was still strengthening the supernatural creatures, but that was not all.

When all of Simon's friends were down and he was badly injured, he warned everyone.

"Don't laugh yet. You think I'm finished? Don't you know the moon is a double-edged sword? We may be fighting here, but no one knows what is happening in town."

"What are you saying?" said William.

"Don't you know that the moon is a double-edged sword?" said Simon. "Think carefully. If the moon strengthens the supernatural, what do you think it does to humans?"

Jamain began to panic. After what he experienced dealing with Lennox, he knew just how cruel a human can truly be.

"What are you talking about? You are a teacher, but I'll tell you what it does. While the moon strengthens us supernatural beings, it brings forth humans' darkest desires, their inner instincts to life."

Michael was at a loss. "Are you saying that the humans are rampaging in town?"

"Yes, I'm saying that the humans are going berserk in town while the rest of the vampires are ripping them apart. Do you get it now?"

The situation was escalating at a rapid pace. They came to realize that there was nothing good about the thousand-year crimson moon. It was a moon of extreme misfortune and horror, which is why it appears every thousand years.

Tired but still with strength, Michael, an awakened Franco, Kylie, and Wally all went into town, leaving Jamain, Wendine,

William, and Eithan to deal with Simon. They knew he still had something up his sleeve, and they were not about to let him get away.

When they arrived in town, it was a total disaster. They saw vampires eating humans, humans going wild and killing them. Sheila, Jeremy, Mandy, and Aaron were also present. With the time they had, they were trying to gather the humans in one place and the vampires in another. They wanted to lock them away from the moon, but it did not work. They needed more hands.

Michael was with them, but he decided to go home and look for Afeisha. Though she was human, it was weird of her not to be a participant in any of the battles, especially seeing how very skilled she was.

As they were gathering the people, Jeremy saw Officer Paul. Ever since the incident that happened at school, they all knew that he was a coward. But for some reason, he was outside, in his right mind, fighting against creatures of the dark without showing any sign of hesitation.

"I guess that's his true nature," said Kylie. "And he deserves it, too. I remember when I was tied up, he came to visit Lennox, threatening to lock him up if he found out he had any hand in my kidnapping." At the same time, Officer Paul saw a vampire heading his way. He had both a gun and a sword. However, he was out of bullets, so he quickly retreated while screaming.

"I stand corrected," said Kylie as they continued to capture the humans and vampires. But Officer Paul was both physically and mentally exhausted. Michael, who went to visit Afeisha at her house, didn't find Afeisha at home. He began to worry that something had happened to her. Searching up and down all around, he still could not find her.

Michael became desperate. He wondered where she could be, especially at a time like this. He remembered her mentioning something about digging up some vital information, so he went to the place where he thought she might be. Transforming into his devil figure for the first time, he went to the places where he knew books and information would be available. But to his surprise, she was not there. He began to get suspicious. For some reason, he went back to the Granchest mansion, which was supposed to be empty, but it was not. Afeisha was inside the Granchest mansion, searching for something, but he did not know what it was.

Minutes after observing her, Michael wondered how she searched for information when there were no lights on in the mansion. Yet the way she moved quickly fascinated him. When he went inside, the whole house was silent. Afeisha stopped her endless search and began to look for the intruder in the room. Michael reverted, not wanting to reveal his dark side to Afeisha. As they both searched for each other, they clashed.

"Aaah! That hurt," Afeisha cried as she rubbed her forehead. Shen looked carefully, and what she saw before her eyes was Michael.

"Why are you here, Michael? I thought you wanted to get back Wendy."

CHAPTER FIFTEEN

Wendy Must Die, The True Owner of The Incasera Sword

“I was searching desperately for you,” said Michael. “Why are you here, and what are you searching for? Don’t you know that it’s dangerous?”

“Slow down, Michael. That is too many questions at a time. Let me answer one at a time.

“Ok,” he rescinded. “First, why are you here?

“I’m here to get some vital information on something.” “Why aren’t you behaving crazily like the others outside?”

“Hey, that is a different question from what you asked earlier,” said Afeisha. “Well, I guess I should tell you. The truth is, when I left my house, I saw people behaving strangely. People who were humble and kind became wild and dangerous. Apart from myself, Officer Paul was the only one who looked normal, but at the same time was not. I do not know what kind of phenomenon it was, but it was indeed something. For some reason, while I was dodging them, my head began to hurt, and before I knew it, I ended up here.”

“Are you saying that the moon didn’t affect you?”

“Of course, it didn’t. Why would it affect me?” she asked.

"The moon strengthens the supernatural while bringing human instincts to life. That is why they were all behaving like that. The last question... why were you searching in the dark?"

"What are you talking about, Michael? The lights are on."

Michael became puzzled. "The lights are off, Afeisha. I've been watching you for some minutes in the dark."

After hearing Afeisha confusing the light and the dark, Michael got up from the floor, helped her to her feet, and flipped the switch. When the light came on, what he saw was beyond him. Afeisha's eyes had gotten clearer, glistening like a pearl.

"Why are your eyes like that?" said Michael.

"I don't know," replied Afeisha. "For some days now, my eyes have been hurting me, and my vision has been improving.

"Well, that explains why you've been searching in the dark, thinking the lights were on. Now I understand what has been happening. Thank the Gods that Wendy was saved from that lunatic Lennox."

"What are you talking about, Michael?"

"I'm speaking about the keys. It was never a crystal necklace but crystal eyes. Because of the way it was written, the confusion between the necklace and the eyes was all mixed up. What he needed was not a necklace but your eyes," said Michael.

Afeisha became scared and hugged Michael.

"No need to worry. Lennox has already left this life, but we have two new enemies: the thousand-year crimson moon and Simon, who turned out to be Franco's dad and the principal. He also wants to obtain immortality, but no one knows that your eyes are one of the keys. So, tell me. Why are you here?"

"Everyone wants to obtain the sword, but it has an owner," said Afeisha. "I just wanted to be sure of the information I saw with my eyes. Do you know who the owner of the sword is?"

"Yes, I do," said Michael.

"The owner of the sword has not yet been born. However, the sword is active because 'sword and claws were met.'"

"Are you saying that Wendy's unborn child is the owner of the Incasera sword?"

"Yes, he is," said Afeisha.

"You also know the gender. Your eyes must really be something," said Michael.

"Ever since my eyes became like this, I've been seeing the impossible, and it's been frightening me."

"I want to ask you this, Afeisha. Who has the power to wield the sword now? The baby is not coming until months have passed, and we need the power to defeat Simon."

"The owner's parents could activate the sword, but it must be done together."

After she told him this, her eyes rolled up, and she saw a premonition.

"You must go back to where the fighting is. Wendy's in trouble. And be careful on the way."

After she said this, she passed out. She was not acquainted with her new powers yet, so it took a toll on her body. Following this, Michael took her up into his arms, rested her on the couch, and went back to where the fighting was.

Meanwhile, Eithan, who had placed Wendy in a safe place away from the battle, was busy fighting Simon until he saw Wendy again. He wondered what she was doing there. What he did not know was that a minute after he carried Wendy off, she awoke and started to walk back towards the fighting ground, as if she were a puppet being controlled by a puppeteer. Something was pulling her back to the battleground.

"Why are you here, Wendy?"

Wendy did not answer because she didn't have one. The fighting was halted once more because Wendy was right in the middle of the fight, which gave room for concern.

The sword that Simon was holding became heavy in his hand. It started to wriggle its way out of his hands until it was loosened. Once again, the sword began to cry. It levitated in the air. Suddenly, it went towards Wendy, pausing mid-air to stand in front of her.

"What is happening?" said Eithan.

The sword came towards Wendy, but for some reason, Wendy did not grab the sword. Simon, who was frustrated at what had just happened, launched towards her with the intention of delivering a quick killing blow. Slow to react, Eithan and the others caught on and headed for Simon both to defend against the attack and protect Wendy, but they were a little too late. Fortunately, Michael arrived there in time and fended him off.

"Where did you come from?" said Simon in anger.

Repulsed by him, Michael said, "I'm here to protect my friends."

The End of the Thousand-Year Moon: A New Addition to the Family

Michael, who was running tirelessly across the forest, made it just in time and fended off Simon's attack, delivering one of his own and temporarily immobilizing Simon. Happy to see him, Eithan went up to Wendy.

However, regaining his strength, Simon hurled himself at Michael, but Wally and Jamain intercepted him, colliding with him before he could reach his mark.

While Wally and Jamain were keeping Simon busy, Wendine and the others were busy taking care of his men, who kept getting up over and over after they had been knocked down.

It was not only the power of the moon. Simon also did something to the men, as if he were controlling them like a choirmaster. Then Wendine realized that the only way to put the men down for good was to annihilate them.

Meanwhile, Eithan was next to Wendy, wondering why she was acting so strangely, but she did not reply.

Wendy's hands wrapped around the sword with certainty, ready to put an end to this repeating nightmare. First, it was Lennox. Now Simon. As she grabbed the hilt, the sword didn't move. Her heart sank to the ground. Her inner turmoil began to take over. Why wouldn't it move?

Michael shouted, "Take the sword, Eithan. You're the father!"

Both their hands wrapped around the blade. Heat emanated from the blade. Now glowing and rising as light as a feather, as if reborn by their bond. It was the color of the moon.

"I guess it needed both of us."

"No, three of us," replied Wendy. She figured it out. The sword was not theirs, but the baby who was lending them its strength.

This made Eithan smile, placing his other hand over her stomach. He swore he felt movement.

Overwhelmed with anger at his ruined plans, Jamain went crashing to the ground, and Wally slumped unconscious. With his eyes fixed on Michael, Simon hurled himself forward once more towards Michael, who returned to his devil form and began fighting him. Michael was on the offensive, powers spiraling out of control, but the momentum shifted quickly to him becoming defensive, as Simon was no walk in the park.

When Jamain saw Simon beating his son, he rose from the ground. With blinded anger, he overpowered Simon for half of an hour. Simon became so focused on Jamain that he completely forgot about Wendy and Eithan, leaving himself completely vulnerable.

That moment of vulnerability was what they needed. As Jamain stepped back, both Wendy and Eithan rushed towards

Simon, piercing his chest with the Incasera sword. Like a knife through butter, the sword went through his body, causing him to bleed tremendously. His eyes widened with fury while the light within the blade burst free, casting shadows over their faces. However, Simon was still alive, being fueled exclusively by his strength and determination.

Wendy and Eithan shoved the blade deeper into Simon's chest. He reeled in pain. With one final gasp, he took his last breath while the world held on, mourning in stillness as nature grieved for the lives that were lost.

Back in town, Franco felt a strange sensation he had never experienced before. As soon as he sensed it, he knew his dad had died. The feeling of loneliness was starting to fill him, so he kept killing the mindless vampires and wolves just to distract himself. After Simon died, the vampires, whom he also controlled, dropped to the ground.

The only problem left was the mindless people in town. After five minutes had passed, the crimson that covered the moon began to fade, and the whiteness of the moon started to re-emerge from underneath. The people in town regained their sanity one after the other, and Officer Paul was a wreck. Everyone present in the battle was tired and drained. All their energy was sapped. Persons who made it out alive that day went home injured, confused, and slept. They did not have the energy to talk to each other because they were all drained.

Wendy snapped out of her daze when the moon went back to how it was. Nights of terror faded into sunlight. Wendy collapsed on Eithan, her body aching yet her soul heavier. He caught her.

"It's finally over," she said. "For now," he whispered.

The next day, Wendy got up from her chambers. She was still drained after a couple of days, but she had made up her mind to forget the dreadful things that had happened. That day, she went down to do her usual morning routine, which was to eat breakfast, but everyone looked tired, and William was not present. Things were quite a mess. Apart from William being gone, Wendine was present at the dinner table with Wally. It was a little uncomfortable for Wally, but he understood.

Elena, who had nearly died, had completely given up on William and decided that when she was released from the hospital, she would move out of the Granchest mansion and start a new life with her son. Fortunately for her, Wally never blamed her or pointed his finger at her because he knew just how blind love could be. He had decided to live with his mother and visit his other family often.

During breakfast, they turned the television on and saw William on the screen. The crowd was demanding that Officer Paul tell them what was going on, but he also did not have the answer. It had been days, and the people were getting restless; they wanted answers. However, Officer Paul was at a loss. It was bad enough that he had to fight a stressful battle the nights before.

All he could think about was going home and taking a nice, long nap. The people's minds were confused. The wreckage from the nights before hadn't been cleaned up, and people who could not remember what had happened needed answers. So, they all turned to the man whom they respected and trusted. Seeing Officer Paul mincing his words, William decided to help him out.

"The cause of this destruction was us," said William. "We were infected by some airborne disease, which made us act the way we did. I don't know a lot of information about it. However, we are asking the doctors to see if they can find a solution."

After William said this, Officer Paul was relieved, and the residents seemed to buy into it.

The people began to repair the town, their houses, the streets, and everything in between. The town became busy and bustling. People were found chatting on their rooftops, others were pushing barrows, and the children found new means to play. They played with corks, bucket covers, and marbles. I guess there is light at the end of every tunnel. The disaster has brought the people closer. School reopened as if nothing had happened, and everyone returned to it. When they all got back, they had intended to discuss the previous events that occurred that night, but Franco and Kylie were still missing. He was now the principal. He inherited everything that belonged to his father. Missing, he was, but no one went to look for him because they knew he needed ample time to recover from the loss.

During that period, weeks passed, and Franco was back to normal. He and Kylie were closer than ever and had started to display public affection, but it was not just them. Michael and Afeisha, too. But the most shocking were Jason and Mandy. Even Aaron and Sheila, along with Jeremy. They were all coupled out. Eithan was the most confused because he had never in his life thought that Jason had those kinds of feelings for Mandy. His curiosity began to burn even more than a furnace.

"How long was it?" asked Eithan.

"How long was what?" Jason replied.

"I'm talking about you having a crush on Mandy."

"It's been a long time. Ever since I met her, I've liked her, but she kept running after you. So, all I had to do was persevere with patience and try to win her over."

Eithan was touched. His curiosity was satisfied, but not with Aaron. He was also confused, but he left that for another time.

Time became peaceful, and everyone enjoyed their happy times while remembering to stay indoors on every seventh day. Though there were a lot of vampires and wolves who were still dangerous, the pace and trouble for Officer Paul lessened, and rumors began to dwindle over time.

Months later, it was time for Wendy to welcome Eithan's and her child into the world. She was having contractions, and her water had burst. She was rushed to the Milly Gates Hospital, where she gave birth. All their friends were present. William also informed Wally, who was living with his mom, about the situation, and he quickly rushed to the hospital with his mom. When they got into the room, they heard the cry of a newborn baby. Wendy gave birth to a bouncing baby boy. Eithan held his son and cried with joy. Despite that, Wally looked more overjoyed than Eithan. If people didn't know better, they would've thought he was the father of the baby. He took the baby from Eithan and held him in his arms.

"Hello, little one, I am your uncle."

The baby reacted to him, and Wally's love for his nephew grew even more.

Everyone wanted to hold the baby. They were all excited, and that made Wendy happy. When the baby returned to her arms, she named him Alex, the masculine version of the feminine Alexa, which means to protect all. After the baby received its name, the sword that William had sealed away began to emanate a purple light. Its owner had finally been born. All her friends became his godparents, and William and Wendine finally became the grandparents they had always wanted to be since they found out she was pregnant.

The room was so rampant that Eithan's family did not have time to enter, but they felt the joy that was shared. As time passed, the baby began to grow up healthy, and he displayed several attributes, such as those of a Vamolf and something else. This became a cause for concern for Eithan, but Wendy knew that he was a special existence that the world had never seen before.

Ever since that night, she knew just how powerful he was going to be and sought to teach him the morals he needed so he wouldn't stray.

Five years had passed, and everyone was busy doing their own thing. At their new home, Alex was playing in his bedroom with his mom. While playing, he unconsciously teleported using his powers to the railing of the porch. This was his first time doing it, and unbeknownst to him, his eyes turned crimson with a hint of purple. It was the exact shade of the thousand-year moon, and inside his eyes glowed an image of a sword in his pupils. Wendy, who began to panic about the whereabouts of her child, rushed towards the living room where Eithan was and told him what was going on. Her voice was cracked, and her face was filled with worry. After hearing what she said, both husband and wife began searching the entire house for Alex. Eithan started to envision the future of his son, Alex, and how monstrous a child he would be if left unchecked. After searching the whole house in less than thirty seconds, they opened the door, only to find little Alex on the railing of the porch, giggling with happiness.

"That's dangerous," said Wendy as she rushed to pick him up. She began to hug him tightly. She then looked into his eyes. Realizing that his eyes had changed color, she called Eithan.

"Honey!" she exclaimed. "Take a look at Alex's eyes and tell me what you see."

Eithan gazed steadily into his son's eyes, and what he saw was not only a shade of crimson but also the thousand-year crimson moon and the legendary Incasera sword located in the middle of both his eyes. Immediately, Eithan knew just how powerful his son truly was.

"Oh no!" said Eithan.

Wendy knew why Eithan said what he said. She immediately assured him that he just needed to learn control, and when he did, his eyes would return to normal.

When she said this, her heart swelled with love and fear.

-The End-

About the Author

The author, known as Weslyn Trimmingham, was born on November 9, 1999, to Wilmoth and Evena Trimmingham. She resides on the island of St. Vincent and the Grenadines and is the second of her siblings, all of whom share a deep passion for the arts. Weslyn spent her childhood in a small village called Francois in Vermont, where agriculture played a significant role in their daily lives, involving activities such as planting food in the mountain, climbing fruit trees and enjoying the river.

At the age of eight, Weslyn discovered a love for anime while visiting her friends, the Lawrences. Series like Detective Conan, Dragon Ball Z, and Fairy Tale captivated her imagination. Detective Conan's influence even inspired her to consider a career as a police officer rather than a teacher. As she matured, her interests expanded to include reading manga and novels, particularly enjoying action, sports, romance, and adventure genres.

Weslyn attended Buccament Bay Secondary School, where she excelled academically and athletically. She recalls, "I remember breaking the 1000-meter relay for girls at one point." Although the assistant physical education teacher encouraged her to pursue football or netball, she declined. Additionally, the principal once suggested a business major for her instead of the arts, a proposal she found compelling enough to follow.

It was not until she began her college journey in 2016, studying entrepreneurship and small business management, that her passion for writing truly flourished. Despite earning an associate degree in her field, her love for crafting her own stories remained strong. The title Crimson Moon" was inspired by a game played by her college friend Shane. This artistic individual enjoys drawing anime alongside her brother, Wesmoth Trimmingham, who is also a jack-of-all-trades. Eventually, Weslyn began to write a story featuring a wolf, a girl, and a forest setting reminiscent of her homeland's natural beauty.

This Caribbean storyteller, with a passion for fantasy, supernatural romance, and dramatic twists, inspired by the mystique of legends and the strengths of the human spirit, weaves powerful tales that blend mystery, danger, and heart. Crimson Moon is her debut novel, the first in the new thrilling saga filled with myth, betrayal, love, and unexpected forms.

Hope you enjoyed the book.

Acknowledgement

Thank you all for the time you took to read this book. The journey of writing 'Crimson Moon' has been filled with challenges, lessons and moments of quiet triumphs, and I could not have completed it without the love and support of those closest to me.

To my family- Your encouragement gave me strength on my days when the words felt heavy and the pages endless. Your belief in me carried this story to completion, and I am forever grateful.

To my cousin Camille- Thank you for bringing this book to life visually with your talent and dedication to the cover and publication process. Your creativity gave Crimson Moon the face it was always meant to have.

To my friends- Your kindness has made the completion of this book worthwhile. You supported and reminded me that stories matter, and for that I'm grateful. I'm especially thankful to my good friend Shane Barrow and my brother Wesmoth Trimmingham. Now, you will finally get the chance to see and read the completed version of this book.

And to every future and current reader- This book is as much yours as it is mine. May you find pieces of yourself in these pages, and may the Crimson Moon whisper its secrets to you, just as it did to me.

With Gratitude,

Weslyn Trimmingham

www.ingramcontent.com/pod-product-compliance
Lightning Source LLC
Chambersburg PA
CBHW061931170626
46813CB00006B/2354